THE BIG PADDLE

Also by Robin Moore

Pitchman
The Devil to Pay (with Jack Youngblood)
The Green Berets
The Country Team
Fiedler
The French Connection
Court Martial (with Henry Rothblatt)
Until Proven Guilty (with Henry Lowenberg)
The Khaki Mafia (with June Collins)
The Happy Hooker (with Xaviera Hollander and Yvonne Dunleavy)
The Fifth Estate
Treasure Hunter (with Howard Jennings)
Phase of Darkness (with Al Dempsey)
The Family Man (with Milt Machlin)
Dubai
Mafia Wife (with Barbara Fuca)
The Washington Connection

THE BIG
PADDLE

ROBIN MOORE
with SID LEVINE

 Arbor House : New York

Library of Congress Catalogue Card Number: 77–90661
ISBN: 0–87795–178–0
Manufactured in the United States of America

Based on an original story by Sidney H. Levine

The authors are indebted to Paul Burke
for such contributions of organization,
administration, insight and special
knowledge that do, indeed, make of him
the third writer of the piece.

1

WITH A FEELING of smug satisfaction Slim pulled the free-wheeling button on the dashboard of his brand-new '33 Pontiac and sat back. There weren't many hills in this part of Oklahoma but when they came, this baby could float right down them without using a drop of gas. Now that was class. Road was pretty good too. Last year it weren't nothing but a damned dust ribbon, but the WPA fixed it up real nice. Turning, he noticed Cliff beside him manipulating a deck of cards with his right hand, deftly transposing bottom cards to the top of the deck then, after a run, reversing the process.

"Are we halfway yet?" Cliff asked, the cards jumping in his hand.

"Better. We should be in Norman in another half hour now." Slim glanced over at his fifteen-year-old son and smiled. "You're getting pretty slick with that one-handed stack."

"I haven't lost a card game, 'cept when I throw one, in a year."

"You're not using any of those moves I taught you to beat your school friends?"

"Naw. I don't have to cheat to win, even when I play seniors at Grove City High."

"That's what I want to hear, pal."

"But it helps to know the tricks. I caught Sam Scruggs dealing seconds last week." Cliff laughed. "His big hands were so clumsy it was a snap to show how he was slipping cards off the bottom of the deck. If he wasn't so big the others would have beat the shit out of him."

"Pal," Slim said solemnly, "I been hustling to make you a class operator since you was hardly old enough to flip a poker chip and let me tell you—never smarten up a sucker by exposing another hustler's moves. It's sure to land you in trouble. And pal, a class operator never uses foul language. That's one thing your mother and I agree upon . . . 'cept of course she doesn't want you to be any kind of an operator."

"I know. I can't even practice flipping cards into a hat without her raising a fuss . . ."

"Now remember, pal, your mother is a real lady. She loves you more than anything." Slim sighed. "She just thought I made my money as a stockbroker when she said 'I do' . . . Lord 'a' mercy, how she went on first time she nailed me scoring on them stocks that was phony as a nigger bishop. . . ."

They drove on in silence punctuated only by the rhythmic flicking of cards moving up and down a fresh deck. Noticing again how his son's hands caressed the deck, Slim felt confident that Cliff was born to the trade. Poor Sarah, her influence never got out of the paddock.

"You keeping up with your golf, Cliff? It wasn't easy for me to get you working in the caddy shack at the Bent Creek Club. They usually don't even look at a nonmember."

"Sure, I'm working. How else would I stake my games?"

"I mean are you playing? Is that pro, Jack Brady, giving you lessons? I put in a bunch of sessions improving his cardplaying, you know—even gave him three decks of cards from Saint Louis Dutch. You can't get decks like Dutch makes them."

Cliff looked at his father, hating to see the snakelike blue veins at his temples and the flushed face. Despite his resolve not to say anything that would hurt him, Cliff heard himself say: "If you were just home more you'd of seen me do the course in par for the first time last week."

A pained expression came over Slim's eyes for a moment as his face flushed even deeper. The veins moving in his forehead, he replied, "I know I've been away too much these past three years, but I'm doing it for you and your mother. You wait and see. Those mineral rights I've been buying are going to make us rich. All I've got to do now is come up with the money to develop them. Once that first hole hits, we'll be set for life." He glanced at Cliff. "Par, huh? That's pretty good."

Cliff smiled suddenly. "A couple of the members at Bent Creek even asked me to go up to Tulsa with them to hustle a tournament. They said I could take down twenty-five bucks easy."

Slim's chagrin dissipated. "No kidding, Cliff. That's really something. My boy a scratch golfer at fifteen."

"Ah, I just had a good day. I haven't done it again but the members figure they'll con a fifteen handicap for me and we'll take about three or four matches before the suckers catch on."

"Hey, I'm proud of you, pal. Really. Look just don't ever tell your mother about the hustle part, though. She thinks golf is just a way to become friendly with the gentry." They grinned together.

A few minutes later, the tents and Ferris wheel of Bill Stember's traveling carnival came into view and Cliff started tingling in anticipation. "Now pal," Slim said, "while Bill Stember and I talk a little business you just watch how the carneys operate."

"I want to see the pig girl!"

"It's for chumps." Slim chuckled.

"I know, but I like it. Least you know I'm not going to be taken by any of those flat joints and wheels of fortune."

"You better by God not. I've showed you how they gaff every one of those games with magnets and weights and tilts and all. You get taken by any one of them and—there's two kinds of people in this world, wise guys and marks, and I don't ever want my son to be a mark. . . . Now, you case the carnival and come back and tell me all about it."

"I'll check out the bare-ass show for you." Cliff darted a look at his father. "If they really show everything they got I'll let you know."

"God damn, if your mother ever heard I let you see such a thing, wouldn't be worth my peace to come home for two months." He winked. "Still and all, if you see something I haven't, let me know."

Gingerly Slim slipped the Pontiac between two battered pickup trucks and, locking the doors, they stepped out onto the rutted dirt lot, Cliff already feeling the excitement. At the red-white-and-blue-striped gate Slim winked at the attendant collecting the dime entrance fee and drawled, "With it." With a nod, they were sent on through.

It was noon and the carnival was spinning in the springtime sun, groups of locals ogling the rigged games of chance, gaudy prizes displayed on the shelves, wheels, shooting galleries, pin games, and dozens of other booths busily engaged in extracting the contents of the suckers' Depression-depleted purses. At the end of the midway just beyond the Test-Your-Strength stand stood a bright red boxcar on wheels, recently deposited by the carnival tow truck.

"That's Bill Stember's office," Slim said. "I'll take you in and introduce you, then you go out and drag the midway for an hour. Okay?"

"Sure. Can you let me hold a couple of bucks?"

Slim grinned and fished them from his pocket, then, placing a hand on Cliff's shoulder, led him up the steps to the door in the side of the boxcar office and, pushing it open, propelled Cliff into the dim interior.

"Well, Slim Thompson, right on time," someone said. "And who have we here?" A fat, smiling, bald man stood up and reached out a hand to Cliff, who took it in a strong grip of his own.

"Bill, this is my boy Cliff," Slim introduced proudly. "I figured I'd bring him along, let him have some fun while we do our business."

Bill Stember's grin widened to reveal an uneven row of yellow teeth. "Hey, Cliff. You have yourself a good time, hear? Don't drop all your money in one place. There's a lot to see."

"Don't worry, Mr. Stember. All these flat joints will get from me is practice." Cliff winked. "I've had a good teacher. Nice to meet you, sir."

Stember watched the boy leave in silence. "Jesus Christ! I'd hate to see that kid when he's twenty-one. He figures to rack up the world!"

"He's all right," Slim allowed.

"Sit down. Sure glad you could get over here today." Stember offered him a cigar. "Pay a nickel for 'em myself. Sell them for fifteen cents with no trouble. . . . Now, let me lay a little biniss on you, Slim."

"That's why I drove all the way here from Grove City."

"This going to be the bes' drive across the goddamn Oklahoma dust you made in a long time." He lit his own cigar. "I saw Roy Brian four days ago in Oklahoma City." He nodded portentously, blowing a stream of smoke at Slim.

"And?" Slim prompted.

"He's interested, Slim. Damned interested. Roy Brian got a lot of money, Slim. Don't you forget it."

"Lot of people got a lot of money, even these days. Important thing is will Brian turn loose some of it?"

"I told him the whole story. How you been in Grove City three years now buying up mineral rights. How those poor Okies been selling so's to move on to California."

Slim nodded. "That's been one thing good about this Depression. Every time I come back from the road after a score I've given the old lady enough for rent and groceries and put all the rest into mineral rights. Now it's time to drill me a hole. Three high-price geologists all say there's oil down there. Now all I need is someone to put up the money to develop."

5

"And I got your man, Slim. Roy'll be right here in. . ." Stember consulted the old bell-top alarm clock on a shelf at the far end of the room, "in 'bout an hour. Now let's talk about where old Bill Stember, who arranged this important biniss conference, fits in. . . ."

Cliff Thompson had been fascinated with carnivals and con games ever since he could remember. As the postcards his father scrawled came in from all over the country, Cliff counted the days until Slim, carrying his black box, returned and he could sit at his father's feet, listening to Slim recount the hustles he had maneuvered on his most recent trip. Then, despite his wife's upset, Slim would deal his son five-card stud or some other game, teaching Cliff all the latest refinements and reconstructing a hand Slim had played in Omaha or Kansas City for a big score.

By the time he was ten Cliff could stack a cooler with the best of them, arranging a blackjack deck so the dealer would win every hand and appearing to shuffle the cards furiously without actually changing their order. Now at fifteen, he had learned just about all the mysteries that Slim's black box could reveal —gaffed dice, missouts, split-outs, tops—all the wondrous tools of the mechanic's trade.

As he walked down the midway a white-haired barker, wearing a pink-and-white-striped shirt with decorated garters around his arms and a straw hat, leaned out from behind a booth loaded with trinkets and said, "Hey kid, did you get the free stamp for the prize?"

Cliff stifled a grin, knowing it was a standard sucker come-on but allowed his eye to be caught, and the carney, seeing he had the mark's attention, shifted into high gear. "Come over, a little closer, I'll show you what I mean. See the twenty-two rifle up there? The beautiful mantel clock, your mom would love it. We got so many prizes we got to get rid of them before we move on. You can get yourself a free prize like I said, you know. Now these prizes where they come from you never saw such stores and like I said, you're due. You gotta go away with something. Just step over here, you'll see what I'm talking about."

As Cliff moved to the stand, the carney leaned across the counter and in a low, confidential tone muttered, "Listen kid, I'm supposed to be busy here. I don't work on commission. I get paid by the week so I have to look like I'm busy. The boss will be back any minute so I want to make him think I'm busy. I tell ya what I'll do. I'll let ya throw these marbles down the shoot, add up your score and it won't cost ya anything. You're doing it just to make me look busy, ya know."

Cliff looked down the track and saw the twenty-six numbered holes at the end. Whichever hole the marble fell into would give him his score. Smiling conspiratorially, the carney handed Cliff six marbles and Cliff rolled them fast—one, two, three—as the carney called out the scores.

"Hey fella, you are lucky! Ya got a forty-one! Let's see on this card what it gives you." After a shifty-eyed glance at the card, the carney called out, "Why, forty-one is worth six points. All you need is ten points for any prize in the booth. You look like a nice kid. I'd like to do something for you. Since this was a free one and you got such a great score, why don't you just pay me the twenty-five cents and I'll let you keep the big score? Then you can give me another two bits for six more marbles and all you need now is four more points to win the prize." The carney stared eagerly at Cliff.

Cliff returned the stare, then with an insolent grin, "Fee-a-zuck yee-a-zoo, I'm wee-a-zith ee-a-zit!" Cliff remembered his father's warning about obscenities, but in carney pig-latin it didn't sound so bad.

"Okay little wise guy," the carney gave him a sour look. "Why don't you do me a favor and take it on the duffy."

Cliff laughed and continued down the midway. He had watched the suckers roll and roll in the Razzle-Dazzle and never get those last four points, paying a quarter each time they put a marble between their fingers. The game kept going on until the mooch was broke or almost broke and no matter how carefully he lined up those high-number holes at the end of the track, he just never seemed to be able to get the amount of points he needed.

Just before leaving the game, Cliff had spotted the outside man approaching the Razzle-Dazzle ready to move in for the kill. After the sucker had lost two or three times, the outside man happened to wander by and offered to put up half the money if the mark would split the pot. He kept going on and on with the sucker, urging him to try one more time—they're both in this thing together—and when the mark was finally busted, the outside man rolled one more time and made the big win. Hey, what luck! Then so as not to burn the mark and make him mad—and perhaps even cause a Hey Rube—the proprietor of the game gave the broke mooch a cheap doll off the rack.

Cliff was approaching the pig-girl show now and could hear the crowd inside the tent screaming in delighted horror. The pig girl, actually some young man picked up along the way, wearing a long blond wig and a dress with two grapefruit sewed into the appropriate places, stood in a pit and grunted and sloshed around in the mud as the spectators watched. The barker explained that the poor girl had the mentality of an animal and was actually enjoying what she was doing so they shouldn't feel sorry for her. With that the pig girl caught one of the snakes that was writhing around in the dirt, picked it up, bit its head off, and threw the head and the body into the crowd. A terrific show—but it was the naked girl part that Cliff liked the best.

He wondered whether he was abnormal being only fifteen and having such a craving to see female flesh. He had learned in moments of temptation to manipulate cards and dice instead of himself, but now here he was outside the tent adorned with pictures of girls in scanty underwear and listening to the squeals of the girls performing inside. "Next show in ten minutes, don't go away," the barker called to him. "Sheba, the Amazon girl, will be out in front to entertain you until the next show starts."

The enticement was strong, but Cliff decided to save the flesh show for the end and turned to case the flat joints for a game he hadn't seen before. As he started to go, however, he almost bumped into a heavyset young man with the unmistakable look of an idiot.

At every carnival he'd gone to, Cliff had seen one or two such mentally retarded youths gawking at the displays and as he watched now, the simpleton made his way up the midway and stopped in front of the Razzle-Dazzle. The barker in his striped shirt and straw hat leaned out and Cliff could almost hear the come-on. Poor dunce, he thought.

Ordering a dime hot dog from a grease joint across the way and paying for it with a nickel and a quick wee-a-zith e-a-zit, Cliff continued to watch, and saw that the carney had already conned the boy into rolling the first three marbles free and now was working on him to build up his score. Cliff found himself growing angry as the defective kept reaching into his pocket, then right on cue the outside man came up and hustled the mark into paying out his quarters until the last one had ended up in the Razzle-Dazzle coffers. A stricken look came over the round moon face and the boy jammed both hands into the pockets of his jeans as though trying to discover another quarter. Then looking as though he would burst into tears, he shambled away, up the midway.

Cliff went up to the carney. "Why the hell did ya have ta take off that poor half-wit? You took advantage of an idiot! You could see he isn't normal. Why don't you stick to taking off people that at least know what they're doing!"

The carney looked down at Cliff and spread his hands. "Hey kid, don't beef at me. I didn't bring him into the world. He wanted to play the game, he played it. I'm not his father."

Cliff flashed a look of disgust, and turning on his heel, said, "That's probably the only good thing that's ever happened to him!" and walked away. Shaking his head at the venality of carnival people, he headed back toward Stember's boxcar.

As he approached the office the clang of the Test-Your-Strength bell diverted him.

"Step right up, men, and test your strength—bang the gong

—yes sir! Three chances for a quarter. Hit the gong three times and—"

A muscular brute of a farmhand accompanied by a stick-limbed, straw-haired girl came into range and the carney aimed his spiel at them.

"Here's a mighty-looking man. Win a beeudeeful Kewpie doll for the lovely lady. Hit the gong three times. Some do—some don't, some will—some won't. How about it, fella? You look like a strong man. Only a quarter to try!"

The beefy young man walked disdainfully to the Test-Your-Strength stand, paid his quarter, took the heavy wooden sledge-hammer from the ground and, hefting it high above his head, brought it down with a mighty blow that sent the bolt streaking up the wire. The gong clanged.

"Hey there, looks like we have a winner," the carney yelled.

Once again the yokel hammered the target and the bell clanged a second time.

"Say, this man sure is powerful. His little lady is going to take home a Kewpie doll!"

But when he wielded the sledge the third time, the bolt flew up the wire—and then fell back down. "Oh, he missed." There was convincing disappointment in the barker's tone. "Try it again. Only twenty-five cents for three chances . . . unless you're running out of gas."

The other young men laughed and the girl giggled.

Red-faced and scowling, the mark took another quarter from his pocket and handed it to the barker, then as an afterthought put down the hammer, took off the handsome leather jacket he was wearing, hung it on the fence that surrounded the Test-Your-Strength flat and went back to the target. He spit upon his hands, raised the hammer high above his head, and with all his strength brought it down so hard his feet left the ground. The bolt clanged against the bell.

"Hey, hey . . . !"

Cliff, who had been taking in the scene, had a notion. Edging over to the fence, he waited until all eyes were fixed on the

10

farmhand's second try, then slipped the jacket off the fence, bundled it up and holding it like a football under his arm, started back down the midway, quickly losing himself in the crowd.

It didn't take him long to find the young man who'd been fleeced in the Razzle-Dazzle wandering lugubriously about the midway. Cliff put an arm on his shoulder.

"I saw what they did to you at the Razzle-Dazzle. How much money did they take?"

"All I got. Three bucks."

"You want to get it back?"

The dolorous face brightened. "Can I?"

"We can try. Follow me." Cliff slipped the outsized leather jacket over his shoulders and led the way toward the Razzle-Dazzle, where the striped-shirted carney was vainly attempting to attract new suckers.

"I thought I told you to take a duffy," the barker snapped.

"This kid's a friend of mine," Cliff announced. The carney groaned.

"I thought I told you— "

"What's the matter with you? You ought to be hip enough to know you never burn a mark. You want this guy to call a Hey Rube and get the sheriff down on you?"

The carney stared at Cliff. Actually the wise-ass kid had a point. He hadn't even let the dunce walk away with a cheap prize, something to show for his money.

"What do ya have in mind?" he asked warily.

"Look, I just won this twenty-five-dollar leather jacket, but I can't use it 'cause it's too big for me. I'll let you have it for five dollars and I'll take care of my friend."

"*Five* dollars? I only beat him for three, why five?"

"Because the jacket is worth more than five and it will stop me from blowing the whistle on you," Cliff answered.

The carney looked from the wise kid to the simpleton and back again. The fundamental rule of a carnival was never get into a Hey Rube you could avoid. After a moment, he said,

"Okay kid," and reached into his pocket, pulling out four crumpled bills. "Here's four." He thrust them at Cliff, taking the jacket from him. "That's all you get and don't let me see you again."

Cliff nodded. "Believe me, you won't." He started to walk away, then stopped and turned. "Oh, nice meeting you, sir."

Back in the crowd Cliff handed the boy three dollars—"Now do yourself a favor, use it to see some shows or buy lunch"— and started back toward the Test-Your-Strength. He arrived just as the beefy mark, despite his girl friend's presence, finally gave up on ringing the bell and looked for his jacket. The bellow could be heard far up the midway.

"Some sumbitch stole my jacket!"

Cliff let the yokel's anger build, then inquired innocently, "Was it a brown leather jacket with straps on the shoulders and silver studs around it?"

"Where'd you see it?" the man roared, his mood further fouled by his failure to win a Kewpie doll.

"Gee, a carney tried to sell me one like that just a couple of minutes ago."

"Where?"

"Lemme think a minute. It was on the midway, one of the games. Oh yeah! I think it was the Razzle-Dazzle. Over there." And Cliff pointed helpfully.

"Yeah? Thanks, kid, thanks a lot."

The redneck strode cursing up the midway, charged into the Razzle-Dazzle counter, spotted his jacket hanging with the other prizes, reached across, grabbed the barker, hauled him into the midway and with one hamlike fist punched him in the jaw, sending him reeling back into the counter, where he slumped to the ground unconscious. Then he kicked over the counter of the booth, took his jacket off the hook where it hung beside the .22 rifle and the kitchen clock, and stalked away.

Slim and Bill Stember were reminiscing about the big scores they'd made when the roustabout burst into the trailer office.

12

"We may have us a Hey Rube, Mr. Stember. Some mark got his jacket stole, claims by Ol' Mac at the Razzle-Dazzle. You better come."

Stember hauled his bulk out of the chair uttering a string of curses. "I thought it was all going too smooth," he said, and started for the door. "Slim, if Roy Brian shows tell him I'll be back directly."

"Sure thing, Bill."

It was only minutes later when a knock came and the door was pushed open. A conservatively suited man with a stocky, muscular build and piercing blue eyes set wide apart under a thick head of black hair parted in the middle stepped into the office and looked around. In his hand he held his straw hat.

"Bill Stember around?"

"You Roy Brian?" Slim asked, standing up.

"Sure am. You must be Slim Thompson." A friendly grin spread across his face. "I've heard a lot about you. Like that lowball game in Lincoln a few months ago."

Slim smiled. "I got lucky on that one."

"I hear you make your own luck." Brian walked to the middle of the office.

"Sit down," Slim said. "Bill just had a little problem to take care of."

Roy Brian took the armchair Slim gestured to and sat down on the front edge of it, skimming the hat onto the nearby table. He was a sharp-looking piece of work, Slim thought, no doubt about it. He gave off the aura of a man with a healthy bankroll.

"Yes, sir. Glad to meet you," Brian drawled. "I understand you and I might be able to do a little biniss. Bill Stember was mighty strong 'bout what you got over in Grove City. Sounds real interesting."

"Could be. I bought up all the minerals for about two square miles around Grove City. I've had three separate geologists make assessments, both real encouraging. Now I need to sink a hole or two. Bill tells me you might be interested."

"We talked about it, Slim. We sure did. I'd like to have a look at your mineral rights, see the ground. Of course I've heard tell Grove City might be sitting on top of a *potentially* lucrative field—"

"Why don't you come around, see what I got, and if you like it we'll cut a deal. I'll put up my mineral rights leases, you put up the cash, and we'll go fifty-fifty on the oil field."

"If we hit on the first hole," Brian cautioned.

"We ought to be ready to go two, three holes," Slim said. "The geologists, the diviners, even some spooky dude said he got the word right from the spirit world, all of 'em claim there's a big pool of oil under Grove City."

"Well, I think you may be right," Brian said, "so I came up with another idea to get the wells drilled. First place, you gotta realize that the money gets controlling interest in a deal like this. You'd get about thirty to forty percent, me and the others putting up the cash would have to have sixty to seventy percent." Brian held up a hand as Slim started to protest. "Let me finish, Slim. What I just said you'll find is true no matter who you go to. But I got an answer that'll solve both our needs." Roy Brian studied the man opposite and noticed the veins starting to throb in his temples. "You want to hear my proposition?"

"I thought I knew what it was. Bill said—"

"Forget what Bill said. This is you and me."

Slim shrugged but kept silent.

"I know an oil driller in Oklahoma City, name of Bull Larsen. Bull is the best driller in the state but he's got a problem. He can't keep away from the cards and dice. He's what I believe they call a compulsive gambler. He'll bet on anything."

Slim nodded. "I know the type. They financed my mineral leases."

"Sure you do." A conspiratorial smile came over his face. "Now I figure an old hustler like yourself, teamed up with me, we could take Bull Larsen off for the price of drilling two, maybe three holes if we don't hit the first time down. I could finance one hole, maybe two, but why not let Larsen do it? And

14

this way, you keep a full fifty percent of that field you've been putting together for so long. . . ."

Slim's feelings were mixed. He knew vaguely that Brian was right about the percentages he'd been talking about, but he'd thought this meeting would result in a straightforward business deal, not another hustle.

Finally he sighed. "What kind of a game are we talking about?"

"Larsen loves skin. He'll go all over looking for a skin game."

"Where do we play?"

"I'll bring Larsen out to Grove City to look over your spread. I'll tell him we want an estimate on putting down three holes and have him bring his contract forms so we can sign a deal on the spot. Then you can mention there's a skin game in town and watch him hit the bait."

Brian could almost read the tired old gambler's mind. This Slim Thompson looked near burned out. He'd come around with a little persuasion. . . . "Think it over, Slim. I'm trying to help you make the best deal for yourself. You keep fifty percent of the deal. I'll take off Larsen with you. Hell! We'll be playing in Grove City your territory!"

"Nobody can win for sure at skin," Slim replied, weakening.

Brian saw the opening and slid in. "I've got a mechanic who can make damn sure we win. He's been dealing skin all over the country, just arrived in Oklahoma City. I've been saving him for just this game."

Brian saw that Slim was wavering. He leaned back in his chair, a look of unconcern on his face as he took one of Stember's cigars from the box on the table beside him and lit it, slowly letting a stream of smoke escape his lips.

"Tell you what, Slim. You think it over and let me know— anytime in the next hour—because if we don't do this one there's another situation near Norman I want to look at before I go back to Oklahoma City. I've got a hell of a lot longer drive in front of me this afternoon than you do."

Slim had been through this sort of situation many times

before. Bet or drop. He felt that queasy weariness start to come over him and he wanted to be out on the midway with Cliff, laughing at the suckers and looking at the girls. He took a last look at his hole card, then sighed.

"Okay, Brian. Bring your man into Grove City. I'll show him my mineral rights and get the game set up."

Roy Brian nodded seriously, then stood up and reached out a hand. "Right, pardner. I'd say you and me are on our way to being millionaire proprietors of an oil field." Slim reluctantly shook on it. "I hope old Bill's got a touch of corn to seal the deal," Roy said, and, heading toward Stember's cabinets, rummaged around until he found a quarter-full bottle of bourbon and two glasses. He helped them both to a glass and then, raising his, cheerfully toasted, "Thompson and Brian, millionaires-to-be!"

As they were finishing off their shots and Roy Brian was eyeing the bottle again, Bill Stember pulled open the door of the trailer office and saw Slim and Roy working his bourbon. A delighted look came over his face.

"Yes, sir," Stember crowed, walking over to the bottle and putting it to his lips, "I see my two friends cut themselves a little ol' piece of biniss." He drank deeply. "Just don't nobody forget ol' Bill Stember when the millions flow in. I'd sure like to get out of this business. Some Rube cold-cocked my Razzle-Dazzle man. Looks like Mac was set up by some son-of-a-bitch."

"We won't forget you, Bill," Roy Brian promised.

"If you gentlemen will excuse me I'd like to go out and find my boy."

"You got a son, Slim?" Roy asked.

"Fifteen years old and already a scratch golfer."

"Great to have a kid. Mine's only six. A girl. What's your boy's name?"

"Cliff. Named after his mother's daddy."

"My girl's name is Kathy. Just a name I liked. Well, looks like we'll all be seeing a lot of each other. I'll send you a Western

Union when I can get Bull Larsen into Grove City. I'll send my dealer ahead so he can get the game set."

"I'll be there," Slim replied. "See you later after I find Cliff. He's probably in the flesh show—might need some help from the old man." Stember and Brian laughed, and Slim stepped outside.

Walking through the midway Slim was hailed by an idle carney. "Hey Fred, did you get the free stamp? . . . Come here. Hey, can I see you a minute?"

"Wee-a-zith," Slim snapped back almost absentmindedly, the deal with Brian occupying his mind. He still wasn't happy about getting into the game . . . but what the hell, it would be his last. He started to pass by the girl show and stopped, watching a gaggle of dazed yokels stumble out. Sure enough Cliff was one of the last out of the tent.

"So you had to stay for the last grind, did ya? If your mother ever found out . . ."

"Hi, pal," Cliff replied innocently. "You want to see the show? It's Gee-a-zorge. George all the way."

"They showed it all, huh? Sorry, but we don't have time to wait for the next show." Secretly, he was pleased, though. Before long it would be time to take his son to visit a very special lady he knew in Tulsa. She was just waiting to properly introduce young Cliff to the first step in being a real man. Teach him good, too.

As they drove along the road back to Grove City, Cliff told his father about the poor dumb kid who'd been taken off at the Razzle-Dazzle. "Anyway, I made a dollar, Dad," Cliff finished the story. "And that carney will think twice before he beats another defective kid."

Slim thought about the story for some moments. He wanted to tell his son that if you're "with," you never do anything to start a Hey Rube, but Cliff was happy with the day and Slim didn't want to spoil that. Instead . . .

"So you made yourself a buck, did you?"

"Sure did."

"And you've still got the two I gave you . . . would you like to try for six?"

"Sure."

"Okay. I'll bet you three bucks I can make you say black."

"You're on, Dad."

Slim pointed out the window. "What's the color of that miserable little patch of grass out there?"

Cliff grinned. "Green."

"What color are the clouds up there?"

"White."

"And that hay stacked up where the steers are feeding?"

"Brown."

"And now, *fast,* what are the colors of the American flag? Quick."

"Red, white, and blue," Cliff replied smugly.

Slim laughed. "You blew it son. Three bucks. I told you I'd make you say blue."

"No you didn't, you said black—" and suddenly, sheepishly, Cliff caught himself and looked down at the floor of the car.

"So you blew your three bucks already. Maybe that goes to prove you shouldn't have taken it the way you did."

"Ah, Dad."

But as they drove along talking about the carnival and the Roy Brian deal—Slim didn't mention the mechanic—Cliff quickly regained his spirits. Things were going to be all right.

"Yes, pal," Slim said as he headed back to Grove City, "I think we're finally going to be set for life."

18

2

SLIM THOMPSON WALKED toward the eighteenth green with Cliff and the Bent Creek Club pro, Jack Brady. Cliff's ball lay two on a par four hole just in front of the sand trap on the edge of the fairway.

"Moment of truth, like them Messicans say at the bullfight," Brady observed. "This kid is a wizard with his short irons, Slim. Couple more years when he gets more distance into his drives he'll be ready for the pro circuit."

Cliff slid the bag off his shoulder, took out his niblick and with a neat snick lofted the ball up and over the sand trap and onto the green four feet from the pin.

"Now there's a golf shot," said Brady. His own ball was twenty feet from the pin and being away he putted first; the ball missed the hole by a foot. "Read that break right and you've got me," he told Cliff. Cliff nodded. Feet together, he stood above the ball and with a deliberate tap sent it rolling toward the hole. It plopped in squarely and only then did Cliff look up at his father, a grin on his face.

"He's playing golf like you deal cards, Slim." Brady tapped in for his par. "I spotted him three strokes and he took me. Next time one stroke, after that I'll be looking for him to give me a stroke."

Back at the clubhouse they all had a Coke and Slim agreed to get Brady another deck of readers from Saint Louis Dutch. "But I'm going out of that field as of tomorrow night, Jack," he warned him. "I'm strictly going to be an oilman from now on."

As they drove back into town, Cliff asked, "Aren't you going to miss being on the road, taking off your scores?"

"No, pal. I sure won't. I used to get a kick out of challengin' the wise guys, taking down another hustler, but no more. Tell you the truth I'm tired, always tired. And I guess I'm losing my nerve. Time for me to get into a regular business. You want to walk around my mineral rights?"

"Sure. If I learn the oil business maybe I could help you, even be your partner someday."

"That's what I'm counting on."

Slim pulled up beside the road at the outskirts of the city and they began walking across a dried-up field.

"This is part of the block of mineral leases I call Grove City Two," Slim explained. "It's more than a square mile represented by five separate leases." He waved an arm at the empty fields of dust. "Someday you'll see oil wells pumping all through here. But first we're going to develop Grove City One, the other side of the main highway yonder."

"How'd you decide that, Dad?"

"The geologists figured we wouldn't have to go down so deep to hit. Grove City Block One isn't as big as Two. I bought mineral rights from old Hiram Jenks when he and the family headed for California, then I bought the Bowens and Mrs. Hawkins to assemble the block. Just three leases. Next thing to do is put them together into a single oil and gas lease."

"When are you going to start drilling?"

"Soon. I've had a couple of meetings with Roy Brian and tomorrow he's bringing in Bull Larsen to look at Grove One. Then we're going to play that skin game and win so big Larsen'll have to drill us a well to settle up. Of course we're going to give him an interest in the oil field so he'll come out good in the long run."

"You never taught me skin," Cliff said. "How do you play it?"

"There's no play to it. It's all luck. They put a deck of cards in a box—they call it a shoe—and each player gets a card and they all bet each other that their card stays in the box longer than the other fellows'. All the cards have the same value."

"You mean like you get a five and another guy gets a king, all you have to do is hope your five stays in the shoe longer than his king?"

"That's all there is to it. Luck."

"If it's just luck you got a chance of losing."

Slim smiled. "No. Roy Brian's sending in a mechanic to take care of that. Thing is, pal, nobody loses if Brian and me win."

Surveying this land always gave Slim a lift. Standing here he wasn't just some con artist out hustling a score. He was somebody, this was *his* His happiness communicated itself to Cliff, already delighted that his father wouldn't be traveling anymore, and by the time they reached the car again, they were in high good humor. Slim started for the driver's side and then turned to Cliff. "Hey pal, you want to drive? Won't be long before you'll be up for your driver's license."

Cliff let out a whoop and charged around the car, pulled the door open and slid in behind the wheel. Slim took the seat beside him and pretended not to be watching as Cliff started the car and pulled away from the roadside, but after they'd been driving five minutes Slim leaned back in his seat and relaxed. "Looks like I got me a chauffeur," he murmured. "We'll get you your license right on your sixteenth birthday, about the time the first well hits."

"When does the drilling start?"

"Soon as possible. Yes sir, I'm going to be a homebody like you wouldn't believe."

Sarah Thompson was standing in front of the white frame

house on the edge of town when the car drove up, pleased to see how smoothly Cliff brought the Pontiac to a stop and at how happy her husband and son looked.

"You boys have a nice day?"

"We sure did, Mom," Cliff answered.

"Sarah, you should see Cliff's golf game. He's a champion."

"You'll meet a lot of wonderful people playing golf," Sarah commented.

"Meet 'em, greet 'em and say how-de-do," Slim chortled, taking Sarah's hand and doing a little dance. "Heck, we might as well join Bent Creek. Now that I'm not going to be traveling anymore I might even take up golf myself."

Sarah laughed. "I don't know how you think the likes of you and me are going to join the club."

"We're going to be rich, Sarah. Rolling in filthy lucre just like the Rockefellers, with servants to make our breakfast and sassiety waiting at the door."

"Well, that certainly would be nice, Slim. Now let's go in the house. I don't know what you two been up to. You're both full of it, for sure. Always scares me a little to see people too happy."

"We're going to be rich, Mom."

"Set for life, Sarah."

"Yes, well, I'll be happy to be set for the next week right now," Sarah replied, but she was beaming proudly nonetheless at her two men.

The Grove City Pool Hall was crowded with people who had heard about the big skin game that Slim Thompson had organized for the two out-of-towners, and several of the more adventuresome townsmen had even asked to sit in on the game. Cliff leaned against the doorframe of the back room where he could watch the play.

He saw immediately why the oil driller was called Bull. Larsen was a gigantic man with stringy blond hair and small dark eyes set close together, giving him a piglike look of perma-

22

nent suspicion. Beside the bulky Larsen and the robust, youthful Brian, his father looked frail, and for a moment Cliff had a premonition, a nervous bad feeling in his stomach. The dealer was a tall cadaverous-looking, middle-aged man wearing a black string tie and garters around his upper arms to hold the cuffs of his white shirt back from his wrists. Long, thin fingers ending in manicured, polished nails expertly cut the tax stamp sealing a box of Bicycles, then, spilling the stiff and shiny cards onto the table face up, removed the extra joker. With a practiced movement the imported mechanic accordioned the spread deck and with a loud riffle dispersed and intermingled the four suits and placed the deck on the table. Bull Larsen reached a paw across the table and cut the cards twice. The dealer picked up the pack, placed the joker on the bottom, thunked the edge against the table and placed the deck in a metal box the size of the cards. Now the cards could only be slid off the top of the deck one at a time and there was no possibility of tampering with them.

Cliff knew he was watching an expert and was glad his father, Brian, and the mechanic were partners in this game. Still, he had this bad feeling.

That morning Cliff had accompanied his father, Larsen, and Brian on a tour of Grove City One and Two. Larsen had read the geologists' reports and pronounced the structure very promising, but he wasn't willing to speculate at his own expense. That's how drillers go broke, he'd said. Slim and Brian had seemed to go along.

A drilling agreement had already been prepared, which only required the signatures of the principals and the down payment to become a valid contract, then Larsen had taken Slim's mineral leases down to the Grove City Town Hall and compared them with the property deeds. Each deed on file duly noted that the mineral rights had been sold to Charles Thompson and the serial numbers had been properly recorded. Then Slim said he knew of a little game . . .

The skin game wasn't fun. It was in fact the fastest way to

win and lose money at cards that had ever been devised short of cutting for high card. The idea was that everybody got a card face up and the dealer dealt the rest of the deck one by one, trying to match the exposed cards. The last unmatched card won.

Cliff watched tensely as the first card, a king, was dealt to Bull Larsen, sitting on the dealer's left. Then a local merchant to Larsen's left got a five, placed a cautious single dollar to the left of Larsen's card and was covered. The third card, a six, was dealt to Slim. He quickly placed two dollars to the left of the local's bet with Larsen and two dollars beside the local's card. All bets covered, a fourth card was delivered to another towns-man on Slim's left, who did the same, and finally Roy Brian, with a jack, placed his bets with each of the other four players.

Now the game got serious. The dealer slid a nine off the top of the encased deck. It was a clean card—none of the players held a nine so nobody's card fell. The dealer placed the nine sidewise in front of him and the players dropped another series of bets.

The next card was a king. Larsen cursed as his card fell and the players collected their bets from in front of him. The dealer placed the two kings lengthwise on either side of the clean card and the betting went on.

An hour and a half later they began the third game. The player on Slim's right dropped out of the game after losing a shocking, for him, two hundred dollars.

"Well, now that the ribbon clerks are out let's step up the betting," Brian boomed.

Slim, watching for the sign, caught the nod Brian gave the dealer and prepared for the showdown game. He and Brian had rehearsed the moves that would be made.

Slim watched the dealer, trying to see how he would put a cooler in the card box, stack the deck so that the three cards matching Slim's would be buried at the bottom. The dealer's long fingers shuffled the cards rapidly and offered them for further shuffling and cutting to the other players, and then, just before Roy Brian's man put the cards in the shoe, Slim saw him pass the deck across his lap. Perhaps, for an instant, the cards had been out of sight, he wasn't sure, but the move had been so swift it was impossible for him to see any exchange of decks. He wondered, in fact, if there had been a switch at all. With Larsen sitting right there, how could the mechanic be sitting with a deck of cards in his lap?

The betting went up. As the cards fell, Slim, with a ten, bet a hundred into the merchant's nine and two hundred dollars into Larsen's queen. The local was wiped out when his card fell for the third time. Only Brian, Larsen, and Slim were left in the game.

Roy Brian pressed his bets a thousand dollars into Slim's and Bull's cards. The dealer slid another card from the shoe. Nobody's card fell but since almost all the cash was already on the table, nobody made a bet. The dealer asked permission to deal again. The three gamblers nodded.

The dealer's thumb went to the top card in the shoe and flicked it onto the table. Roy Brian's deuce fell and his bets were distributed into the two mountainous stacks of cash in front of Larsen and Slim. Everything was on the table now. This was the moment Slim and Brian had planned.

Slim looked across the round table at Bull. "What do you want to do, split the pot? Or go on?"

Larsen glared back at him. "I'm going all the way."

"How much you want to press?"

"Make it easy on yourself."

Slim, coldly, "Do you know what you're saying?"

"Try me."

Slim breathed deeply, sat up straighter in his chair and reached into his inside jacket pocket. "Okay, my mineral leases against your drilling contract."

Bull nodded. "Mister, you just made yourself a wager."

It was all Cliff could do to keep himself from yelling to his father not to do it. Slim gave the dealer a hard look. "I need a pen, so does Mr. Larsen."

The dealer stood and passed a pen across the table. Slim took it. Obviously nothing in his lap. Slim began signing the pile of leases one by one and then passed the pen to Larsen, who signed the contract, acknowledging receipt of payment and validating the drilling agreement.

"Write a spudding-in date," Slim rasped. "I want to have it clear when we start drilling."

Bull Larsen shrugged. "Is one week from today soon enough?"

"Write it in." Slim watched the date being added. Then, with the contract covering the pile of leases beside Bull Larsen's card, both men nodded to the dealer.

Roy Brian pushed his chair back from the table.

The dealer, his cheeks appearing even more sunken than before, thumbed a card onto the table. A five. Dead card.

"Card!" Larsen commanded, staring down at his queen. The last king dropped. Slim's ten and Larsen's queen stood.

With no more bets to come the dealer took the remaining cards out of the shoe, placed them face up on the table, and fanned them out. With a rodlike finger he stabbed at a ten close to the top of the deck, then tapped a queen farther down with the forefinger of his left hand.

"The ten falls. The queen's the winner," he announced.

Bull Larsen reached for the mineral leases before raking in the cash. A horrified look on his face, Slim turned to Roy Brian, receiving back a shrug of surprise.

"Guess I got me some mineral rights to drill," the Bull said softly, tucking the leases securely inside his jacket pocket.

As Cliff watched, sick to his stomach, his father placed his hands on the table and pushed himself to a standing position, his veins twitching, his face growing bright red. "You double-crossing son of a bitch," he shouted and with both hands outstretched threw himself across the table at Brian. Suddenly, as his fingers found Brian's throat, he let out a loud squawk, his brain snapped and exploded with the stroke, and his son looked

26

on in terror as his father's eyes protruded, the cords in his neck distended.

"*Dad,* dad, what's wrong—"

The force of Slim Thompson's lunge had carried his body across the table and it collapsed now in a heap, rolling off the table. Cliff caught his father in his arms.

"Dad! What's the matter? Dad, please . . ."

Gently Cliff lowered his father to the floor of the pool hall as Bull Larsen and Roy Brian began to back away. It didn't require a doctor to recognize that Slim Thompson was dead.

Cliff got up to a standing position and looked at Roy Brian. "You did it, Brian. You took off my dad deliberately. You killed him for his minerals sure as if you pulled a gun and shot him."

"No, young man, that's not true." Brian began to talk fast as the locals moved closer. "It was a fair game, someone's gotta win, someone's gotta lose. Slim's a professional. He knows that You can't win them all." And he made a quick exit.

Through his misery and anger Cliff watched him leave and saw the dealer follow, tall and thin, walking in a peculiarly stiff-legged fashion out the back room of the Grove City Pool Hall. Then he turned and forced himself to look at his father. The terrible, pitiful expression on Slim's face as he had made for Roy Brian would be branded forever on Cliff's memory.

After Slim Thompson's small funeral Bill Stember sat in the parlor with Sarah and Cliff. Cliff wasn't sure whether Stember had been in on the conspiracy against his father, but he doubted it. The man wouldn't have dared show his face here.

After sitting and talking for an hour about what a fine man Slim had been and drinking several cups of tea, Stember stood up. "Well ma'am, I'm afraid I'll have to get on my way back to Norman. We're packing up our rigs there, moving on. Slim talked a lot about you. I sure am deeply sorry when we finally met it had to be under these circumstances. 'Deed I am." He turned to Cliff. "Like to walk out to the car with me?"

Cliff nodded. Outside, he said, "We appreciate your coming, Mr. Stember. Not many of Dad's friends did. . . . You know Roy Brian cheated my father and caused his death."

"Yes, son. That's why I wanted to talk to you away from your mother. When I introduced Slim to Roy Brian I honestly thought we were putting together a legitimate oil deal. Wasn't until the other day when Brian and Bull Larsen came to see me I realized what must have happened."

"What was that, Mr. Stember?"

"Roy told me about the game and your father's sudden passing, then he offered me five hundred dollars for making the introduction." Stember caught Cliff's look. "I didn't take it. My deal with your father was for a piece of the oil field. I wasn't taking five bills from Brian for setting him up. I feel real bad I brought them together."

"Well, Dad wasn't exactly ducking the meeting," Cliff said.

"There was a time Roy Brian and I were good friends, partners in some things. I never knew how much he changed. He's got greedy, thieving greedy, and that can ruin the best. I know, I've seen it happen." The carnival owner spread his hands. "What are you and your mom going to do? I don't suppose Slim had anything left after the game?"

"A gold watch he won in a game five years ago. The house is paid up, at least Mom made him see to that." Cliff shook his head. "I can't understand how my father got taken by Roy Brian. I just can't figure out how they did it."

"I wouldn't know, son. I'm not much of a card man." He put a hand on Cliff's shoulder. "Look Cliff, any way I can help you or your mother you let me know, hear? You need a job, I'll always have something for you. You can always find where my carnival is in *Billboard.*"

"Thanks, Mr. Stember. But don't worry about us, we'll make out. Only one person better worry." Cliff's face hardened.

Stember worked his bulk behind the wheel and started the engine, then giving a wave, pulled out of the driveway. Cliff

28

watched him drive away, turned and went back into the house.

His mother was in the kitchen as he climbed the stairs to the second floor and then the next flight up to the attic. He pulled a stool up to the black leather valise his father had always carried on his hustling tours and sat staring at the bag for a while.

Then he opened the valise and pulled out a deck of readers from the Dutchman in East Saint Louis. He went through the deck, backs up, reading each card and turning it over for confirmation, then reached for the skin shoe and studied it. Maybe if this shoe had been used in the game it might have turned out differently, he thought, testing the spring that pushed the cards against the frame at the top of the silver-plated metal box.

Turning his attention to the dice stick with the hollowed-out handle, he scooped a pair of missouts from a tray and, holding them in the same hand with the stick handle, he alternately hid them in the recess and brought them out for play.

"Cliff!" Sarah's voice startled him into dropping the dice in mid-move. Looking round, he saw his mother's weathered face, the severe lines around her lips, and the sad eyes focused on the valise, symbol of that part of her dead husband's life she hated. She climbed the remaining steps to the attic.

"Why are you up here alone?"

"Thinking, Mom."

"Cliff, I don't want you ever again to touch that bag. It's evil. It drove your father to his grave."

"It wasn't the stuff in this bag that killed him. It was Roy Brian."

"Cliff . . . please, listen to me. I know what you're thinking. But your father lived by that bag, and he died by it too. He made his choice. I just don't . . . you don't have to follow him. I'll find a job. I want you to concentrate on your studies, on *making* something of yourself. I want to be proud of you. Your father's gone now, and we have to start new. Let's begin by throwing out that bag, right now—"

"No, Mom, it was his, I want it. It's all I have left to remember him by . . ." He saw the look on her face. "I don't want to be a hustler, Mom. I just want Dad's bag. It *means* something to me." He stood up. "Honest, Mom, you *will* be proud of me."

Sarah looked into her son's eyes and saw a determination there, a strength she could not remember finding in her husband. This boy suddenly seemed so strange to her, so strange . . . her eyes filled with tears and she could feel Cliff putting his arms around her and holding her tight.

Like a man.

3

THE CHAOTIC SCENE at the Fort Bragg Induction Center that cold February of 1943 was pretty much what Cliff Thompson had expected. Permanent Party personnel were everywhere, making themselves feel important by shouting at the recruits who paraded past in bewildered confusion on their way to becoming part of the United States Army.

But Cliff was anything but bewildered. Coolly taking in the scene in the long supply warehouse, he carried his six feet with an air of confidence that belied the fact that he was as new to the army as any of the inductees around him. As his eyes settled on the soldiers slapping equipment at the timid recruits and then scrutinized the noncoms hovering in the background, he heard a voice shout: "Hey you! Yeah *you.*"

Cliff turned his gaze on the round-faced youth on the other side of the long table piled with equipment. "What's your problem, soldier?"

"My problem? Wake up, dummy. You're holding up the line. Get your ass moving or you'll spend your first day in the army in the guardhouse."

Cliff stared at the soldier for two beats but said nothing.

31

Then, indicating the recruit in front of him struggling with an armful of equipment, he said, "No hurry, let the guy get his gear together—"

"Move out," the soldier yelled and pointed to the upper sleeve of his khaki shirt. "This stripe says that's an order!"

The recruit ahead had finally organized his load and shuffled forward, so with a grin, Cliff moved on to receive his duffel bag, shelter half, and helmet liner. From the corner of his eye, he noticed a corporal watching him.

At the next station another processer was asking the recruit what size he wore. Dazed, the slight young man said he wore a size 36 suit with a 28 waist. A uniform was pitched at him. He put down his load to examine the pants and jacket.

"They're too big. They'll fall offa me—"

"Move on!" the noncom called out sharply. Then turning to Cliff, "Next. What's your size?"

"I have my clothes made," Cliff said. "I don't know." The corporal who had been following Cliff's progress down the line was joined by a buck sergeant, a sandy-haired older man Cliff judged to be in his mid-thirties. The two noncoms watched as a set of uniforms was tossed across the table. Cliff set his equipment down and picked up the uniforms, inspecting them. "I can't wear this."

The sergeant nudged the corporal, who walked up to Cliff. "Problem, soldier?"

"Not if you can get me to a good tailor."

"At twenty-one dollars a month it's going to take you a long time to save the price of a tailor-made job."

"I can handle it."

The corporal caught a nod from the sergeant and leaned across the table. "Tell you what, I'll meet you at the end of the line and give you a card to the best tailor on the post."

"I'd appreciate that, corporal," Cliff replied.

Half an hour later as he walked out of the supply warehouse, a heavy duffel bag balanced on one shoulder and his black valise in the other hand, Cliff found the corporal waiting for him. He handed Cliff a card. "You give this to Mr. Sills. If you got the money he'll make you look like a general. Just say Corporal Jenkins sent you."

"Sure. How much of a cut do you get for steering me?"

Corporal Jenkins grinned. "If you don't got the money, don't go."

"I got the money."

"You know"—Jenkins' tone became confidential—"you seem like a man who appreciates the better things in life. Do you also maybe enjoy a little sport?"

"What kind of sport?"

"Ever shoot craps?"

"Some, when I was in college."

"Well, if you feel like a friendly soldiers' game I could put you into one."

Cliff replied innocently, "I guess it might help me fill up evenings until basic is over here and I go to OCS."

"You're already set for officer training, are you?"

"I'm a lawyer. Had three months in the Raleigh D.A.'s office after North Carolina Law School before the army called their marker on me."

"Oh, well, I was wondering how a guy your age had kept out so long. What are you? Twenty-five?"

Cliff nodded. "Good guess."

And a long ten years it had been since his father died back in Grove City. Slim hadn't left Cliff and his mother any money, but what he did leave was more valuable than money. As a teenager Cliff had been in great demand among golf hustlers in the Southwest for "father and son" tournaments and it was the money he earned hustling that put him through college and law school and supported his mother in reasonable comfort. His mother disapproved of the money he gave her, knowing how it was earned, but Cliff had promised her faithfully that when he graduated from law school and started earning a living as a lawyer he would never hustle again. And he never had.

33

Of course now things were different. He had been drafted into the army even though he was his mother's sole support. It was his firm conviction that the promise not to hustle anymore did not hold under these circumstances. Besides, he had to admit it—the straight life was boring. . . .

"Okay, Thompson. I read all about you on the forms while you were processing. You're a lucky guy. Sergeant Pete White told me to invite you into his game tonight."

Jenkins turned and pointed back at the supply warehouse. "Tonight and every night in the quartermaster's shed over there behind the warehouse. A little friendly craps."

"Tell Sergeant White I accept."

As Jenkins watched Cliff walk off to the barracks, Sergeant White appeared at his side.

"There goes some kind of a wise guy," White said. "So he wants to know your cut from Sills. And he talks about the army calling markers."

"He's a live one, Pete."

"How many of those cards did you get out?"

"About six."

"So we found us six we know have green in their pockets. I spotted a few others. But that last one, don't lose him when you pick up their bags for shipment. And, Jenkins . . . keep your eyes open around him. He's no ordinary mark."

4

FOR A MOMENT, amidst the crap shooters' love talk to the tumbling dice in the dimly lit supply shed, Cliff felt a twinge of nightmare as he saw once again his father's face staring at him from the grimy floor of the poolroom. . . . Then he determinedly shut it out and stepped into the cone of light made from the shaded light bulb hanging from the ceiling.

A pleasant-looking sergeant, his sandy hair combed straight back from a high forehead, looked up and signaled him over.

"New shooter coming up," Sergeant White called out. "The dice are hot tonight. Don't know if we're going to be able to bank this action much longer. Take it or lay it, we'll pay it. It can't go on all night like this, I guarantee you."

Cliff grinned at the hoary spiel and for a moment was back in Grove City, Oklahoma. Again, the vision of his father came, and went.

"How've they been, gentlemen?" Cliff asked.

"Cold as a hooker's heart . . ."

"Yeah, the sergeant's full of shit, no mother's son here can hit . . ."

"Well, maybe we can warm things up some," Cliff said, as

his practiced fingers held first one die and then the other by opposite points. "The dice have to come to the shooter some time."

As far as he could tell, the dice didn't seem to be loaded. Cliff knelt down to the Indian game, craps rolled on a G.I. blanket stretched out on the floor, the far end tucked under a footlocker.

No way a man could control dice bouncing them against the locker. He shook the cubes and cast them onto the blanket, watching them bounce against the wood and roll back toward him. Five and three. Eight and six were easy points. Only three-to-two odds against the shooter. The G.I. who worked the game with Sergeant White scooped up the dice and threw them back to Cliff.

"Hard eight?" the sergeant called, ready to cover all bets from the thick roll of green in his right hand.

A discouraged-looking G.I. threw ten dollars onto the blanket. "Shee-et, might as well get rid of it all now as later."

The sergeant covered it with forty dollars although the odds were actually ten to one on a hard eight—double fours—coming up before a seven, and Cliff rolled the dice again as the G.I.s betting with him chanted, "Eighter from Decatur."

"Twin fours," the hard-way bettor implored. Cliff tried to put a little spin on the dice, but the bounce destroyed it, and he threw a six, followed by a nine, then another six and finally made his point. Hard Way sighed dejectedly at the six and two. The sergeant picked up and paid off and Cliff let his money stay.

Now he had twenty dollars on the blanket. His next roll came up seven. Forty dollars. He began to feel more relaxed. After all, this was no bust-out joint, just an army crap game.

Cliff dragged twenty bucks and rolled. Another pass. The men began getting excited and as Corporal Jenkins, acting as the sergeant's receiver, picked up the dice and rolled them back to Cliff, they began riding with the hot shooter, throwing hundreds of dollars onto the blanket. The sergeant regarded the play warily. Cliff rolled . . . a six. Roar of approval. Easy point.

The side action picked up dramatically as Sergeant White started taking hard-way bets, and then Cliff reached for the dice again, shook them and let them go . . . a four and a three. Losing seven. As the sergeant's man picked up the dice for the next shooter, Pete White gathered up the money, adding the bills to the roll in his hand and Cliff moved around to make room for a new shooter.

For the next two hours Cliff lost himself in the G.I. crap game. The bitterness that had come into his life when his father died, the worry about his mother, even the anger and hunger for revenge against the man who had hustled his father into the grave was forgotten in the clicking of the dice and the age-old prayers and imprecations of gamblers being taken off.

As it came Cliff's turn to roll again, White announced that ten minutes remained until the new G.I.s had to be back in their bunks for eleven P.M. bed check. With mutters of "chicken-shit army," the size of the bets suddenly increased and Cliff, who was perhaps twenty dollars behind, laid a twenty-dollar bill in front of him, picked up the dice and rolled them across the blanket. Seven. With forty dollars piled in front of him now and the players shouting encouragement, he rolled again and came up eleven. The G.I.s couldn't get their money down fast enough. Cliff bet the eighty, shook the dice . . . five.

"Fever, little fever," Cliff intoned. Three times he rolled the dice, three times they escaped seven, and on the fourth roll he hit a four and one.

Sergeant White added eighty dollars to Cliff's pile and, hawk-eyed, watched the receiver throw the dice back. Cliff kissed the dice and, shaking them, could almost feel the cubes giving off heat. Next pass—seven. The crap shooters yelled their approval as White paid off. In the last few minutes of the game the bettors had drawn at least even with the house, perhaps ahead. With three hundred and twenty dollars in front of Cliff, there may have been as much as twenty-five hundred dollars around the blanket as every player waited for Cliff's next roll.

Cliff pretended not to watch Corporal Jenkins' hands as, with a clumsy move, they picked up the dice and rolled them back. This guy would never last in a back-alley game, Cliff thought. He looked around the blanket at the sweating, red-faced inductees, country boys all. These shit-kickers didn't stand a chance.

Picking up the dice and, clicking them together, he watched as the stump-jumpers let their winnings ride on Cliff's next roll, and out of the corner of his eye saw Sergeant White staring at him closely. Casually mindful of everyone's gaze, he reached down and fingered the pile of money in front of him for a moment, then pulled two hundred and twenty dollars from his stakes. He continued shaking the dice and the shouts grew impatient—"Shoot 'em," "Roll 'em"—and finally Cliff shrugged and let the dice go hard down the blanket. They bounced back and from the sound of the groans, he didn't have to look to know they'd come up snake eyes. He'd crapped out. Quickly, Jenkins started picking up the money.

Cliff knelt, staring directly at White, who began a nervous patter. "All right guys, this is it. One more shooter and the game's over. I don't want to be responsible for any man here missing bed check and getting K.P. for a week. Tomorrow's another game."

The house had beat the players for at least a couple of thousand dollars that night, Cliff thought. After another seven or eight minutes of desultory shooting, Sergeant White closed the game and sent the players on their way, but Cliff hung back until all the other players, muttering about their bad luck, had gone. Finally he was alone with White and Jenkins.

"You better get going, soldier. You miss bed check they'll put four more days of K.P. onto your regular duty, you know."

Cliff ignored him. "What do you think I am, *Sergeant?* One of those red-necked shit-kickers? If you want to throw tops in the game you better get a mechanic better than stump-jumper here—" Cliff jabbed a thumb into the receiver's chest.

White spread his hands. "When you gamble someone's got to lose. You lost your money trying to win mine. Everyone who loses thinks they've been cheated—"

"Bull. You threw in tops. Supposing I'd told those yokels what you've been doing to them every night. I could have started a real Hey Rube here. That bunch of hillbillies would have lynched you on the spot."

White started to answer but closed his mouth. Cliff went on, "Now I showed some class. I waited until after your play to tell you you cheated me. When I saw Jenkins make his move I could have dragged everything and passed the roll. Then the guys would really have got the message. Now why don't you show some class too and give me back my money?"

"You didn't lose any money, you won tonight—"

"I want the hundred dollars back that I rode with. Let me tell you, when I was in knee breeches I was rolling tops better than this sad ass of yours."

Realizing he was beaten, White started to peel twenty-dollar bills from his thick stack. "Where you from, Thompson?"

"Grove City, Oklahoma. Now give me my money."

White handed Cliff five twenties. "How'd you learn craps? Taking off rig monkeys?" White laughed. "Look, kid, you're okay . . . I know class when I see it. . . . Come on over to the main NCO Club on Reilly Street about five tomorrow. I'll buy you a beer and we'll talk some. Okay?"

"Sure. Nothing better to do."

"Okay, see you then. I might be able to use you . . . help you, I mean. . . ."

5

THE TEN DOLLARS extra Cliff handed Mr. Sills produced fast results. At five o'clock the next day, Cliff arrived at the NCO Club in a tailored uniform and found Pete White waiting for him at the door. They picked up two beers and made their way to a table.

"You know, a thought came to me last night after you left," White began.

"Yeah?"

"Yeah. I've heard about Grove City."

"We pump a lot of oil there."

"It was something else. George the Greek from my hometown, New Orleans, wound up with some phony mineral rights that a guy dumped on him—"

"What? What was the name of this guy?"

"Let's see . . . Bruce . . . Brian . . . yeah, Brian, I think it was. Why? You know him?" Pete asked.

"No, no. Go on."

Pete gave him a quizzical look and continued. "The way I heard it, seems this Brian clipped some yokel from Grove City out of his mineral rights, then put the Greek in the deal. But

40

the rights weren't worth shit and the Greek got taken for a bundle."

"What do you mean?" Cliff's smile was grim. "Those rights were worth plenty . . . and the yokel from Grove City happened to be my father. The old man had a stroke right after and died."

"Yeah? Your dad? Small world." White took a long swallow of beer. "He got a tough break."

"Yeah, you might say . . . a great guy, and he taught me everything he knew. And I've learned a little since then."

White whistled. "Well, I never thought I'd get a guy like you in one of these shit-kicker crap games. I been in the army almost two years and you're the first pro I've come across."

Cliff shrugged.

"So, here you are, what are you going to do now?" Pete asked. "Me, I really found a home in the army. I thought it was the end of the world when I was drafted. Thirty-three! What was I going to do? Then I realized in the army I was safe from the Turk and a few others I owed money to—they were out to break my legs—and now I'm making more money than I did outside." He laughed. "If the war just lasts ten years, I'll be able to retire. Three squares a day, thousands of marks, a good score every night, what more could you want?"

"Those G.I.s over in Italy probably wouldn't agree with you," Cliff commented.

"Ah, come on, you know I don't mean the fighting." Abruptly, White changed the conversation. "You've got a lot of class, Cliff. Just like I heard your father did." He leaned across the table. "Would you like to put in with me, kid? We could take off some big scores together."

Cliff took a pull on his beer. "It took me seven years to work my way through college and law school. I'm heading for OCS and a slot as an army lawyer. Then I'll take care of Mr. Roy Brian. All nice and legal."

"Look, if you need someone to play the outside, I could be a big help to you," Pete said. "I've learned a lot about the Army—"

41

"Then how come you're only a buck sergeant?"

"Hey, that's the best rank there is—not too much responsibility, I'm Permanent Party here at Bragg, with plenty of free time. I take care of the right people and they let me run my game. If I need it they give me protection. It's cheaper than the ice, the police protection, I paid for in civilian life and I'm making more. . . . We could have a lot of good action, Cliff. And you got to cut your teeth pretty sharp if you think you're going to build a paddle big enough for Roy Brian's ass. You need a lot more practical experience even though you did nail me rolling tops into the game. That's just small stuff. You get me transferred to wherever you're sent as an officer and we could do real well for each other."

Cliff thought about the proposition.

"I've checked your records, Cliff," White said. "You're being assigned to limited basic training because you're going direct to OCS, but after basic you'll wait around Fort Bragg, could be a couple, three months to be assigned a class at OCS."

"That long?"

"They wait until they get enough for a complete class before sending you down to Benning. What I'm saying is . . . right after basic I can get you assigned to Supply on permanent detail until you're transferred."

"Sounds tolerable to me."

And Sergeant Pete White was good as his word.

"First thing we're going to do," Pete said when Cliff reported for duty seven weeks later, "I'm going to give you a little tour of Fort Bragg in my car. A friend of mine, Joe Lipwitz, is in a Signal Corps outfit," Pete smiled. "Couldn't have picked a better assignment. Joe was a great wire man before the army got him. He could signal a player's hand faster than a hooker blows a fifty-cent john. We've got a hustle almost ready to work. You interested?"

"Lead the way . . ."

. . . two days later, it was after supper, about six-thirty, but the mid-September light was still strong. A group of twenty or thirty G.I.s, their pockets full of paratroopers' pay, were waiting in front of the Airborne Supply headquarters for darkness to fall and their crap game to start. Across the company street stood the loft where the parachutes were hung after a drop to be re-rigged and folded for the next jump.

As the paratroopers waited, they stared up at the flat roof of the hangar where the usual covey of pigeons perched, cooing and clucking, staring back down at the G.I.s. There was some talk of getting a .22 rifle to see how many pigeons they could pick off before the birds flew out of range.

Into their midst drove Pete White in his 1940 Ford. As he stepped out of the car an Airborne sergeant called out to him, "What's the matter, White . . . the action so slow with you straight-leg ground-pounders you got to come to our Airborne crap game? You want to see some real shooting, huh?"

But Pete was staring up at the pigeons, ignoring the sergeant. "Them fuckin' birds," he muttered loudly. "They get bird shit all over my car. You know, coming over here two of them missed my car by about an inch. I damn near had two of 'em splattered all over my windshield. Ought to be some way to get them fuckers off the post altogether."

Cliff, who had been milling around with the others, put in with, "Ah, Sergeant, you're full of bird shit yourself. Those pigeons wouldn't come near a hundred yards of you or your car."

"Like hell they wouldn't. I tell you I goddamned near hit two of them," Pete shouted. "Them fuckers is a menace to this post."

Another soldier disagreed, and within moments everyone was arguing about how close pigeons would come to a human being. As the talk heated up a corporal from the Signal Corps took Pete's side. "Sure them birds will get near people," he said. "I've seen them birds land on a man's shoulder sometimes—"

A chorus of hoots met Joe Lipwitz's statement, and in a minute Joe was heatedly insisting that if he wanted to he could get one of those pigeons in his hand in five minutes.

Pete raised his voice. "You're going to get a pigeon in your hand in five minutes?" He looked over at the hangar. "What are you going to do? Climb up a ladder and grab one?"

Cliff took it up. "No way you gonna get one of them birds in your hand in five minutes 'less you shoot him and pick up the body." More hoots from the paratroopers followed.

"No, goddamn it, I tell you I can have a pigeon alive, one of those pigeons right up there, in my hand in five minutes"—his face reddening, he pulled out a thick wad of bills—"and this here bankroll says I can. Now put up or shut up!"

"I'll take the sucker's money," Pete yelled, and pulled out a twenty-dollar bill.

"I'll take twenty of that too" Cliff said, and in moments there was a stampede of G.I.s waving their money as the pigeons made mocking noises from above.

"I'll hold the stakes," Pete said. "We'll all get a piece of the sucker's money. Put your money down here on the company street in front of him. I'll make sure he covers every bet." Within two minutes there were neat little piles of five- and ten-dollar bills on the edge of the street, each one covered by Joe Lipwitz as Pete stood over the stakes watching them.

When all the bets were covered Pete suddenly shouted, "My God, I'm going to get a little bit more down on this. This is too good to miss," and threw another twenty dollars on the street. Before that flurry was over, almost a thousand dollars more had been shaken out of the paratroopers.

"That poor son-of-a-bitch isn't going to be playing any craps for a long time," one of them said as Joe continued to cover all bets with his thinning bankroll. Cliff estimated there was now at least fifteen hundred dollars riding on Joe's ability to get a bird in hand. And not so to speak.

Satisfied that he had shaken all bets possible out of the crowd, Joe walked toward the hangar across the street, taking his time. "Ten seconds down," a soldier called out. Moving up close to the hangar, Joe let his eyes wander up to the roof, then let out a strange series of warbling whistles, and suddenly one of the birds on the roof flew up into the air and descended, landing, incredibly, on Joe's right shoulder. Gently, Joe reached up, took the bird in both of his hands and petted him. As the dumbfounded men watched, Pete scooped up all the money on the company street into a heavy sheaf of bills, and, holding it in both hands, walked over to Joe.

"Okay, Corporal. You win. Take it, it's yours. Us wise guys lose." Pete handed the money to Joe, who took it, stuffing it into his shirt. A mutter could be heard from an Airborne sergeant, "I'll be a go to hell son-of-a-bitch . . . how could that happen—?"

Abruptly Pete did a double take. "Hell, I'll tell you how it happened. Look, he's wearing a Signal Corps patch, those guys work with birds all day—"

An angry growl went up and Pete turned on the corporal. "Okay, so you beat us fair and square, but it was still a trick. Take your dough and get the hell out of here and don't ever let me see you getting into any of my games."

Some of the heavier losers began moving menacingly at Lipwitz, but Pete diverted them with, "Any of you guys see him around again, you'll know what to do. So he beat us this time. He'll never pull another scam on us. Right?"

While the troopers muttered agreement, Joe was already in his car, parked behind the hangar, and heading back to Signal Corps H.Q.

Later Pete said to Cliff, "First thing I learned as a punk hustler in New Orleans, always notice something different or unusual that you can put to your advantage. You never know when it will come in handy. Like Joe Lipwitz, and his trained pigeons."

He allowed himself a smile.

6

As the weeks went by, Cliff and Pete became a formidable team.

Cliff had learned to deal three-card monte at the age of nine and could slide the three queens around the tabletop with the dexterity of an old carney.

"Three whores stranded in Shanghai," Cliff chanted as he flipped the queens face down across the tabletop. "One's a brunette, the other two redheads, just show me which is the brunette. Just tap her on the back for me."

In back rooms and barracks around the post, Cliff and Pete put on their act, but they especially liked the Airborne area. That extra fifty a month jump pay seemed to make impetuous bettors of the paratroopers.

At first Cliff's clumsy moves allowed the troopers to follow the "black lady" and turn it up whenever they wanted, but when they actually started betting there was no way they could follow him. After losing several times, they realized the futility in trying to watch Cliff's hand, and just took a chance on betting one of the three cards. Once a three-card monte game became hot, Pete would play the outside to Cliff, come in, win a few, lose a few . . . and at this point the G.I.s with larceny in their hearts were in real trouble.

It was damn near a set piece: Cliff allowed his attention to be diverted—"Hey there, soldier, your fly's open, the bird's going to fly out of its nest," Pete laughed, and indeed Cliff's fly was open and Cliff, chagrined, looked down and buttoned up. As he did so, Pete reached over and made a tiny crimp in the corner of the black queen, winking broadly at the other players. When Cliff straightened up again he started his spiel, shuffling the cards. "Three whores ready to be taken. Who wants the brunette? Who thinks they know where the little black one is?"

Pete threw a ten-dollar bill on the table. "I say the middle card."

The soldiers closest to the table could see the slight crimp in the corner of the card and threw down their money, and when Cliff turned the middle card over, sure enough it was the black queen.

"Well whatcha know? Someone here's got sharp eyes." Cliff paid off and started shuffling and spieling again. "Three little ladies here give up whoring, want themselves a husband. They'll take any man who can make an honest living. In fact the little brunette there will take a man who can make any kind of living. She don't care whether he's a pimp, bank robber, or even if he's Airborne." Appreciative laughter from the winners. "Find the little brunette, find the little brunette."

Once again they studied the cards and when Pete threw another ten-dollar bill on the table, several others did the same. "Okay, the black queen is on the right," he said, stabbing his finger down onto the card, and sure enough he was right again.

Cliff appeared to be flustered. "We got a man with *real* sharp eyes here, must have been a three-card monte dealer himself somewhere." Cliff looked up at Pete. "You a carney boy, by chance?"

"No, not me. . . . Like you said, I've just got sharp eyes."

Cliff looked around the group as though asking them to bear witness to his misfortune. "I don't know where this sergeant came from. Guess I'll have to move the old cards a little faster. . . . Can't lose all my money or I won't be able to get into the crap game . . ."

By now the word had spread and the paratroopers, eager to take advantage of the amateur, were crowding around, showering their money on the table. When the bets were all in—about six hundred dollars—Cliff picked up the three cards and, caressing them, moved them face-side down around the table, throwing one in the middle, two on each side. Finally he let the cards lie still. "All right, gentlemen, is the black queen going to hide from you devils or is someone going to find her and have his *way* with her?"

A master sergeant pushed himself through the crowd and threw a fifty-dollar bill on the table. "Can you cover my action?"

"We cover them all or we cover our face in shame," Cliff replied, throwing a fifty on top of the sergeant's. The paratroopers, meanwhile, were staring down at the backs of the three queens, craning to spot the crimp.

"All right, who's going to pick the black lady?"

The soldiers looked at Pete. Pete winked back at them and a sergeant who had been standing up close all during the game reached down, put his finger on the card with the tiny crimp and turned it over. It was red.

A burst of angry shouts went up as Cliff scooped up the money, and the sergeant who had turned over the card whirled on Cliff. "You bastard, you *cheated* us—"

Cliff shook his head. "Hell, no, I didn't cheat you, but you sure as hell tried to cheat me! . . . You marked the black queen when I wasn't looking. After I lost a few I noticed where you made the little crease with a fingernail. So what did I do? I straightened it out with my thumbnail and put another one in the red queen. Okay? So the cheaters got taken. What you got to say to that?"

The sergeant began looking around. "Yeah, well, none of *us* crimped the card. Where's that buck sergeant?" But of course

48

by now Pete had wisely faded from the scene.

Cliff tucked the money in his pockets. "Okay men, I hope you learned a lesson. You built the paddle for your own asses—as the man says, 'You can't cheat an honest man. . . .'" And the reverse was even truer, Cliff knew. The dedicated hustler, the scam artist who thought he knew all the angles could be the biggest mark of all. The wise guys were often their own best customers . . . a piece of wisdom Cliff was counting on to help him when the day finally came for him to put his big paddle to Roy Brian's murdering ass.

7

NOT LONG AFTER, Cliff received orders to report to Officer Candidate School in Fort Benning, Georgia, and ninety days later, Cliff Thompson became an officer and a gentleman, assigned, as he had hoped, to the judge advocate general's office. Which was how he happened to find himself, after a period of training in Washington, D.C., at Fort Devens, Massachusetts, in the fall of 1943.

Fort Devens took immediately to Cliff. Warmly welcomed by Brigadier General Paulus Lymanner himself, the reserve commander of the judge advocate general's office and a well-connected Boston lawyer in civilian life, Cliff was immediately put to work as a defense counsel at courts-martial, working to get G.I. malefactors spared the stockade or Leavenworth. There was one small hitch, however. General Lymanner's efficiency and that of his immediate subordinate Colonel Elliott Stein, the chief prosecutor, was based upon the number of convictions they secured. When Cliff lost a case, which was most of the time, both Lymanner and Stein clapped him on the back, and with great joviality wished him better luck next time . . . but on the few occasions when the defendant was so patently inno-

50

cent that even the court-martial board could not bring itself to convict, their hostility fairly glowed. A conundrum for sure.

The easy thing for Cliff would have been to relax, play golf —which these military gentlemen so favored—and not take the trouble to prepare the cases he was asked to defend . . . but Cliff discovered something about himself. Some games he couldn't play, not these *gentlemen's* games, even if the army said he was now one of them. So he worked hard to win every case that came to him—and while he was at it combed the post law library for texts on petroleum and mineral rights.

Because Cliff Thompson *never* lost track of his main course in life, which was to destroy Roy Brian.

As Pete White had said back at Fort Bragg when Cliff got his orders to report to Fort Benning for OCS, Cliff could have stuck the whole army out at the supply room, could have gotten Permanent Party and the two of them could have hustled until the end of the war. But Cliff had told Pete his one goal in life was to get Roy Brian, and, "I'm not going to do that spending the war hustling. I intend to come out of this army a respected judge advocate general officer, able to go anywhere in the whole country with some clout behind me. Which I'm for sure going to need to build my paddle for old Roy. . . ."

Now he was at least on his way, but it was on the golf course that Cliff started to build his clout. General Lymanner, it turned out, was an excellent golfer, as was the post commander, Lieutenant General Arnold Johnson of Houston, Texas. Cliff let it drop one day that he was known to play, and from that point on, they included him in their foursomes—Cliff taking care not to beat the generals except on rare occasions. He declared his own handicap at ten (theirs was eight) and was very careful to play to it, developing a slice or hook on a moment's notice if needed.

When Cliff had developed sufficient influence with Johnson and Lymanner, he used it to have Pete White transferred from Fort Bragg up to Devens, and shortly after his arrival Sergeant White was promoted to Staff Sergeant White, assigned as supply sergeant in the new recruit's area, where he happily settled in as the proprietor of Fort Devens' most lucrative permanent supply room crap games. Soon he added another stripe and then a third, and by the time Pete had been at Fort Devens for a year he'd become a master sergeant, supervising all gambling action throughout the post. He was well aware that he owed this good fortune to Cliff and the tacit understanding was that when the war was over the two of them would team up going after Roy Brian and Pete would split his take down the middle.

Meanwhile, though, Cliff was finding it increasingly difficult to present a cheerful face to Colonel Stein and Brigadier General Lymanner—every time an innocent, or at least not seriously guilty, soldier was sent to the stockade Cliff resented it and was upset. There was no such thing as military justice, he quickly learned, just military expediency. Still, by holding his counsel and cheerfully losing on the golf course, his influence increased and he soon became a captain. And then a major— by late 1944, Cliff had become such a good defense counsel Lymanner transferred him to prosecution and found a new lieutenant to handle defense. Cliff found he preferred trying to prove a man innocent than guilty, but he went along. It was actually corporate law that interested him most now. Corporate law that would be a weapon in his pursuit of Roy Brian.

It was in early '45 that he received word that his mother was in the hospital and not expected to live. All his leaves and furloughs had been spent with her in Grove City and now he got an emergency leave to be by her side. After a torturous trip on military-clogged transport, he finally reached Sarah Thompson's side a few hours before her death.

After he'd arranged a simple funeral he still had a week of his leave left, so he introduced himself to several geological-survey companies in Oklahoma City, Tulsa, and the Grove City area, finally hiring the best of them to make a complete survey of Block II of the Grove City field, where his father had accumulated the leasehold for oil development that Roy Brian had skinned him out of.

52

The next stop was the Grove City Courthouse. Cliff had been a constant visitor there since he was old enough to understand the legalities of mineral rights and knew that a landholder could sell his mineral rights to a developer and the sale would be duly recorded on the deed. If the owner of the rights sold them to someone else, the transfer would be noted too.

Cliff had seen the five deeds to Grove City Block II reflect first Roy Brian's name, and his address—Delray Beach in the Miami area—then, one by one, while he was in college, the names of others. At first it had puzzled him but then he learned that Roy Brian's oil development company, after making a fortune on Block I, had sunk several dry holes and had given up on Block II, and so they had been sold. Before returning to Fort Devens, Cliff again checked the names on the deeds. Five names. Five sets of mineral rights. And one of them was George the Greek's. At the appropriate time Pete White would be very helpful.

With his mother dead and buried, Cliff felt himself completely released from the promise not to avenge his father's death. More than ever he was determined to go after the man who had betrayed Slim Thompson, and caused his death.

By spring of 1945 it was obvious that the war in Europe could not last much longer and when Germany fell in April and Japan started looking shaky, Cliff and Pete began thinking seriously of the future. Then V-J Day arrived, and by early fall the army began giving out discharges.

As the troops returned from Europe, their wallets swollen with overseas pay, combat pay, jump pay and flying pay, Pete's crap games reached near-epic proportions. Since Master Sergeant Pete White was also a reasonably efficient supply sergeant, the overtaxed Fort Devens administration was only too happy to allow him to stay on and reap his profits. Cliff elected to stick around too for a little while longer—but with a different target.

All through the war, the golfing zeal of General Lymanner and his associates had not abated. With the first snowfall in early December, they were still playing, using red golf balls which could be easily found in the snow. The stakes were as high as ever and in a few weeks all handicaps would be canceled. The time had come, Cliff decided, to hustle Lymanner, post commander Johnson, and Stein out of everything he'd let them win from him—plus overage.

On a Thursday afternoon in December with relatively mild temperatures of forty-eight degrees predicted, General Lymanner suggested to Cliff that they play their final game of golf before giving in to the rigors of winter.

"With no handicaps I guess I'll just have to play over my head, sir," Cliff replied, grinning ruefully.

"Winter hazards make everybody about equal, major," Lymanner replied breezily. "So, since this is our last game why don't we play the Boca Raton Special?"

"Sir?"

"It's named after the Boca Raton Club in Florida, where it was invented. We play a foursome, each man for himself, ten dollars a hole and ten dollars a stroke. What that means is, on each hole the winner gets paid ten dollars by each of the three losers. Runner-up on the hole is paid ten dollars by each of the two men who scored below him and the third man down is paid ten dollars by the fourth man."

"It sure doesn't pay to be fourth man, does it?"

"Well, as I said, with winter rules we're all reduced to about the same circumstances, major."

"I expect you're right, sir. Like I said, I guess I'll have to play over my head. What about the ten dollars a stroke?"

"That means at the end of the game the winner takes ten dollars for each stroke he's ahead of each of the other three players. In other words, if you beat me by two strokes I owe you twenty dollars. If you beat General Johnson by four strokes, he owes you forty dollars, and if you beat Colonel Stein by six strokes, he owes you sixty dollars. This is on top of the ten dollars a hole for each winner. You get it?"

"Yes, sir. You gentlemen are out for my blood, which those stakes are too rich for."

General Lymanner smiled. "Well, Major, we could never win the kind of money from you that Sergeant White has hustled since he's been here. You got him transferred to this post, as I recall. Let him bank your game. . . . Are you ready to play tomorrow?"

"Of course, sir . . . and when you put it that way, perhaps you'd like to get a bigger piece of action from me." Cliff stared levelly at General Lymanner.

"Not a bad idea, Major. Quite sporting of you, really, considering that we're all playing without handicaps. I'll talk to General Johnson and Colonel Stein. What would you say to doubling the stakes, making it twenty dollars a hole and twenty dollars a stroke if the others agree?"

"What about making it twenty-five?"

Lymanner suppressed a smile. "You really think the winter rules are going to help you that much? Okay. I'll take it upon myself, Major, to commit the others. Twenty five dollars a hole, twenty-five dollars a stroke. The Boca Raton Special, we'll tee off at twelve noon. It's warmest then."

At 11:45 A.M. the next day, generals Lymanner and Johnson, Colonel Stein, and Major Thompson were standing on the first tee with their four noncom caddies. Since everything was in the open now, Cliff had chosen Pete White to caddy for him, a move that caused the other officers to raise their eyebrows but they said nothing.

There were some snowbanks on both sides of the first fairway, so all the golfers immediately chose red balls for their drives. They teed off according to rank—General Johnson, the post C.O., hitting first. As always, Johnson's drive was strong and lofting and dropped two hundred twenty yards straight out from the tee; Lymanner went second with a two-hundred-yard drive and Stein managed to get one hundred ninety on his. Cliff, who had never been seen by them to drive more than one hundred eighty to two hundred yards at the most, stood up to his ball, hit it—and everyone watched as it sailed a good thirty yards beyond General Johnson's: a solid two-hundred-fifty-yard drive. The generals looked at each other and whistled, then started down the fairway. On their next shots, Stein managed to get his second just under the first green and both Lymanner and Johnson used their five-irons to loft their balls close to the edge of the green. Cliff walked up to his ball, one hundred fifty yards from the pin. He studied his lie a moment, pulled the seven iron from his bag and with a neat snick lofted his ball over the edge of the green, where it fell with a thunk on the near-frozen ground, a mere ten feet from the pin. It took Stein three more strokes to get down for a one-above-par bogey, and Lymanner and Johnson two putts to make par. . . . Cliff sank his ten-footer for a birdie three.

As they picked up their balls and started for the second tee, Cliff smiled at General Lymanner. "As I said, sir, I'm going to have to play over my head today if I never did it before." The second, a tricky dog's-leg par-four yielded three bogeys to Lymanner, Johnson and Stein. Cliff birdied the hole for a three. He was now two holes and three strokes ahead of Lymanner and Johnson and four strokes ahead of Stein. The generals nudged each other as they approached the third, a par-five hole that had come to cause Cliff trouble—at-first-purposeful trouble. The tee seemed to rise out of the edge of a huge lake around which the golf course was built, which Cliff would say caused him psychological problems. Of course the generals didn't realize that his seemingly inevitable slice into the lake had been manufactured when he'd first started playing with them so that he wouldn't foul up and get too far ahead of them: he'd slice into the lake and take a two-stroke penalty. Now he worried that his artificial bad habit would be for real, and took pains to compensate . . . he'd close his stance and move his right hand over, which ordinarily might cause a hook.

It was Cliff's honor, and as he walked up to the ball General

Lymanner said, "Don't forget, Major. Just because the lake's frozen doesn't mean you can walk out there and hit the ball off the ice." He winked at Johnson. Cliff nodded grimly, glanced down at the lake's edge less than ten feet from where he stood. The others noted his apprehensive glance and grinned as he addressed the ball, made his adjustments (too subtle for them to notice), waggled once and hit. The red ball sailed out over the fairway two hundred sixty yards straight ahead. The other three gasped—and gasped even more when Cliff's next shot, a booming three-wood from an improved lie—permitted by winter rules—sailed two hundred twenty-five yards onto the green thirty feet from the pin . . . almost a sure birdie, possible eagle.

"Damn it, Thompson, we've been playing almost two years and I've never seen you do *that* before," Lymanner said.

"It's amazing what fear, pure fear can do for a man," Cliff replied. Stein distinguished himself with a two-over-par seven, both generals came in with bogey sixes and Cliff two-putted for his birdie four.

As they went on, the three officers became increasingly demoralized, falling further and further behind, their problems compounded by the special hazards of winter golf . . . such as when the ball lands on icy, frozen terrain the blade of an iron can't hit under the ball as it does on turf and so it's necessary to slap the ball off the ice with a near-perpendicularly bladed two-iron instead of with the other more lofted irons designed to take a divot out from under the ball. Although a new technique to Cliff, he'd privately mastered it, and now found himself using the two-iron more and more as they finished the first nine and encountered a larger accumulation of ice on the fairways.

Discouraged though far from beaten, the other officers all made fine drives out into the frozen fairway of the par-four, three-hundred-eighty-yard tenth hole, each man using his two iron, all getting on, although Cliff's ball was closest to the pin. Each player handed his caddy the club and strode down the fairway. This time they all parred the hole, which made for a new spirit of friendliness from the generals and Stein. Thompson, they decided, had simply played over his head on the front nine but now real class would win out.

The eleventh hole was a five-hundred-twenty-yard par-five ribbon of icy fairway into which all four players made creditable drives. Cliff's ball was the farthest out and after the others had addressed their balls and slapped them off the ice, Cliff studied his lie and asked Pete White for the two-iron.

As the others watched, Pete rummaged through the golf bag, shook it, and then looked up blankly at Cliff. "Major, your two iron isn't here."

"What the hell do you mean it isn't here?"

"It must have dropped out back there."

" 'It must have dropped out,' " Cliff repeated acidly. "Okay, hustler. All bets between us are off on this hole. Now shag your ass back and get my two-iron. I'll have to hit with the three." He gave Pete a baleful glare. "What are you waiting for. Move. Leave the bag here, dummy."

Pete dropped the bag and trotted back along the fairway to find the lost two-iron while Cliff took out his three, walked over to his ball and looked down at it sitting on a plate of ice. He looked up at the other three officers, all of whom wore broad grins. None offered to lend him a two-iron. Strict rules of golf prohibited this anyway.

Cliff swung. The bottom edge of his three-iron caught on the ice, sending the ball a disastrous one hundred yards. He looked up in annoyance. "Sergeant White is a hustler, you know. He's been betting against me all the time he's been caddying today."

"How're you doing with him?" Johnson asked.

"He's down a thousand dollars, and was obviously trying to get even."

It wasn't until Cliff was lying five on the edge of the green that Pete, the two-iron under his arm, caught up with him— the others were all lying four and much closer to the hole. General Johnson parred the hole and Lymanner and Stein were down in six. Cliff finally holed out for a double bogey seven, and after some well-chosen abuse at Pete went on to the twelfth tee with three hugely encouraged competitors.

This was the last time Cliff was to lose a hole. Shooting birdie after birdie on the treacherous winter terrain as the others only occasionally made par and usually went down for bogeys or double bogeys, Cliff ran up an alarming score in the game which Lymanner and Johnson themselves had made cruelly expensive.

By the time they'd reached the eighteenth hole generals Lymanner and Johnson were not speaking to each other and both were snapping at Colonel Stein, who had the misfortune to be lower-ranked. As they walked off the eighteenth green toward the clubhouse, all three officers were glaring at Cliff.

"I'm going directly back to my quarters, Major," Johnson said, biting off his words. "I'll send you a check tomorrow."

"Yes, sir," Cliff replied. "That would be seven hundred dollars. Four hundred dollars for sixteen holes at twenty-five dollars a hole and, let's see"—he consulted his scorecard—"twelve strokes at twenty-five dollars a stroke, that would be three hundred dollars. Seven hundred dollars total. Correct, sir?"

"You'll receive my check in the morning." Tight-lipped, looking neither to the left nor to the right, General Johnson, post commanding officer, strode toward the staff car waiting for him.

"You'll have my check tomorrow also, Major," Lymanner said through clenched teeth.

"Right, sir. That would be three hundred twenty-five dollars for thirteen strokes plus four hundred dollars for the sixteen holes. Seven hundred twenty-five dollars. Correct sir?"

With a stiff-necked nod, General Lymanner marched off the golf course to his own car.

Cliff turned to Stein. "Now let's see, Colonel—"

"I never thought I'd be hustled at the officers' golf course!" Stein said. "And by a lawyer at that. A disgrace. You called your caddy a cheap, hustling crook. I'd say it was the other way around."

Cliff ignored him. "In your case, sixteen strokes . . . that's four hundred dollars on strokes and four hundred twenty-five for seventeen holes—eight hundred twenty-five dollars."

"You'll get it all before your discharge—"

"Fine. Nice to have met you, sir."

Stein gave the outrageous major a fierce look, turned on his heel and stalked across the club grounds.

"Hey, Cliff?" Pete asked, "why'd you tell me to lose your two-iron?"

"Tell you later. It's cold out here."

8

AT 0900 THE FOLLOWING MORNING Master Sergeant Peter White presented himself to the command sergeant major, a bulldog-like hulk of a man sitting in a posture of malevolent protectiveness outside the door to General Johnson's suite of offices.

White was wearing the sharpest tailor-mades he owned, sporting his Good Conduct Medal and a VFW ribbon—he'd already joined the Veterans of Foreign Wars to give him a second ribbon to wear. He was greeted with a pained look. "Sergeant, you know procedure better than to ask for an appointment with the commanding general. If you really feel you need to see General Johnson put your request through the normal channels. It will be evaluated and you'll receive a report in due course—"

"Now, goddamn it, Mulvaney, don't tell me about 'due course.' I gotta see the general. A bad thing has happened he should know about before it happens again. Bad for him, bad for me."

"White, you just simmer down. I don't know what you got

the red ass about so bad but the general don't want to hear about it."

Pete's face, red with anger, confronted the sergeant major's at close range. "I guaran-damn-tee he's going to want to hear what I have to say. You can make book on it."

"Last time I got into one of your games I lost half a month's pay."

"You left too soon. I was all ready to hand you a big pot. Come in tonight you'll get it back three times. Now get in there and tell the general that Major Thompson's caddy from the game yesterday needs to see him on a very important affair."

Mulvaney looked closely at him. "You better tell me all about it, and anyway, I'm not letting you in till you cool down. . . . What happened?"

"The general got taken off yesterday. So did I. I want him to know. Look, Mulvaney, if you don't get me in it'll be your ass because next time he's going to get taken off even bigger and it'll be your fault because you wouldn't let him get protected."

"You want me to tell the general that?" Mulvaney asked incredulously.

"Yes. Right now, goddamn it."

With a worried look, Mulvaney finally heaved his bulk to a standing position and started for the door.

"Now just control yourself, Sergeant," Johnson said, "and tell me what's so vital that you had to by-pass all the proper channels to get in here?"

"Yes, sir. But every time I think of how we were hustled yesterday I get so mad—"

"We have all come to the conclusion that Major Thompson took us in, but what has that got to do with you, Sergeant?"

"In the first place, sir, my loyalty is to you and this command. I know that Major Thompson helped get me transferred here, but I've tried to do a good job for you, sir, in keeping some kind of order on this post in supply and recreation."

Sergeant White's euphemism for his crap games brought an

inadvertent smile to the general's lips. "Your activities have flourished only with my tacit approval, Sergeant, because I am persuaded that you run honest . . . recreational facilities. Although, to be candid, I had some doubts after yesterday afternoon."

"I know, sir. That's what made me so angry I damn near busted in on you."

"You have known Major Thompson for some time. Would you call him a hustler, to use the vernacular?"

"Until yesterday I didn't think so, sir. But yesterday, by the time we hit the ninth tee I could see he'd been setting you up for that game. I sure didn't know he was a professional."

"So I gather. I believe Major Thompson mentioned you were betting against him even though you were caddying for him."

"When it comes to making a buck, General, I never let sentiment overrule my better judgment. I thought Major Thompson was just a smart lawyer. I never thought he'd beat you and General Lymanner."

Johnson was skeptical. "How does it serve you to come in here and tell me all this?"

"I didn't want to be tarred with the same brush as Major Thompson, sir."

"You mean, you didn't want to lose your license to provide gambling on this post, Sergeant. . . ."

"I didn't want to see you hustled by Major Thompson the way we were yesterday, sir. That's why I dropped his two-iron, I thought it might throw him off his game—"

Johnson leaned forward. "So that was deliberate, eh?"

"It was the only hole he lost but he still took me for a grand. That's why I came to see you today. Major Thompson is a professional golf hustler. Don't play him again unless you get half a stroke a hole."

"I think we all agree. You lost too, eh?"

"Yes. But I'll get it all back, in spades. Major Thompson's golf game with you is going all over the post. But now he's got in over his head. He's made some crazy bet and this is one I know he can't win. Anyway, sir, I was so mad at Major Thompson for that hustle, and making it look like I might be part of it that I couldn't think straight until I'd come to you. Thank you for seeing me, sir." An anxious look came over his face. "You won't ask me to stop providing recreation for the casuals coming through, will you, sir?"

Johnson let out a sudden burst of laughter. "Your survival instincts saved you again, Sergeant. I might well have closed you down today, I was that mad. No, no, continue as you are. . . . Now, what were you saying about some bet Major Thompson is offering?"

"Well, sir," Pete replied, "after you left I was mad but I congratulated the major on a great game of golf. He said to me, 'You haven't seen anything . . .'" Pete stopped as though reluctant to go any further.

"Yes, yes, yes, Sergeant, tell me about this bet."

"Well, sir, Major Thompson said that on certain days in the winter the air gets dense and extremely buoyant. He wanted to bet me that he could drive a ball six hundred yards from the third tee. Now I never heard of anybody driving a golf ball five hundred yards, much less six hundred so naturally I took the bet—five thousand dollars."

"*Six* hundred yards?"

"That's right, sir. He showed me how the third and fourth fairways are lined up perfectly and how six hundred yards extends about halfway down the fourth fairway from the third tee in a straight line. Like I said, I never heard of anybody driving six hundred yards . . . he was talking about floating a ball on some damn carpet of density, he called it, in the winter atmosphere. . . ."

General Johnson laughed. "That is the most crazy improbable bizarre thing I ever heard. I happen to have a master's degree in science and I know he's crazy."

"I thought so too, sir. But he's betting on it."

"The bugger must have some trick," Johnson muttered.

"No, sir. As you know, I'm a gambler and I pinned him down to all the conditions. He told me very clearly that he would drive a golf ball off the third tee at least six hundred yards. I said, 'Oh, sure, you'll drive it into a jeep and drive the jeep six hundred yards and then let it fall out,' and he said, 'No, Sergeant, I will hit the ball, it will go up in the air, it will fall down and when it stops it will have gone at least six hundred yards.' "

General Johnson thought about this for a few moments and finally looked up at the sergeant. "White, I want you to tell this . . . this hustler that you have some friends that would like to take a piece of that bet. Do you realize that Major Thompson took us for twenty two hundred and fifty dollars? . . . This is just the time to get even, before he gets out of the army. There isn't a man in the world that can drive a golf ball six hundred yards. . . ."

Two days later Cliff reported to General Lymanner, who fixed him with a hostile glare. "I have heard that you claim to be able to drive a golf ball six hundred yards. Is that correct?"

"That is correct, sir."

"You realize, of course, that no man in the history of golf has ever done that."

"Well, sir, it took quite a few years to break ten seconds in the hundred-yard dash."

"All right, Thompson, what's the catch . . . some special souped-up ball—?"

"No, sir, you can buy any box of professional high compression golf balls you want, pick the ball you want me to drive, put it on the tee and that will be the ball I'll hit."

"Impossible."

"Sir, as you may have noticed last Saturday, I have devoted a considerable portion of my life to playing golf." Lymanner nodded sourly. "I've been told I could go on the pro tour if I wanted to, but I have more important things to do with my life—"

"All right, Major, General Johnson doesn't believe you can do it. Are you prepared to cover a large bet from a group of senior officers?"

"Yes, sir."

"There's one more condition. There will be a board of judges consisting of General Johnson, Colonel Stein, myself, the sergeant major and at least one more general officer. All will have to agree that you drove a golf ball six hundred yards within the conditions of the bet."

"That will be all right with me, sir."

Lymanner hesitated a moment, took a deep breath, and finally said, in the manner of a man who has just made one of his life's most fateful decisions, "Major Thompson, you've got yourself a bet. When do we settle it?"

"The only thing I ask is that you let me pick the day. I'll cover every bet anybody wants to make, all wagers to be put in an escrow account until the day comes, then be drawn out of the bank and taken to the third tee, at which point I will attempt to drive the ball at least six hundred yards. If I fail, the money will be apportioned out to those who have bet against me."

"Supposing it turns out to be two or three months before you decide to try this?"

"If I don't attempt it by the end of January of 1946, I lose. Fair enough, General?"

Cliff's confidence somewhat unnerved Lymanner, but at this he could only nod his agreement, and add, "In the meantime I'd be pleased if you did not come around this office anymore. Consider your army duties terminated. Your only obligation now is to accept all bets . . . and incidentally, the commanding general and I will be the only people that can withdraw the money from the escrow account. Fair enough, Major?"

"Absolutely. As long as that cash is at the third fairway when I'm ready to make my drive."

During the next few weeks Pete White and Cliff studied weather reports and watched the sky as bets flooded into the escrow account. Within three weeks the story had gone through the entire First Army and thousands of dollars were wagered and covered. As the days went by Pete became more and more concerned. "Jesus, Cliff, we're going to walk out of the army broke if you can't do it—"

"I'll do it. We just have to have the right day. That one perfect day. Should be before the end of January."

"Supposing we don't get it?"

"Then I'll lose."

"You lose?" Pete said. "*I* lose. Everything we've made is going to cover the bets coming in. There'll be more generals and colonels watching this drive of yours than it took to win the last five wars."

"No general ever won a war," Cliff said. "It was won by G.I.s who got their asses shot off."

"Well, you sure didn't get *your* ass near a place where it could get shot off."

"I've got my own war," Cliff said, and walked away.

More days passed, and Pete was offered the chance at a Christmas furlough.

"Go ahead and take it, Pete," Cliff said. "I know you want to see your girl friend in Miami."

"Yeah, Carol says the war's over and if I don't come down . . . well, she's pretty annoyed."

"You better go then . . . but if the right weather comes, I'm going to have to call the bet. If you're not here you won't see it."

"Yeah . . . damn." Pete shrugged. "Well, I guess she'll just have to hold her water. She'll never understand, but maybe someday I'll be able to straighten her out. . . ."

Pete and Cliff had Christmas dinner together in Boston at the Copley Plaza Hotel. The weather still wasn't right. They also spent New Year's Eve together in Boston. "Son-of-a-bitch,"

Pete said. "I could have been with Carol and now I've lost her. Do you realize we've only got thirty-one more days left for you to win the bet?"

"I know, Pete. Hang in there. Things have got to work out sometime in January. I tell you I'll win if the weather conditions come up right—"

"And if they don't, we lose everything. All the money I've made hustling for the last three years. You know how much we've got bet on this thing? Besides my five thousand dollars against you which got General Johnson into this hustle in the first place, you and I have over thirty thousand dollars down and more going out every day."

"Pete, will you listen to me? You still don't think I'm big enough to make the paddle for Roy Brian's ass, do you? Maybe you'll change your mind when you see what happens. Trust me. If I don't come through on this one you don't have to help me with Roy Brian. And I realize it would be damn hard to make the paddle without you."

"Oh hell, Cliff, I'll stick with you, even if we lose everything. Shit, I lived it up in the army, no man ever had a better time than I did. I can always go back to New Orleans. I'm still in at the racetrack there. But hell, Cliff, we got to win!"

On the second of January it started to rain and the temperature rose to an unseasonable thirty-eight degrees. Cliff visited the meteorologist's office every day.

"I think we can set the bet for four or five days from now," he told Pete on January tenth. "But don't tell anyone yet. I've got to watch the weather."

"Can you *please* tell me what the gimmick is?"

"Don't worry, I know what I'm doing. Trust me."

"I'm trying. But we've got forty-six thousand dollars in bets now. Why *can't* you tell me?"

"Just call it superstition."

The driving rain continued for two days then abruptly ceased and suddenly clear skies covered northern New England. With the clear skies came a cold snap, temperatures dropped to below zero overnight, and the next morning Pete found himself shaken awake with the announcement, "Okay, let them know we go tomorrow at eleven. That'll give everybody who's betting against me a day to get here. Be sure all the money is out of the bank and down there at the third tee. D-day, old buddy."

At 10:30 the following morning a hundred assorted generals, colonels, light colonels, majors, and master sergeants from army posts all over New England and as far south as Governor's Island and Fort Dix, New Jersey, managed to get themselves to the Fort Devens officers' golf course. The clear, bright cold weather was perfect for flying and every officer with any influence at all had been able to commandeer an airplane to take him to Fort Devens. There had been no snow for almost three weeks and the golf course was bare of winter obstacles, its chief feature now the G.I.s with marker flags spread out one hundred yards apart. Perched firmly at the end of the fourth fairway was the six-hundred-yard marker.

Cliff arrived on the third tee at 10:45 carrying a one-iron in one hand and a battered black leather valise in the other. There was a lot of comment about his using an iron instead of a normal driving wood—the iron would give maximum roll to the ball, of course, and the hard surface of the fairway would help that, too . . . but six hundred yards? Impossible.

At 10:55 Cliff put his satchel on the ground, and worked a long tee into the frozen earth. Then, his driving iron under his arm, he motioned to General Lymanner, who walked over to him with an unopened box of high compression golf balls. Cliff took the box and opened it. Another officer took a ball out and placed it on the tee.

Although the temperature was hovering at twenty-four degrees, Cliff shucked off his parka and with only a loose sweater for warmth addressed the ball. At the far edge of the tee stood Lymanner, Johnson, Stein, the commanding general of nearby Westover Air Force Base, and the commanding general of Governor's Island in New York.

Standing ramrod straight and expressionless beside General

Johnson was the provost marshal, one hand holding the handle of the attaché case containing the stakes, the other resting on the butt of the .45 automatic pistol holstered at his side. There would be no diversionary tactics here. Cliff would have to win his bet or Johnson could refuse to allow the armed officer to pay off.

Over a hundred spectators were clustered around the third tee, and as Cliff stepped up to the golf ball everyone knew there was ninety-two thousand dollars riding on this one drive. Twice Cliff stared out across the fairway marked by the red flags and waggled at the ball. He started his swing and then stopped it in midair. He stepped back from the ball and looked up the fairway again. The bettors stood stone still. Then suddenly, as though he were a ballet dancer, Cliff pirouetted, faced out directly across the frozen lake, its surface glazed and shimmering in the sun, and with all his strength walloped the ball. It shot straight and low through the air for what looked to be at least two hundred and eighty yards before it finally landed on the ice, and then it started to roll . . . and roll. In hypnotic fascination the spectators watched the ball as it moved across the new, near-frictionless ice.

The officers let out a roar, as though a referee had just given the ball game to the other side on the world's worst bad call. Pete noticed the provost marshal's knuckles whiten as he gripped the case, and General Johnson's lips compress to thin lines, as the ball continued to roll, and roll, across the sheer ice of the lake.

Unnoticed by the bettors, whose attention had been focused on the fourth fairway, another group of flag-waving G.I.s stood far out on the ice. Ostensibly they had been fishing for lake trout underneath the ice, but when Cliff made his drive they immediately jumped to their feet and raised their red flags. It took very little depth perception to see that the six-hundred-yard marker on the ice was the same distance as the six-hundred-yard flag on the fourth green. The ball slithered across the ice like a tiny

70

curling stone, beyond the six-hundred-yard mark and on, and on, and on.

The onlookers' mutterings were distinctly threatening now, and Pete suddenly knew he had to make the move of his life.

In a rage he stalked up to General Johnson. "No!" he yelled wildly. "It's a phony, he cheated us. Five grand I bet! He was supposed to drive down the fairway."

Johnson and the other officers were taken aback at Pete's hysterical performance. "You're not going to pay him?" Pete screamed. "You *can't*. I told you he was a hustler. Fuck him! Don't give him the money."

"Sergeant White, get a hold of yourself," Johnson said.

Cliff was just lowering his iron, having watched the entire flight and roll of the ball with his club in finishing position. He stared coldly at Pete. "Six hundred yards," he announced, "and still rolling."

Pete turned from the general and rushed at Cliff. "You're a cheat, a hustler, a bullshit con man. A miserable fucking disgrace. . . ." Grabbing Cliff by the sweater, he had it half ripped off before Cliff dropped his club, grabbed Pete by the arms and pushed him toward Johnson.

"You're not going to pay off?" Pete continued to yell. "The man cheated us—"

Johnson looked out over the ice a moment and then back to his fellow officers. "We were deceived, no question. As a matter of fact my first reaction is not to pay—"

"There you go, sir. Screw all that military honor shit. You're not going to let some West Point code make you pay off just because he hit the ball six hundred yards across the *ice.*"

"There was no specification about what direction I had to hit the ball," Cliff said quietly.

"My five thousand bucks says he doesn't get paid," Pete insisted.

"Sergeant, if you don't quiet down I'll have you removed," the general said in a severe tone. "Major Thompson did what he bet he would do. I would like to hold the stakes and consider the case further, of course."

"Right, sir," Pete said. "Don't give him his money. You officers, if you'll forgive me, sir, worry too much about this honor shit. If you got the muscle not to pay off a bet, God bless —don't!"

A grim look came over General Johnson's face. He pulled himself to his full height, fixed the other officers about him with a stern look and announced: "However, despite the protests of this sergeant, a gambler himself with a substantial bet on this performance, I am forced to concede that Major Thompson drove a golf ball"—he paused and looked out over the ice again—"seven or eight hundred yards, beyond the six he bet on. Therefore"— he turned to the provost marshal—"Colonel Marks, you may hand the stakes to the winner . . . and Major Thompson"—his look was withering—"your final discharge papers will be ready for you to pick up this afternoon."

Stiffly the provost marshal walked over to Cliff and opened his attache case. Cliff picked up his own black leather valise and opened it wide. Unceremoniously the provost marshal dumped the piles of ten-, twenty-, fifty-, and hundred-dollar bills, neatly packaged, into the black satchel. When his attaché case was empty he snapped it shut, turned and left Cliff holding his father's old traveling valise—which he'd kept with him since his first day in the Army—stuffed with ninety-two thousand dollars in cash.

"No-o-o-o!"

Pete threw himself at the valise, trying to work it out of Cliff's hand. "This tinhorn hustling cheat ain't getting my money. He's trying to screw us with his cheap-jack bullshit tricks. . . ."

With extreme distaste the officers cleared the area as General Johnson called out, "Provost marshal, please restrain that man."

The officer tore Pete away and, as the others went off, removed him from the scene.

Cliff, alone on the third tee, gripped his valise and said quietly after the retreating general, "Thank you, sir. Nice to have been in your army."

9

THE BRILLIANT FEBRUARY sunshine danced off the waves that lapped the sands of Miami Beach and reflected from the rippling swimming pool of the Roney Plaza Hotel. It was a joyous contrast to Fort Devens. Cliff had been out of the army exactly one day after taking off the generals and, splitting the lush green contents of his old valise with Pete, had settled down in Boston for a week to await Pete's discharge. Now, with a brand-new wardrobe from Brooks Brothers, he was ready to begin.

It was eleven in the morning as Cliff and Pete lounged in the spacious parlor of their posh two-bedroom suite. Pete was still gloating over the record score they had taken off at Devens. ". . . And General Johnson even sent me a letter of condolence over my loss! I'm going to have it framed. Is that some kind of a monument to an outside man?"

Cliff winced slightly as he looked at Pete, his conservative tastes affronted by his friend's outfit. For all their teamwork together, they held markedly different views, especially about civilian clothing . . . still, they'd both been anxious to get out of the northern winter and there'd been little time for further shopping before catching the Silver Meteor to Miami—and, hopefully, Roy Brian.

Cliff turned toward the window. "I think we'd better think carefully about the fact that we're sitting here with close to ninety thousand in cash between us. There must be a hundred heist men who'd love to stick us up if they knew what we had. And I sure couldn't afford that . . . I'm going to need all the loot I've got to build that paddle for Roy Brian's ass—"

"Hey!" Pete interrupted. "I thought we made a deal. It's all the money *we* got that's going to build that paddle. Remember?"

"If you still want to go through with it. . . ."

"You can guaran-damn-tee I do. Now . . . we've had us some fun, made out with those broads last night, done a little drinking. . . ."

"Time we got down to business, right?"

"Right. Where do we start?"

Cliff reached for his father's valise on the floor beside him and, lifting it to his lap, took out some papers.

"Okay. Here's the geological report on Grove City Block II, and here"—he handed Pete a typewritten page—"is a list of the five people who now hold the mineral rights to Block II."

Pete took the list and stared at it, letting out a loud whistle. "Hey, Cliff, you just hit the jackpot. I know every mother's son on that list. They're all hustlers." He paused, grinning at the sheet in his hand. "Well I can say one thing for Roy Brian. He's a fair man."

"Fair? How in hell—"

"He played no favorites, he fucked them all."

"Or thought he did." Cliff retrieved the list.

"One of them is right here in Miami," Pete continued. "Nate Burger. He owns the best card room in town. He's also been one of the biggest players here for the last ten years. Mehmet Mamonis is in New Orleans. That's the Turk, the guy I told you about I owe five grand to. He was after my kneecaps until I got in the army." Pete looked at his partner thoughtfully. "Cliff, what do the mineral rights have to do with the paddle?"

"I haven't really figured that out yet. But I want the rights back. They were my father's. And if we develop them right, with those new deep-drilling rigs they've got now, they could put us on easy street—don't forget, Roy Brian got rich on Block I."

"Cliff," Pete cautioned, "you gotta remember, even though the people on your list think those rights are worthless, when we start going after them they're going to figure we know something they don't and they'll be hard to get."

Cliff nodded. "We've got a job ahead of us."

Pete stood up. "Okay, Cliff. First we put the money in the bank. Then I got to find my Carol. I haven't heard from her since I didn't show up for Christmas. All my letters come back 'Return to Sender.' "

"And I've got to start reaching out for Roy Brian," Cliff said. "Carol . . . she's a singer, right? And you said she could steer the players to the tables better than anyone you ever knew?"

Pete nodded. "You bet your ever-lovin' ass."

"Good. Her talent we can use. What do we do, make the rounds of all the joints?"

Pete shook his head. "I'll come up with an easier way. Right now, what about the bank?"

"First stop. Any particular institution of finance appeal to you especially?"

"Whichever is closest, old buddy."

"Okay, and we'll take out a joint account, two signatures for all checks."

"Thank you, *partner,*" Pete said, and meant it.

One hour later, they left the Lincoln Bank and Trust Company just up Collins Avenue from the hotel, Pete proudly tucking their little black book into the breast pocket of his loud sports jacket. "Man, I finally feel like a southern gentleman!"

76

Cliff eyed his partner. "Southern gentlemen wearing checks this year?"

They both laughed.

As they walked along the beachfront, they saw the local bookmakers busy tacking up their scratch sheets and entries for the day's racing programs, sun worshipers strolling over from the water's edge to check the odds and place bets, cigar counters and cabanas crowded with excited vacationers handicapping sure things. It was the first peacetime winter season in Miami for five years and the lotus eaters were out to make up for lost time. Overhead the speakers were blasting out the morning line. Pete nudged Cliff. "See what we've been missing? You forget what life is really all about after five years in the army. And I thought I'd found a home." He looked about at the action surrounding them. "*This* is home."

He strolled over to the scratch sheets. "Hey, Cliff! We just got time to make it out to Hialeah in time for the daily double. . . . We can see who's in town, get acquainted again, get the lay of the land. . . . What do you say?"

"Lead on, partner."

For Pete, it was old home week at Hialeah—he hadn't just been boasting about knowing his way around tracks. Racing had never been part of Cliff's education in the art of the hustle, and this was the perfect opportunity to begin remedying that gap in his education.

As they walked through the stands, Pete was kept busy greeting track regulars, all of whom seemed to be pleased at seeing their old colleague back from the wars and admired his threads, telling him he never looked better.

"We've gotta show class out here," Pete said in an aside to Cliff. "Don't go near anything but the hundred-dollar window."

"I didn't come out to Hialeah to lose it all," Cliff protested.

"You won't. Just bet weights and odds. That way you figure

it out on the program before you hit the hundred-dollar window and look like a real handicapper."

"Weights and odds?"

"Here, I'll show you. Take the first race. You just add the weight of the jockey to the odds on the horse. See. Here's Osage. Six to one. The jockey weighs 115 pounds. So you add six to 115, comes out 121. Now do it for all the horses in the race and the horse with the lowest number you bet to win. Odds are you won't do worse than break even and, like I say, you can show a lot of action working on the program and at the hundred-dollar window."

As Cliff used the system for the first race, Pete continued to meet and greet and tell his old buddies about his millionaire oilman from Oklahoma "over there at the hundred-dollar window." To his surprise, Cliff won on the race and as Pete went with him to the payoff window he pointed out some of the local wise guys and out-of-town gamblers who had come south for the action.

"Things haven't really changed much since I was drafted in forty-one," Pete said. "Look, there's old hunchback Jake, the paper inspector, working his shift." Pete pointed to a stooped-over ancient, a baggy suit hanging from his body, staring intently at the concrete floor. "That's Jake. There's always some sucker who throws away a winning ticket. Jake just shuffles through the tickets, kicking them over with his foot. And damned if he doesn't find enough winners to keep him going. Been doing it for years. He can't stand up. His whole life is spent in that position."

By the sixth race, Cliff was ahead three hundred dollars, and as they made their way to the hundred-dollar window—they'd won on Flamboyant at six to five—Pete suddenly nudged him. "There's Karl Eddy, the best peat man in the business."

Cliff looked at a short, middle-aged, bald man. " 'Peat man?' "

"Safecracker. He can can-opener anything. I wonder what

job he's casing around here. Well, no doubt we'll read about it in the papers."

"Let's meet him."

Pete shrugged. "If you want . . . I don't know what good he can do us—"

"Hey, you were the one who taught me to keep an eye open for the unusual . . . he looks unusual, I'd say."

Casually Pete changed course, and a minute later almost bumped into the older man. He stopped. "Well, hiya, Karl, what's new?"

"Ah, Pete White, my friend from New Orleans. Yes? And how are you? My God, it is a long time I don't see you."

"I was in the army."

"Oh yes, the war," Karl said vaguely in a curious, middle-European accent. "I am so glad the war is over."

"This is my friend Cliff Thompson," Pete went on. "We were in the army together. We both just got out."

"I hope you kill many Nazis. I would like to have helped but I was too old. Although"—his voice rose and a cheerful expression came to his face—"I was able to be of some help to our government using certain skills I possess. I am, at the moment, what you might call, persona most grata with the FBI you will be glad to hear."

"Where you staying?"

"I am, as they say, beating the winter at the Biscayne Hotel in South Beach. I'm always there after the last race. Maybe I see you sometime, yes?"

"I'd like that," Cliff said.

Later that day, after long, leisurely showers and changes of clothes, Pete and Cliff met in their shared parlor at the hotel. Pete was now wearing multihued striped slacks and yellow suede shoes.

"Jesus," Cliff said, "you look like a mark going to a Polish wedding. Tomorrow, my man, we are going to buy you some

clothes that'll make you look like a successful working stiff. We've got some paddles to build in the next few months."

Pete glanced down at his raiment and pretended hurt. "I thought it was pretty sharp myself." He grinned. "Come on, m'lord, let's check out the lounge."

Sitting at the bar of the Bamboo Lounge, his eyes darting about the room appraising the women for late-night possibilities and the men for potential marks, Pete suddenly said, "Hey, Cliff, see that bass player? That's Henry Sergeant."

"Looks like he's humping his instrument," Cliff said.

Pete laughed. "That's what he was famous for on Bourbon Street. People came in to watch him get his rocks off against his big fiddle. You know, sometimes his trio backed up Carol . . ." Pete walked over to the small stage.

"Hey man, where you at?"

Henry Sergeant smiled. "Everything's solid, man. Fine as wine."

"You still can't let that thing alone," Pete laughed.

"My trademark, man."

"Say, you remember that cute blonde I used to go with? Carol? Sang at the Monteleone Hotel?"

"Nobody could see her gonna forget Carol . . . she's here, Pete. Got a gig at the Beachcomber Club. Doing the late show startin' at eleven."

"No kidding. Hey thanks, man, I'll have to catch her act."

"You do that, babes, and tell her old Henry says hello."

When Pete returned to the bar, Cliff was making light conversation with a well-put-together lady perched on the barstool beside him.

"I found where she is," Pete reported.

"Let's go, then."

"It's only seven o'clock. She doesn't go on until eleven." He nodded approvingly at the girl. "We've got four hours to kill."

"Then why don't we have some dinner here and go over to Nate Burger's."

"Good idea, Cliff . . . of course Nate's will be there tomorrow and you might have something better to do with your time tonight." He winked at the girl.

"We'll go to Nate Burger's."

"Do they have a show?" the girl asked.

"It's stag only," Cliff said.

"Oh . . . one of those."

"It's a place where you play cards," Pete told her.

"Have dinner with us anyway," Cliff said.

"Well, it's very nice of you to invite me. By the way, I'm Margo Swanson. I just arrived here and I don't know a soul. . . ."

As Pete and Cliff entered Nate Burger's place, Pete was saying, "Hey, Cliff. She was ready. What's the matter with you?"

"She'll keep. I've lost enough time as it is. Let's not forget what we're really here for. Okay, partner?"

Nate's card room was class all the way. Situated above the Five O'Clock Club on Collins Avenue, it was not actually a private club, but only professional gamblers, prominent men-about-town, and a sprinkling of celebrities were admitted.

At the far end of the room was a large, round, green-felt-topped poker table, a red velvet sash surrounding it to keep the kibitzers away from the gamblers. Seven players were concentrating on their cards, while at smaller tables along the wall the sports were dealing short cards—games like gin rummy, pinochle, klubiosh, and casino, which required only a few minutes to play a hand—and in the center of the room larger tables accommodated bridge, hearts, and pan players. The Western Union ticker intermittently clacking out sporting results merged with the well-ordered tumult of professionals dealing cards. "Jeeze," Pete breathed, "there wouldn't be an unsolved crime in America if everyone in this room told everything they know."

Cliff looked over the scene. Here was where it was all about to begin. As they walked over the thick red carpeting, Pete said, "First I'll introduce you to Nate."

A short, balding man walked toward them from the door behind the poker table, his eyes flicking around the room, taking in all the gamesters, seeming to know what was happening at every table. He wore a neatly cut pinstripe suit and floral pattern tie. "Hiya, Nate," Pete said, "remember me? Pete White from New Orleans."

"Sure, Pete. 'Course I do. What's doin'?"

"This is Cliff Thompson. He's from Oklahoma and he's come down to catch the winter action."

"Pleased to meet you, Mr. Thompson . . . you a player?"

"I enjoy a game now and then. I'm a lawyer by trade. Specialize in oil."

"Well, good, Mr. Thompson, we'll sure try to give you some action." Nate's voice was hospitable, but his eyes kept moving. "Matter of fact there's a seat open at the poker table now."

"Fine. Haven't sat in a game for a long time."

Nate looked at Pete. "You too?"

"No, I'll just watch."

Cliff sat down at the poker table and for the next two hours, playing conservatively, lost a hundred dollars. Twice he called for new cards, watching the old black porter leave the card room and enter the door to the back office, quickly returning with the fresh Bee brand deck.

"Cliff, it's eleven o'clock," he heard.

"Sorry, Pete. The time got away from me, I guess." Cliff stood up and another player immediately slipped into his seat.

"Come again, Mr. Thompson," Nate Burger said as they left.

"We sure will, Nate. You've got a real nice place here."

Out on the street, Pete's tone was sympathetic. "You didn't do so good, huh Cliff?"

"On the contrary, I did very well." He flashed the cards he had palmed. "My father used to do a lot of business with Saint

82

Louis Dutch. Puts together the finest packs of readers in the country."

Pete nodded. "We going to pull a nice-to-meet-you-sir operation?"

"Something like that. I still have my dad's best gaffs in the old black bag but we're going to need some special equipment for this hustle. We'll leave Nate Burger for later. . . ."

The Beachcomber Club on Dade Boulevard off Collins Avenue was divided into two sections—a large dining area featuring a dinner and supper show and a cocktail lounge open until the early hours of the morning where you could catch a singer and pianist.

When Cliff and Pete entered the lounge Carol LaRue was in the middle of her act. "Well, there she is, Cliff. That's my Carol." Pete was clearly excited.

Cliff nodded in appreciation. "And you left *that* alone on Christmas just to watch me hit a golf ball?"

"C'mon Cliff, don't even bring it up."

"Sorry . . . but seriously, you got yourself one beautiful woman."

"Yeah"—Pete sighed—"I hope so."

They were led to a table in the center of the room that wasn't big enough for two, much less three, but with a well-placed ten-dollar bill, Pete secured a larger, more private table against the bamboo-matted wall. Upon the slightly elevated platform, Carol started her new number, "It Had to Be You."

"Hey, that's our song," Pete said. "I wonder if she saw me come in." Cliff didn't have to point out that as Carol sang, she turned to the pianist every few bars and sang the words directly to him while the young, shock-haired accompanist smiled mistily back . . . "I wandered around, finally found, somebody who . . ."

"Who, Pete?" Cliff asked.

Pete stared morosely into his drink until Carol's set was over, then he was on his feet, pushing through the tightly packed tables toward her. "Carol. Baby!"

Carol turned and saw him coming toward her, leaving a row of disgruntled drinkers in his wake. "Hello, Pete." It was a very small hello. "You finally made it."

"Baby!" Ignoring the stares and catcalls he stepped up on the stage, put his arms around her and kissed her . . . and as she tried to take a step backward two serious-looking gentlemen suddenly materialized on each side of him.

"Shall we show him out, Miss LaRue?"

Carol paused long enough to make Pete's heart flop over, then, "No. I hate to say it but I know him." The bouncers retreated, and Carol allowed herself to be led back to Pete's table, this time by a longer, more circuitous route that didn't endanger the drinks on the small tables.

"Cliff, meet Carol," said Pete. Cliff was on his feet and holding a chair. "I've been looking forward to this pleasure for three years, Carol. You are Pete's main topic of conversation and now I see what a limited vocabulary my friend has."

In spite of herself Carol laughed, and the ice was at least cracked. "Pete wrote to me about you too," she said. "Especially when he stood me up for Christmas."

"Aw Carol . . ."

"Yes," Cliff said, "I am very sorry about that, really, Carol. It was my fault," and tried valiantly not to look at her breasts, barely contained by the tight plunging bodice of her gown. He decided to concentrate instead on the wide blue eyes which stared unblinkingly back at him. "We did, however, manage to conclude a business deal which will benefit all of us."

"Don't look at me when you say us," she said.

"Aw, please, baby, I can explain—"

"Don't bo—" Carol was winding up for a blast when a waiter arrived with a silver cooler and a bottle of champagne. Cliff inspected the vintage carefully and smiled at the waiter.

"Dom Perignon 1939. Very nice." With a quick wink at Pete, he turned back to Carol. "After your lovely performance I thought you might like a good champagne."

The cork burst from the bottle with a satisfactory pop. "You taste it, Carol and tell us if it's all right or whether it should go back."

Obediently Carol picked up her glass, large eyes fixed on Cliff, and sipped. "It's just marvelous, Cliff . . . I love real French champagne."

Cliff signaled the waiter to pour, satisfied that his performance had achieved its effect. By now Carol was relaxed and smiling and for a moment even reached out her hand and took Pete's in hers. Relieved, Pete sat back in his chair.

"To our very good fortune at finding you, Carol," Cliff toasted, holding up his glass. Carol and Pete lifted theirs, clinked rims and drank . . . and Cliff began his story. He told her everything, about the dice and the cards and the golf, the pigeons and the paratroopers, saving for last the story of how they took off the generals of Fort Devens for ninety-two thousand dollars.

By the time he had finished, Carol was doubled up laughing, wiping the tears from her eyes. Slapping Pete hard on the back, she said, "Okay, you rat, I forgive you. Jesus, what a story!"

"When you're through tonight we'll go back to our suite at the Roney and really celebrate," Pete said, delighted.

Carol suddenly became serious. "I can't, Pete . . ."

"What do you mean, you can't?"

"I promised Alex we'd get together after the show."

"Alex?"

"My accompanist."

"You're not *going* with him . . . a crumb-bum *musician* . . .?"

"Look, Pete, he put my act together in two weeks for this place. This is a high-class place and I needed high-class arrangements and material. He really helped me—"

"Hey, you can *forget* all that now, baby, we've got real, *serious* dough and we're going for a lot more. Forget this Alex."

Carol's face hardened. "Alex had this job lined up for the two of us in mid-December but because I was expecting you to come to New Orleans any day I turned it down. Then when you didn't come I was alone Christmas and out of a job. I called Alex. He'd already found another girl but he paid her two weeks' notice out of his own pocket and gave me another chance. I'm just going to dump him?"

"But it's just business . . . isn't it? I'm not saying you should quit the act. . . ."

"It started out just business," Carol said softly.

There was a long pause which Cliff tried to cover by filling everyone's glasses. "Drink up, folks, more on the way—"

"Look, Carol," Pete began again. "I'm here, out of the army. We'll be together all the time now. Cliff and I got eighty-seven grand between us—well, minus five thousand. . . ."

"Why minus five?" Carol queried.

"I gotta go back to New Orleans some time and pay the Turk the five grand I owe him from before the war. Otherwise I won't get to enjoy my money."

"The Turk? That dirty old bastard is running a whack-out joint right here on the beach."

Cliff suddenly became alert. "Mehmet Mamonis is in Miami?"

"Yeah, the Turk, if that's his name. He looked me up. Wanted me to steer some suckers to his tables. Offered me twenty-five percent of whatever he took them for."

"The cheap crook. You shoulda got fifty."

"What's the difference? I said no anyway."

Cliff sipped his champagne thoughtfully as Pete continued his importunings. Finally Carol glanced at her watch and stood up. "Time for my next set."

"You'll be back after . . . ?" Pete asked, unintentionally making it sound like a question, and holding onto her hand.

Carol nodded. "Sure, Pete."

"You tell Alex you have to see an old friend when this place closes. . . ."

"I'll see what I can do, hon."

After she'd gone, Pete turned uneasily to Cliff. "Those musicians are a hard act to follow, they're all muff divers, you know."

"Nobody ever died from it. I'm going to make a telephone call," Cliff said. "Meet you back at the table."

It was four in the morning when the Beachcomber Club cocktail lounge closed and by that time Pete, Carol, and Cliff had finished off the better part of a third bottle of champagne. A sullen, sulky Alex had not let them out of his sight after Carol's second set, even when he played the piano, and as they stood up to leave, Pete said, "That creep gives me the creeps."

"Stop it, Pete . . . I'm going back with you two, aren't I?" Carol was feeling no pain from the champagne. "It's a good thing there are two of you . . . I told him it was strictly business."

Outside the club they found a waiting taxi and when they arrived at the hotel, Pete grandly threw open the double doors of their parlor. "Well, this is it, the Presidential Suite."

"Oh no!" Carol said. "Not more champagne."

And indeed a bottle stood in an ice bucket on the coffee table. "I thought we might have it for breakfast if you aren't in the mood now. . . ."

"I'm in the mood for something else." She looked Pete up and down, hands on her hips, legs apart, then turned to Cliff, a grin on her lips. "You'll understand if I insist on my Christmas present right now?"

Cliff grinned back. "I wouldn't understand anything else."

Carol reached out one hand and securely tightened her fingers around the bulge in Pete's trousers. "Which door is Pete's?" she asked.

"To your right."

Carol headed toward the wrong door, a bemused Pete following.

"Your other right, Carol," Cliff advised.

Carol hiccoughed. "Thanks," and with Pete firmly in tow

87

strode to the correct bedroom door, opened it and led Pete through. Pete had the presence of mind to push the door shut behind him.

Cliff looked after them, smiled, and thought, a dynamite lady. She will be very, very useful.

10

CLIFF HAD BEEN SACKED OUT on a chaise longue soaking up the Florida sunshine for over an hour when Pete and Carol appeared. Carol had on a brand-new one-piece bathing suit that revealed even more of her than the dress she'd been wearing the previous night.

"I see you've been shopping," Cliff remarked.

"Yeah, we started out the day making someone happy . . ." Pete said.

"I couldn't very well walk around in what I was wearing last night." Carol smoothed the fabric about her hips.

"If you're going to spend money there's nothing better than a beautiful lady to spend it on," Cliff said as Pete and Carol lay down on the long beach mats and faced up at the sun. There was a contented silence for some moments, then Cliff turned over on his side toward them.

"Something we were talking about last night . . ."

"The Turk?" Pete suggested.

"Right."

"Are you really going to pay him that five thousand?" Carol asked. "It was five years ago you owed him."

"If it was fifty years ago and the Turk was alive he'd be looking for his money—with a baseball bat!"

"Pete's going to pay him," Cliff said. "Tonight. And off the top of our mutual fund."

"Hey, that's my private problem, Cliff."

"Don't worry. As you'd say, I guaran-damn-tee we'll use that payoff to our advantage."

That evening before show time Pete and Carol arrived at the Palm Isles Club on Collins Avenue, far to the north of the Roney Plaza Hotel, and stared at the neon signs blinking on and off in the windows.

"Some joint," Pete said.

"The terrible Turk's coming up in the world. Shall we go in?" Holding her head high, her chest thrust forward, Carol walked through the door . . . the bartender mixing a drink looked up and an ounce of whisky overflowed the five-eighths-ounce cheat jigger . . . the patrons, almost entirely male, stared at her and momentarily lost the thread of their game. Affecting a super cool to the stir she was causing, Carol walked over to the bartender with Pete. "We'd like to talk to Turk," Pete said.

The bartender, eyes all over Carol and without looking at Pete, said, "He's up there," gesturing toward the stairs.

One flight up, Pete knocked briskly on the door. They heard Turk's gravelly voice. "What'ya want? I'm busy."

Carol called through the door, "I just wanted to see you for a minute, Mr. M. It's Carol LaRue."

The tone changed abruptly, "Carol! Just a minute, baby." A chair scraped and the door quickly opened. "Well, what a surprise—" and then he saw Pete. The Turk's long, cantilevered black mustache twitched and his eyes narrowed under his bald scalp. "What do you want?"

"Can we come in?"

Turk frowned but gestured inside his office.

When they'd sat down, Pete said, "As you know I've been

in the army five years, Turk. And I've been saving up just for this day."

Turk stared at Pete. "You telling me you came here to pay off?"

"Correct, Turk. Five big ones." He reached into his inside coat pocket, withdrew a fat envelope and, standing up, began counting fifty- and hundred-dollar bills onto the desk in front of the amazed Turk.

"There it is," Pete said proudly. "Five grand—five—count it."

Turk shook his head slowly. "I wouldn't believe it if I didn't see it. I figured I'd really have to reach out for you."

"Like I said, five years I've been putting aside dough for this day. Now"—he sighed—"it's Tap City for me. But it's worth it." By which Pete made it obvious that he was aware of the stories around New Orleans about how the Turk dealt with deadbeats.

With almost a respectful gesture, Turk picked up the pile of green bills, squared the edges and put the stack in his desk drawer, then looked up at Pete. "I've got a nice place here, I'll show you the casino. It happens I can use a new stickman— wouldn't take you long to sharpen up again. The job's yours if you want it."

"Thanks, Turk, I'll think about it. But I was planning to go to New Orleans and try to get in the action."

"You're better off in Miami, Pete. We're having one hell of a fine season . . . the town's full of suckers trying to get rid of money. You could take off a score here anytime." He turned to Carol. "Been giving any more thought to that proposition I gave you—?"

"I've been pretty busy getting my act in shape . . ."

"Pete, old buddy," Turk said, "here you're back from the army, you've found Carol again, she's doing great in Miami, getting to be a real celebrity these days"—he literally beamed

91

at her—"and you're telling me you'd leave her here in Miami without you?" Being sure he wouldn't.

Pete appeared torn. "Between the both of you," Turk pursued, "you could make some serious money for your future together. All Carol has to do is show up with a couple of players a week. Her twenty-five percent of the house score would add up to a nice bonus—"

"Which is half what she's entitled to," Pete said quickly. "Fifty percent is what she should get for a steer."

Turk leaned across his desk. "But it's only half as tough for a beautiful dame like Carol to lug a mark as it is for some monkey like you." Turk winked at Pete.

"There *is* that fellow that was buying champagne last night," Carol began tentatively.

"That's the idea," Turk said. "What about him?"

"He's from some rich oil family in Oklahoma."

"Rich, huh? Bring him around."

"Fifty percent," Pete said.

"Come on, Pete," Turk replied affably. "It's just a hobby for her."

"He seemed so nice." Carol looked genuinely remorseful.

"You're doing him a favor. He's rich. He wants some action. He might even win."

Carol looked alarmed for a moment and Turk laughed. "Don't worry, sweetheart, your twenty-five percent is insured. Nobody wins here unless we want it that way."

Carol looked at her watch. "Gee, time for me to get back to the Beachcomber Club and dress for the show." She stood up.

"When are you two coming back?"

"We'll be in touch tomorrow," Pete promised. "I appreciate the job offer."

"You can start tomorrow night if you want."

"We'll get back to you. Soon." Pete took Carol's arm and led her toward the door, Turk jumping to his feet, scurrying around his desk and opening the door for them.

92

"Pete, that was a real class gesture. I ain't gonna forget something like that. I'll be waiting for your call."

While Pete and Carol were paying their planned visit to Turk Mamonis, Cliff was allowing himself a far more pleasurable pursuit—the delicious Margo, now fully recovered from her disappointment at not being with him the previous night.

". . . it was just madness to come down here from Washington, I know," she was saying, seated on a banquette in the Bamboo Lounge, "but I simply had to get away, see some new scenery, get warm, and I've heard so much about Miami night life. . . ."

. . . it occurred to Cliff that he had never really known a woman, any woman. His love life had always been take, enjoy, maybe even give a little, but always move on, don't get stuck. He couldn't afford to be otherwise. Ever since he'd been old enough to know what to do with a woman, there had been only one thing totally on his mind . . . total ruination of Roy Brian Only when that was behind him could he start thinking about putting down roots . . . finding a woman to settle down with. But for now . . .

Cliff casually slipped an arm over Margo's shoulders and she snuggled closer to him. "I'm so glad I met you my first night here, Cliff. I didn't really know what I was going to do at Miami Beach."

"You're going to have a good time."

"Right!" She smiled brightly and looked up at him. "It's so nice to have someone to share things with . . ."

Cliff smiled back and ordered another drink.

Later they danced and then Cliff took Margo to dinner at the Beachcomber Club, where they danced again, Margo holding Cliff's hand tightly and pressing her cheek against his. For a brief moment Pete and Carol flashed by. "Do we have a lot to tell you!"

"Tomorrow," Cliff appealed. On the beach. At noon.

"We won't be back 'til after the late show. By the way," Pete said, "that bottle of champagne is still up there."

Then Cliff escorted Margo back to their hotel, and wordlessly they rode in the elevator to Cliff's floor, Margo waiting, her arm through his as he opened the door to the suite.

"What a beautiful room," she said, entering and swirling around in the parlor, her chiffon skirt rising above her thighs. "It makes my room look so dinky."

"My pleasure, madam. Shall I open the champagne?" Room service had provided a fresh ice bucket and glasses.

"Please."

The pop of the cork drew a murmur of pleasure from Margo, and wrinkling her nose, she slowly drank the glass offered her, never once taking her eyes off Cliff. She put the glass down, and Cliff reached out for her, drawing her close. For a moment Margo pulled away. "Now don't rush me, Cliff. I haven't had all that much experience with men," she whispered, and then pressed herself against him.

Minutes later, Cliff was closing his bedroom door.

It was an unsteady Cliff Thompson who emerged from his bedroom at about noon the next day and collapsed on the sofa beside Pete and Carol. Margo had proved to have had considerable experience with men after all. What's more, she really *enjoyed* herself. A considerable woman. . . .

The two looked at their enfeebled leader and laughed.

"How did it go at the Turk's?" Cliff asked, trying to pull himself together.

"How did it go with you last night?" Pete asked, and Carol put in, "Don't tell us, you don't have to."

Then seeing that Cliff was not about to be diverted from his question, Pete finally said, "Well, Turk was plenty surprised when I paid him off. Even offered me a job. Offered us both jobs. Lugger and stickman."

"Congratulations—"

"Yeah, but he's still only going for twenty-five percent of

what he takes off Carol's marks. And me, stickman? Better he should have asked me to shill. I can't go in and out with the dice like you need me to if I'm holding a stick in my hand."

"There's something I want to show you, Pete." Cliff stood up and walked back into his bedroom. Margo, a swirl of black hair on the pillow, was deep asleep. Picking up his father's black valise and bringing it back into the living room, he reached to the bottom, pressed a catch to reveal a secret compartment under the false bottom.

"Now I'll show you something you haven't seen before." Carol and Pete drew closer as Cliff pulled out a bamboo stick, curved on one end, a handle on the other. "Here's a dice stick like none you've ever seen before."

"Feels like any other stick," Pete slapped the curved end against his hand.

Cliff smiled mysteriously, took it back and then holding it straight up pressed his thumb on the forward part of the handle. A hollow appeared under his thumb and a pair of dice fell into his hand.

"You can go in and out with *this* stick, partner."

Pete whistled and taking back the gaffed stick, slid the dice in and out of the handle, a delighted grin on his face.

"With a little practice you can go in, out, any damn thing you want with that stick," Cliff said. "Completely control the game. My father had it made specially."

Pete laughed. "By God, Cliff. I believe we do have the paddle to Turk's ass."

"And Carol, you're going to start drawing your twenty-five percent of your first mark's earnings tomorrow night."

"Why wait?"

"Let the Turk want you a little more, get hungrier . . . tonight's your night off, right?"—Carol nodded—"okay then, it's settled. Tonight"—he spread his arms wide—"we celebrate, at the fanciest, best, most expensive, restaurant in town."

And for now, he decided, he'd rest up and try to get in shape for the matinee he anticipated Margo would be expecting.

He was right.

A considerable woman.

As they walked into the Blue Danube restaurant, Margo gasped. Confronting them was the most opulent setting they'd ever laid eyes on, a sea of rich crimson-red plush and discreet dark wood. Onstage an orchestra floated Strauss waltzes out over the crowd, while expensively dressed couples danced on the parquet floor.

"Good evening, sir," the headwaiter, white tie and tails, greeted them. "You have a reservation?"

"Thompson. Four," Cliff told him.

The headwaiter stared at his chart for some moments as though having difficulty locating the name. Cliff pulled a five-dollar bill from his pocket and palmed it to His Elegance—instantly the name was located.

Threading his way through the diners, the headwaiter showed them to a fine table for four and, as Cliff ordered a bottle of Bollinger brut champagne, they eased back in their seats and basked in the atmosphere.

Carol nudged Pete. "Hey, you know who that is at the table next to us?" nodding at a group of distinguished-looking diners. "The guy calls himself Count Zoltan Lazlow. Claims to be a real count and sure has the money for one. He comes around to the Beachcomber all the time and buys drinks for ladies he takes a shine to."

"What else does he do?" Cliff asked.

"I don't know. Whatever counts do, I guess."

They had just ordered their filet mignon and a second bottle of champagne when Count Lazlow noticed them and within moments was standing behind Carol's chair.

"Carol, dear girl, you are not working tonight? No? Then I shall not take my group to the Beachcomber Club."

Eyeing the vintage Bollinger and Cliff's expensive suit, he went on, "May I borrow Carol a few moments? Mr. Clegg Hoyt is with my party, the president of the Boca Raton Club, and he

96

is most anxious to meet this wonderful talent. Do excuse me."

Carol stood up, introduced the others, and with a whispered, "It's good for business," followed Lazlow to his table, where she seemed to make quite a hit, even with the ladies.

Margo left for the powder room just then, and Cliff leaned over to Pete. "Who do you think that count-of-no-account's mark is?"

"Count, huh! . . . Outside of Hollywood this is the only place in the country where that kinda dodge could work."

"He's a sharp hustler all right, lots of class . . . did you hear him say the president of the Boca Raton Club?"

"Yeah. Some joint north of here."

"Exactly five miles from Delray Beach," Cliff said. "You know who lives in Delray Beach? Or at least did. Roy Brian. . . ."

"Brian? I know what you're thinking already." Pete took a long sip of champagne. "Jesus, Cliff, can't I order bourbon and ginger? This stuff is starting to taste like old cheese."

Cliff laughed. "Yes, sure, go ahead No point in your trying to fake too much class, partner—drink your poison and save the champagne for the girls." He looked over again and studied the president of the Boca Raton Club.

A few minutes later their main courses arrived and Count Lazlow stood up and escorted Carol back to her table. "When you have finished dinner you will please all join our table? We are so fortunate I have been able to teach the chef here how to make a Hungarian flaming tart. Very special. My treat, eh?"

Cliff smiled graciously. "It will be our great pleasure to share the fruits of your culinary wisdom."

Count Lazlow's eyes squeezed shut in apparent pleasure. "I feel sure, Mr. Thompson, that a man of your obvious refined taste will appreciate the years of European gastronomical experience that is required to produce so delicate a dessert. *Bon appétit,* my friends."

Pete stared after Lazlow's retreating figure, then turned to Cliff. "Jesus, I don't know which of you bullshits worse."

Cliff grinned. "What did you tell him about me, Carol?" he asked quietly. "Your count is making me for a mark unless I'm very much mistaken."

"That you're from a *very* wealthy Oklahoma oil family and are considering setting up a law practice in Miami."

"Good girl. Let's play this one all the way."

Thirty minutes later, they were at Count Lazlow's table and being introduced all around. "We hear you're considering settling down here with us in Florida," Clegg Hoyt said affably. Hoyt was a bluff, vigorous fifty-year-old whose face had obviously seen as much of the outdoors as of corporate offices.

"I like the area." Cliff shrugged. "I suspect that Miami or even farther north, say Fort Lauderdale, would be a good place to practice law."

"What's your specialty?"

"I specialized in petroleum law—for family reasons—before going into the service." The veiled allusion to wealth was not lost on Lazlow, Cliff noted. "But as a major in the judge advocate general's office I was of course involved in courts-martial and developed an interest in criminal law. I think that's the area I'd like to go into now."

As he talked he became aware that Hoyt and the others were obviously puzzled by the seeming contrast between himself and Pete. Even their girls were markedly different: Margo a rather demure—with her clothes on, at least—quietly dressed young lady and Carol a flashy blonde. Cliff decided he'd better clear up their questions.

"I'm fortunate," he went on, "that Mr. White, who was my investigating sergeant in the adjutant general's office, is knowledgeable about the Miami area and has agreed to become my chief investigative assistant in my new practice."

"How fascinating," said Mrs. Hoyt, a refined-looking, gray-haired lady. "Mr. White, you are the first, can I say private eye?"—Pete grinned and nodded—"the first private eye I have ever met."

"You don't come across too many of us," Pete agreed. "But

98

every lawyer who works on criminal cases needs us."

"And now," Count Lazlow pronounced dramatically, "may I introduce to you a special treat, *Egapplacheenta,* Hungarian flaming tarts made from an old family recipe, from the time when my grandfather served the Archduke Franz Joseph Hapsburg—as his foreign minister."

Somehow Cliff managed to keep a straight face as the tarts were brought on, flames dancing, by the chef himself, while a white-haired waiter ceremoniously poured brandy and Benedictine.

"Your family must be very old," Margo said, meaning it, to Count Lazlow.

His eyes squeezed together again in an expression of delight. "My dear, the Lazlow family is so old in the courts of Bohemia that we consider King George of England *nouveau.* When King Charlemagne and his horses invaded our lands, back in the Middle Ages, it was the Duke of Lazlow that met him and turned him back."

"I thought it was in Spain, the Pyrenees, where he was finally driven off," Cliff said almost as an aside.

"Listen, Charlemagne was all over the place. And there was Lazlows in Spain too."

"I've never met real royalty before." Margo gushed. And you still haven't, Cliff thought. A natural straight, she might prove more useful than he'd thought.

Clegg Hoyt turned from the count, his credulity obviously strained. "Are you a golfer by any chance, Mr. Thompson?"

"Yes, I enjoy the game. Of course a wartime army isn't exactly the ideal place to keep one's game sharp."

"Well, we'd surely enjoy having you come up to the Boca Raton Club for lunch sometime. Maybe we can work a game in. You have a home course?"

"I play at the Tulsa Country Club when I'm home . . . which reminds me, now that I'm out of the army I'll have to switch from a military to a regular member again."

"When do you think you might come up?"

"You know, that's a funny thing," Cliff said casually . . . "I'll be in your area tomorrow."

"Then it's settled! One o'clock?"

Cliff nodded, darting a look at Margo. He'd have to be out by ten-thirty latest, he estimated. "Perfect. You can meet some of the members—"

"I am going to be there myself," Count Lazlow joined in.

"Good, Zoltan. I'm sure we can persuade Cliff that there's no place better for him to start his law practice than here with us—"

"We'll all give you our business, I'm sure, Cliff," Mrs. Hoyt added quickly. "Of course, we hope we won't need a criminal lawyer." She laughed wickedly.

Cliff smiled, nodded, and decided he badly needed a breather. He reached for Margo's hand. "Would you like to dance? A shame to let all this music go to waste."

As Margo flowed into him on the dance floor, Cliff half-muttered a note to himself . . . "Better leave a call for nine A.M."

"So early?"

"That'll be eight o'clock in Tulsa. I have to talk to my old buddy, Jack Brady, the golf pro there. Used to coach me at the Bent Creek Club in Grove City."

"What do you want to talk to him about?" Margo asked petulantly.

"Golf, darling. What else?"

11

AT ONE O'CLOCK on the dot, Cliff emerged from the chauffeur-driven limousine he had rented at the Roney Plaza and entered the Boca Raton Club, a long, low, pink stucco building covered with jacaranda, jasmine, and poinciana blossoms. He was greeted at the door by a porter and immediately escorted into the grill room, where Hoyt, a pleased expression on his face, stood up and introduced Cliff to the other members seated around the table.

"You fellows had better get to know Cliff Thompson," he said jovially. "You may need him someday. He's going to be practicing criminal law around here." There was much good-natured joshing regarding which members would be requiring Cliff's representation first, after which drinks were ordered around the table.

A man named Pierce Lovell, originally from Sewickley, Pennsylvania, said, "I'm told you have a background in petroleum. Any truth to the rumor you might be interested in buying up mineral rights in Florida?"

"I hadn't thought too much about that, sir . . . just two weeks ago I was still a major in the adjutant general's office. But oil has been the family business. . . ."

Another member said, "I hear that some geologists think there may be oil in southern Florida."

"I've heard that," Cliff replied, caution in his tone, as though he were reluctant to admit he might be interested. Interest, however, clearly picked up all around the table. Here was a wealthy young man about to become even wealthier . . . right in their own backyard.

"We'll have to introduce Cliff to one of our members who isn't here today," Hoyt said.

"I have already made arrangements." Count Lazlow quickly staked his claim. "When Roy gets back I will take Cliff to his home for dinner." The count turned to Cliff. "We are talking about Roy Brian—"

"Hey, isn't Brian from Oklahoma?" Pierce Lovell asked.

"Brian . . . yes, I think I've heard of him," Cliff said. "He hit oil in Grove City . . ." So the address on the mineral rights was still good . . . he could barely contain his excitement.

"Yes, we've all heard him talk about Grove City," Hoyt replied. "But now as for Florida . . . maybe we can put a little syndicate together right here. You never know . . ."

A trim, exceptionally attractive young brunette walked through the grill room just then, dressed in a short white tennis skirt.

Count Lazlow smiled, his eyes closing a moment. "Will somebody tell me how it is my timing is always so perfect." He tapped Cliff on the arm. "We were talking about Roy Brian who, it so happens, is in Veradero Beach, Cuba, with his wife Eleanor. The beautiful young lady that just walked by is his daughter, Kathy."

"I'll introduce you to her, Cliff," Hoyt offered.

"I will make the introductions," the count announced imperiously, stood up and walked over to the table where Kathy was sipping a tall glass of iced tea.

"The old goat," Lovell grumbled. "How that leftover piece

102

of European decadence ever got into this club—"

"Oh, come on, Pierce," Hoyt said, "the count's the only good laugh we get around this club some days. And he came in handy during the war, remember—we needed every active member we could get just to help pay upkeep on the grounds."

Count Lazlow had now turned toward them and was gesturing to Cliff, who stood up. "Excuse me a minute, gentlemen."

As Cliff approached the table, the count said, "Cliff, I want you to meet Kathy Brian. I was just telling you about her father, my good friend Roy."

Kathy put out her hand and Cliff was surprised at the strength of her grip and the directness of her gaze. "Kathy, this is Cliff Thompson. As a matter of fact he is from Oklahoma too, just as your father is."

"Oh, really? Can you sit down Cliff?"

"For a few minutes. I'm having lunch with some other people—"

"They will wait," Lazlow declared. "Sit. . . . Cliff is considering staying here in Florida. We are all trying to convince him that he will like it here."

"I certainly think I will." Cliff looked at Kathy. "This is a lovely club."

"Yes . . . do you play tennis Mr. Thompson?"

"Golf is my game, but I can give someone a little exercise, I guess."

"After lunch you should try a game with Kathy," Lazlow suggested. Once a shill, always a shill. "She's our women's champion."

"Then I'm sure she's too good for me, but I'm sure I'd enjoy it anyway."

"You come out to court one," Kathy said. "I've got to give a lesson to a group of the younger girls but when that's over—"

"You can give me one," Cliff finished for her.

Kathy smiled, finished her tea and stood up. "See you in about an hour, right, Mr. Thompson?"

"Look forward to it, Miss Brian."

Back at the table, during the course of the meal, they set up a golf match with Cliff for one-thirty the next day. Cliff laughed and chatted with them, but his mind was elsewhere. Her name was Kathy Brian. . . .

Kathy was a champion all right, Cliff quickly discovered as they rallied, warming up. She had a forehand drive like a man's and her backhands rocketed across the net. "Are you ready to start, Cliff?" Kathy called out.

"No, but I'll never get any better."

"Rough or smooth?" she asked.

"You go ahead and serve."

Wearing the white ducks and polo shirt he'd brought along in case of a golf or tennis match, Cliff crouched in the ready position, expecting the bullet serve she uncorked, but still unable to get his racket on it.

Fifteen-love. They changed courts.

Cliff managed, with an awkward darting stab, to get her serve back on the second point and even managed to sustain a short rally before she slammed a high shot directly back at his feet. Thirty-love. Two more serves and a sheepish Cliff turned to Lazlow, Clegg Hoyt, and Pierce Lovell.

"Love game. Like I said, I'm a rusty ex-soldier. But no excuses. The lady is a champ."

"I told you so," Lazlow called out. After she'd won three more games running, Kathy turned off some of her steam and Cliff managed to win a couple of games. And now that she had demonstrated her unmistakable superiority over Cliff on the court, she settled down to enjoying the game, joking with Cliff, congratulating him on his good shots, and giving him tips.

"What do you charge for lessons?" Cliff asked as they changed courts after the first set. "I'll owe you when this is over."

"Please, Cliff, this is on the house. . . ."

Let's hope we can get down to business later, Cliff thought. Meanwhile, Hoyt and Lovell were exchanging knowing smiles—as Cliff of course intended—figuring that if he was this awkward playing a woman, however good, in tennis he would surely be no big threat the next day. Lazlow, too, was wondering how high he could push the stakes on the golf game, but that wasn't the only thing on his mind. He saw how Kathy and Cliff played, obviously enjoying each other. By the time they'd finished the second set, they were clearly far more interested in each other than in the game. When Roy Brian returned from Cuba, Lazlow decided, he would make sure he approved of this young Thompson. Brian was always interested in meeting wealthy men he could take off . . . and if the count brought him in there might well be some cash in it for himself.

It was four o'clock when Kathy and Cliff finished their mismatch and Lazlow duly noted the way her shoulder brushed against his, and his arm went briefly around her waist, as they walked through the narrow gate of the court.

"You were magnificent, my dear," he told Kathy and smiled at Cliff. "Now, you two, you must have cocktails and dinner with me this evening. I told Roy and Eleanor that I would look out for Kathy while they were away and I can't think of any better way to do it."

"Sounds great to me," Kathy said.

Cliff shook his head sadly. "Count Lazlow, I really wish I could. There's nothing in this world that I'd rather do"—he looked at Kathy—"but unfortunately I have a dinner appointment in Miami Beach. . . ."

Kathy's disappointment was obvious—as was Lazlow's. "Can I have a rain check? Any other time at all . . . say, tomorrow?"

Kathy hesitated. "I promised the Leighton Smiths I'd go to their party . . . but maybe I can work something out. You're coming out tomorrow to play golf, right? I'll see you then and let you know. Okay?"

"Sure." He picked up the bag with his clothes in it. "See you tomorrow."

As Kathy made for the women's locker room Lazlow accompanied Cliff to the parking lot. "I know about your appointment tonight . . . and I am sure your lovely Margo is extraordinary in many respects. But, my friend, don't settle for a ham sandwich when a gourmet banquet awaits you. . . ."

Cliff smiled. "I assure you, count, tonight's appointment *is* business."

"Yes . . . well, I urge you not to miss this opportunity. Kathy Brian is the most sought-after young woman in the city . . . and not only for her beauty."

"I believe it. I'll see you tomorrow, count."

"Meet me at the cashier's desk at noon. Till then, my friend."

"You betcha, count," Cliff said to himself as he got into his limousine and headed back to Miami Beach.

At nine that evening Cliff, dressed in his Brooks Brothers suit, arrived at the Palm Isles Club with Carol LaRue on his arm. The Turk was at the door to greet them.

"Nice to see you again, Carol."

"Turk, I want you to meet Mr. Cliff Thompson. He's been a regular at the Beachcomber and I told him about your place and he just couldn't stay away."

"Carol here says you have the best room in town if a fellow wants a little action," Cliff said.

"Nice of her to say that." Turk gave Carol a nod. "We get a lot of action from all over. It's upstairs, please follow me."

At the top of the stairs Turk knocked on the door to the casino, a small window slid open and the door swung inward. A crap game was going full blast along with two blackjack tables, a poker table and a roulette wheel. Girls in short skirts and bare midriffs were passing out drinks, and as Cliff walked in the dealer's voice at the crap table boomed out, "Eight the point and winner pay the line, same good shooter."

"That's five passes in a row," one player said excitedly to another.

"Yeah, the dice are smoking tonight."

Cliff smiled at the shills' patter, knowing he was probably one

106

of the few real players in the room. Most of the patrons were there to provide a front for the marks who would be taken off. As Carol led Cliff to the dice table, the shooter conveniently sevened out, and in one smooth gesture the stickman called out, "Seven the loser, the last come on the outside, new shooter coming up," then scooped up the dice with his stick and handed them over to Cliff.

Cliff didn't bother to test the dice. This wasn't the night for the big score, just a preliminary round. With Carol encouraging him, Cliff began rolling, betting twenty dollars a throw, cash on the table. His first roll came up nine and he bet another twenty at odds of three to two. He made the nine and had ninety dollars in front of him, let it ride and came out with a seven. Now he had one hundred eighty dollars. He bet fifty on the line, rolled a ten and took double the odds for a hundred, then with the "players" roaring encouragement, came up with a six and four. "Big Dick from Boston. Ten the winner pay the line," the stickman intoned, and Cliff had five hundred and thirty dollars in front of him. He placed two hundred dollars on the line and came out with a six and five. "EEOOLEVEN, a natural. This man is really hot!"

Cliff put an arm around Carol and kissed her. "Hey, baby, you're bringing me luck. Here, blow on these, make them talk sweet to me."

Turk grinned and nodded to Carol, who kissed Cliff back and blew on the dice.

By the end of an hour Cliff was four hundred and fifty dollars ahead. . . . "I've got to leave you here, Cliff," Carol said as Cliff walked away with her from the crap table. "Time for me to go to work."

"Maybe I'll go with you."

"But you're doing so well and you wanted to come here. Tell you what," she said as the Turk came up to them, "you stay here and I'll come back after the last show. By then you should have a fortune and we can go out and spend some of it."

Cliff took the drink a waitress had handed him, gulped half of it down and said, "I already got me a fortune, baby, and I'm ready to spend it on you right now."

"Now, Cliffie, you know I gotta work—"

"I told you, baby, tell me how much they pay you and I'll double it for two weeks and you take a vacation with old Cliff."

"Hey, I just might take you up on that, be careful . . . now you stay here and I'll see you in a couple hours."

"Just don't forget, baby. I'll be waiting and rolling."

"I'll send her in one of our cars, Mr. Thompson," Turk offered, "while you do some more damage at the table."

"I'll be waiting," Cliff called, and then returned to the crap table.

"Nice piece of work, Carol," Turk said approvingly at the bottom of the stairs.

"But he's winning."

"We send him out a winner tonight and he'll come back and lose everything we can take off him. Unless, of course, you think he might take it and run."

"Cliffie baby? He's loaded. And hooked. I told you he's from a filthy-rich oil family." Carol looked around elaborately to see if anyone was listening, then bent her lips close to Turk's ear. "He's going to be around Miami for a while, he's buying up oil all over Florida."

"You mean he's buying mineral rights?"

"Yeah, that's what he calls 'em. He's buying these mineral rights all over."

"He's from Oklahoma?"

"That's right."

"Okay, kid, thanks. And remember you get twenty-five percent of everything he loses."

"Thanks, Turk. Pete can collect for me."

"What about Pete? He coming in?"

"You said the job starts Wednesday, that's tomorrow. He'll be in."

Turk put Carol into a house car and sent her back to the

Beachcomber, then returned to the casino, where Cliff was betting high on each roll of the dice. The temptation to take him off was finally too much. He gave a nod to the stickman.

In twenty minutes Cliff lost four hundred dollars, and by the time Turk came back to inspect the table, he was ready to leave. "Well, Turk, I had an interesting evening—"

"There's a lot of it left."

"No, when Carol left I guess she took my luck with her. Besides, I've run out of cash." Cliff smiled. "Hell, I'll get even tomorrow night. And then some."

"That's the spirit. We'll be looking for you, Mr. Thompson."

"Call me Cliff. My daddy was always Mr. Thompson. I'll see you."

Cliff went outside the Palm Isles Club to the waiting limo, and by eleven-thirty he was back at the Roney Plaza, where Margo was waiting for him in the Bamboo Room. "I hope your business was all that important," she said impatiently. "I'm starving—"

"I told you to grab a bite, honey."

"I'm starving for *you*, Cliff."

"So we'll eat in and sack out early. I've got a big golf game coming up tomorrow . . ."

"Umm, but first you've got to handle, as I believe you call it, my action.

He smiled. A considerable woman.

12

COUNT LAZLOW, a welcoming smile spread across his face, was waiting for Cliff at noon the following day in front of the cashier's cage at the Boca Raton Club. Cliff handed the cashier the five-thousand-dollar certified check he had picked up from the Lincoln Bank and Trust Company that morning and waited while the cashier examined it, put it in the safe and gave Cliff a receipt. Lazlow took the receipt from Cliff.

"I'll take this out and show it to Clegg and Pierce before you arrive. That way it will not be embarrassing, eh?, and they'll know the money is on deposit before they set the stakes."

"Did the club pro get my handicap from Jack Brady in Tulsa?"

"Yes, yes, all taken care of."

It was obvious that Clegg Hoyt and Pierce Lovell were golf nuts—they had the look: powerful hands and wrists, weather-seamed, suntanned faces. They also gave off the aura of security and self-confidence that went with the very rich. They welcomed Cliff to the foursome with cheery good humor. "You don't mind if we make this game interesting, Cliff, do you?" Lovell smiled suggestively.

110

"Can you take one hundred dollars a hole and one hundred a stroke?" Hoyt added.

"Fine with me. I find concentration falls off unless there's a little fear in the game."

Followed by good-old-boy chuckles. And as the guest, Cliff was given the honor on the first tee.

The first hole was a par four, straight away from tee to the green four hundred thirty yards away, a green guarded by four bunkers. Cliff pushed a drive one hundred eighty yards out, almost in the rough to the right of the fairway.

"Well, you're in the fairway, Cliff," Clegg Hoyt boomed encouragingly as he drove his ball two hundred twenty yards down the middle. He stood back from the tee, nodding in satisfaction as Lovell came up and proceeded to drive his two hundred thirty yards straight down the fairway. Count Lazlow's drive landed between Hoyt's and Lovell's. Being away, Cliff would shoot first. He selected a three-wood and managed to hit his ball fifty yards short of the green. The other golfers, who had observed his relatively poor drive, were surprised at what he'd accomplished with his three-wood. Both Hoyt and Lovell were on the edge of the green with their second shot; Lazlow managed to catch a bunker.

Hoyt and Lovell nodded to each other, satisfied with the way the game was shaping up. Cliff's Tulsa pro had rated him with a fifteen handicap over the telephone, and they had promptly said theirs was twelve (actually it should have been seven or eight). Still, it gave Thompson three strokes, but even with this advantage they were confident that he was not going back with any part of that five thousand dollars he'd deposited in the club safe.

Cliff, still away, now selected a wedge and neatly lofted his ball high into the air. It stopped within ten feet of the pin. Hoyt and Lovell winced, then congratulated their guest on a fine shot.

Cliff shrugged and thanked them.

Count Lazlow made a bogey five. Hoyt and Lovell both two

111

putted for pars, and Cliff sank his for a hard par.

The next hole was a long par three. In view of Cliff's sorry drive on the first—and the unlikelihood that his wedge had been anything more than a lucky shot—Hoyt and Lovell both pressed him on the second hole to double his belts, figuring to make up lost ground, but it only got them deeper into trouble. At the end of nine holes the recklessly doubling duo were close to five thousand dollars behind Cliff—the count had wisely resisted any impulse to press his own bets—and on the tenth hole they started to come apart completely.

Cliff was aware of their growing anger, but decided there was nothing he could do about it . . . yet. Because of the various handicaps, this became the most complicated round of golf he'd ever played—if he didn't mathematically calculate each hole precisely right, he could blow the whole thing then and there. . . .

It was a disgusted, wrathful Clegg Hoyt and Pierce Lovell who stalked off the eighteenth green studying their scorecards. "We're going to the locker room," Hoyt threw over his shoulder at Lazlow and Cliff. "We'll settle in the bar."

Lazlow directed a baleful glare at Cliff. "Come with me, my new young friend," his voice dripping sarcasm, "follow me."

Cliff followed the count off the eighteenth green to an empty practice green, at the far end of which he abruptly turned on Cliff. "So you had us all fooled, even *me*. I must really have been going soft these past few years to be taken in by a hustler. Well you can congratulate yourself, Mr. Thompson. You may be the first golf hustler to take off members of the Boca Raton Club right here on their own course. We try to guard against this sort of thing—"

"I don't know what you're talking about—"

"You don't know what I am talking about? What I'm *talking* about is your beating the president of the Boca Raton Club and two other members for five thousand dollars this fine afternoon. You think I don't know a hustler when I see one?"

112

"You're way off base, Lazlow," Cliff said carefully, "I don't even know the word—"

"He doesn't know the *word*," Lazlow called up to the sky. "Well let me tell you, if there's anybody knows a hustler when he sees one, it's me. Count Lazlow. I have taken off the richest marks in Europe. I even helped the Duchess of Fairleigh hustle one of America's richest industrialists out of half a million dollars, which the lady and I split. I don't know a hustler? Where do the Lazlow family recipes come from? From my years as *maitre d'* of the finest restaurants of Europe. Golf? You think *I* don't know a golf hustler? I've played courses from Japan to France to South Africa. I knew you were a hustler on the third hole. No, I knew it on the *first* hole when I saw your second shot after that pulled drive. You didn't see *me* pressing any bets. Where do you think I got the money to belong to this club? You are an amateur, a neophyte compared to Count Lazlow."

Cliff stared at Lazlow, a look of innocent surprise and hurt coming over his face. "I really don't know what this is all about . . . if anybody was—to use your expression—being taken off I guess it was me. I'm the one that lost today the way Hoyt and Lovell were pressing me."

Now it was Count Lazlow's turn to show surprise. "What do you mean, Thompson?"

"Just what I said. I lost. I don't know what's bothering Pierce and Clegg. They certainly didn't say much to me when they walked off the eighteenth hole."

"Thompson, what in hell are you talking about?"

Cliff tapped his scorecard. "Well, look at the scores, hole by hole. They both had twelve handicaps and I had scratch. They certainly came out ahead of me."

"What are you trying to pull, Thompson? Your home pro in Tulsa gave you a fifteen handicap. Why do you think Clegg and Pierce are so sore?"

"A *fifteen* handicap?" Cliff said incredulously. "I haven't had a fifteen handicap since I was fifteen years old. I was a scratch golfer when I went into the army. If anyone should be sore it's me. Hoyt and Lovell obviously play to a six or seven handicap—not the twelve they went out with. So, count, if anybody was taken off today it was me. They were after blood. And they got some."

Lazlow's mouth was open, and then it stretched out into a broad grin. "Come on," he said, suddenly buoyant, and led Cliff to the bar where Hoyt and Lovell were glumly studying their scorecards.

"Gentlemen, there's been something of a misunderstanding here," Lazlow announced jovially.

"Yes, I guess there has," Hoyt said, staring at Cliff with ill-concealed hostility.

"You don't understand, Clegg," Lazlow hurried on, "you and Pierce won today, I broke even—"

"What do you mean we won?" Clegg Hoyt tapped the score-cards. "The way I figure it, Mr. Thompson, with his fifteen handicap, beat us out of about three thousand dollars each this afternoon."

Lazlow squeezed his eyes almost shut, an enormous smile spreading across his face. "No, no, Cliff just told me he's a *scratch* golfer. With your twelve handicaps you easily beat him."

Hoyt's scrutiny of Cliff was filled with new interest. "You're a scratch golfer? Then how come you went in with a fifteen handicap?"

"I can't understand it," Cliff said. "Somebody must have made a mistake. As far as I'm concerned I went in with no handicap, and incidentally, speaking of handicaps, if you fellows don't mind me mentioning it, you certainly play a superior brand of golf to any twelve handicap players I've ever come across."

Lovell and Hoyt looked at each other, grinned sheepishly and consulted their drinks. Then, all his former heartiness returning, Clegg Hoyt called out, "Waiter!" and turned to Cliff. "What are you drinking, Cliff?"

"First let's get this handicap of mine settled," Cliff answered tensely. "I want to telephone Jack Brady and see what he actually did tell your pro, if you don't mind."

"Oh, don't bother, our man must have misunderstood. Whatever, it's a pleasure to have a gentleman like you at our club. You could have taken us for a lot of money."

Cliff shook his head, "I expect to make my home here and I certainly wouldn't want to be thought of as indulging in any —irregularities? After all, gentlemen, I'm an attorney, not—to use the count's term—a golf hustler."

"You certainly are not," Lovell quickly agreed.

"So let's go over to the pro shop and find out what really did happen," Cliff urged.

"Cliff, forget it," Hoyt said.

"Yes, Cliff!"—from Lovell—"it's not worth it. Say, you should become a member of this club. I'll put you up, Clegg will second you, right, Clegg? We'll get you a guest card right now until your membership comes through, you're definitely the sort of man we want around here. And we'll play another game so you can win back the money you lost today."

"Or we beat you out of," Hoyt amended.

"Sure," Cliff laughed, "as long as you guys revise your handicaps four strokes down."

"You got us, Cliff," Hoyt beamed. "But no hard feelings, eh?"

"Well, since I only lost what?"—he studied his card—"two hundred dollars to each of you, I guess I can't ask for murder one."

When they had finished their drinks Cliff suggested they go over to the tennis courts and Lazlow promptly ushered them all across the lawn. Kathy Brian was at court one playing singles, and with a wave called out, "I'll be through in about fifteen minutes, Cliff. Buy you a drink?"

"You've got a deal," Cliff called back.

Count Lazlow instantly evaluated the scene. "Ah, yes, now tonight you and Kathy *must* come out to dinner with me—and the Hoyts and Lovells too. It will be a wonderful party, yes?" There was a chorus of agreement, but the count, Cliff noted, was suffering. He smiled to himself, thinking of the emotional confession the old fake had made to him not an hour ago.

Leaving the tennis courts Cliff, Hoyt, Lovell, and Lazlow went down to the men's locker room to shower and dress. The count opened his locker and glanced at himself in the mirror on the back of the metal door.

He looked at the wide, clean-shaven Slavic face, the nearly bald head, the hooded, evasive eyes. "You idiot," he whispered to himself. "You have exposed yourself."

He banged his locker shut and the clang of metal resounded throughout the locker room, startling the other bare-assed gentlemen.

13

AN UNCHARACTERISTICALLY SUBDUED Count Lazlow hosted the small party that evening in the dining room of the Boca Raton Club. To his right at the round table sat Kathy Brian and Cliff, to his left Amy Hoyt, Pierce Lovell, Clegg Hoyt, and Lovell's young second wife, Nancy.

The consuming interest at the table, indeed throughout the room, was the apparently building romance between Kathy and Cliff. Kathy's wealth and beauty made her a natural subject for gossip, but now the rumor mills really had something to work with . . . a handsome, mysterious young man, oil fields in Florida, an astonishing golf match.

"Tell us how it happened, Cliff," Nancy Lovell urged.

"Well, it's not so exciting. My father was a great sportsman" —Cliff felt he wasn't stretching things too much using that expression—"and when I was twelve decided he wanted his son to become a scratch golfer, so when I was fifteen my age was my handicap."

"I wonder what you were like at fifteen. . . ." Kathy mused softly. And for a moment the strong image of his father's face haunted him as Cliff was reminded of the father of this lovely girl, of Roy Brian's skunk treachery . . . and he imperceptibly shook his head, and threw it off.

"Mostly," he said, turning to her, "I was interested in golf and my father's business."

"I wish I could say the same for my son," Hoyt said. "We can't seem to interest him in anything but flashy cars and women."

"Now, Clegg, you know he'll grow up," his wife put in.

"Anyway, Zoltan told me what you all thought." Cliff smiled at the count. "It's a good thing you didn't walk off and leave me on the eighteenth hole. I never would have known what I was supposed to have done."

Count Lazlow breathed a deep sigh of relief—obviously Cliff was not going to give him away. He felt his old confidence returning, and with a smile observed Kathy's almost unconscious gesture as she reached out for Cliff's hand and held it tight in an act of loyal confidence. How could anyone think this sincere young man would ever do something dishonest? she seemed to be asking herself. Nancy Lovell and Amy Hoyt appeared to be thinking the same thing.

Exuberantly, the count stood up and called the headwaiter to the table. "Jarvis, I have it—just the thing. I will make Budapest Flamers for my guests tonight!"

Jarvis winced, but in the tradition of all good maitre d's with valued customers, smiled bravely.

"That will be an experience for your guests, sir."

"Yes, yes, you will love it. Listen, this drink was invented by my great-great-grandfather, the duke—to titillate the princess he later married!"

"Oh, my God," Kathy giggled, and Hoyt rolled his eyes up to heaven, but everybody was having too good a time to spoil it. As Lazlow ordered ingredients, Cliff tapped Kathy on the arm, nodding toward the orchestra, and in unspoken agreement they rose and walked out to the dance floor.

"Looks like Roy and Eleanor are going to have a little surprise waiting for them when they get back," Lovell said, a broad grin on his face, as they watched Kathy and Cliff sweep across the floor, barely aware of the stir they were causing.

When they returned to the table Count Lazlow was in command, meticulously pouring the ingredients of his flaming cordial into a silver bowl, imperiously ordering the maitre d' to hand them to him one by one.

"He's awful," Kathy laughed.

"He's the floor show," Cliff agreed. "How long have you known him?"

"Oh, ages—my father and Count Lazlow are old friends, I really don't even remember when I first met him. My father was the one who got him into the Boca Raton Club though . . . you know, sometimes I wonder who he really is. Dad always just gives me a mysterious look when I ask and says 'Zoltan and I have had some interesting experiences together.' "

"I'll bet they have."

Kathy gave him a quick look. "What do you mean, Cliff?"

"Nothing . . . Just that I'm sure anything Zoltan has done in the past has been intriguing. . . ."

With a flourish, Lazlow proclaimed his creation ready and, waving a match, touched it to the concoction. A bluish-yellow flame leapt from the bowl, attracting applause from some of the diners, and with a bow to the room, the count ladled the flaming savory coffee into cups.

When they had all finished and pronounced it excellent, Kathy put her hand on Cliff's arm and said, "It's warm in here. Would you mind, I'd like a little fresh air." Taking her hand and asking to be excused for a few minutes, he led her from the dining room. The eyes of every club member in the room watched them leave.

Outside, they walked slowly, arm in arm, over the grounds and past the tennis courts. After a while, Cliff asked, "When are your mother and father coming back from Cuba?"

"In about five days I think. Of course they could decide to

stay longer—Dad's interested in buying some Cuban real estate. It's practically like buying property in the United States when you go to Cuba."

"Maybe."

"I can hardly wait for you to meet Mother and Dad. I know they're going to love you. Especially Dad—you've got so much in common . . . the oil business, Oklahoma, and all. And my father plays a great game of golf. Not the way you play, of course . . . they talk about hustling golf," she laughed. "My father and some of the other members are really merciless when it comes to playing strangers for big stakes. He's not bad at tennis either."

"Tennis . . . that reminds me"—Cliff reached into his pocket —"I went by a jewelry shop this morning and saw something that made me think of you." He handed a small black box to Kathy.

"Cliff, you didn't have to do something like this." Opening it, "Oh Cliff . . ." Nestled in the box was a small gold tennis racquet hanging from a delicate gold chain. "It's adorable, Cliff, I love it."

"I managed to get an inscription put on it while I waited."

Kathy raised the gold charm closer to her eyes and in the bright moonlight read, "To Kathy—the only beating I ever enjoyed—Cliff." She read it again, "Cliff, thank you. It's really . . ." She laughed. "I'll bet you don't get beaten at anything very often . . . help me put it on, Cliff."

He took the chain, opened the clasp, and, putting his arms around her neck, slipped it on. They stood a moment silently looking into each other's eyes, then slowly moved closer together until she was against him. After another long moment Cliff bent his head forward and kissed her.

It was more like the kiss of two teenagers, Kathy thought, simple, very tender, undemanding. She wondered if the fifteen-year-old Cliff Thompson had kissed a girl this way back in Oklahoma . . . well, not quite this way, she decided, as the

120

excitement took hold of her and she put her arms around Cliff's neck, pulling herself tight to him. Some moments later they parted and looked at each other for a while, until Cliff blinked, a small crooked smile coming across his lips. He took Kathy's hand and together they turned back toward the clubhouse, slightly overwhelmed at how fast things were progressing. . . .

They entered the dining room just in time to see Count Lazlow ignite still another batch of his Budapest Flamers. "Oh no," Kathy whispered. "Look, Cliff, I know a marvelous lounge about a mile from here where we can hear some great music. Let's go, huh?"

Cliff smiled, his fingers interlocking with hers, "I'd love to, Kathy," and then the smile faded. "No. Oh, Kathy, I'm sorry I can't. I almost forgot I have a very important meeting tomorrow morning at seven o'clock. The man came in from Oklahoma just to see me and he's leaving town at ten—and what's more, I have to brief myself for at least an hour tonight before I hit the hay." The look of hurt and disappointment was plain on Kathy's face. "I am sorry, Kathy. I just wish we'd met before I got involved in these damned business meetings. . . ."

Kathy nodded and tried to smile brightly. "I understand, Cliff."

He leaned closer. "I'll make it up to you . . . next time. . . ."

"You know where to find me, sir."

"Is that an invitation?"

"Maybe. . . ." she said and started back to their table. "Now you'd better go . . . your limousine may turn into a pumpkin."

Cliff followed her back and said his good-byes, protesting his early morning appointment and thanking his host, and was waved farewell with a chorus of boozy cheer. Amy Hoyt and Nancy Lovell watched him leave.

"That's quite a new beau you've got there."

"I think it's a little early to use that word," Kathy said, but her friends saw a distinctly new excitement in her eyes.

Nancy reached over and patted her hand. "Don't worry, dear. Your father will just love him. . . ."

14

As THE LIMOUSINE sped away, Cliff relaxed in the spacious backseat, his thoughts turning immediately to Kathy. He wished like hell he could be with her, but tonight was the night: step one of the paddle.

His father had always counseled him that luck was the most elusive lady known to man and anyone who counted on her to make his way was a pigeon. Nonetheless, the last two days had presented him with a remarkably fortunate circumstance: Roy Brian had a beautiful daughter whom Cliff had never known existed before. Still, he reminded himself, if he hadn't instinctively felt that going to the Boca Raton Club would get him closer to Roy Brian he never would have met Kathy. The biggest problem now was how to use her without becoming so emotionally involved that he lost his objectivity, and promptly thought of that satisfying kiss on the beach after he had fastened the gold charm around Kathy's neck . . . the sort of thought he'd have to be careful about. Still . . . he wondered if Kathy had experienced the same feelings he had. Probably not, he told —reassured?—himself. She was beautiful, sought-after . . . plenty of men must be trying for her. . . .

Five days left, he thought to himself, four more nights before Roy Brian would return from Cuba. Could he handle both Kathy and the Turk within that time? He had to. There was no margin for failure now.

The limousine proceeded south through Fort Lauderdale and Hollywood, and as it approached northern Miami Beach he reached behind his head and found the package he had left on the ledge below the rear window. Unwrapping the brown paper, he took out the dice stick he had showed Pete, a string now tied around the crook at one end. Stretching his legs in front of him, he unbuckled his belt, pulled his pants open and pushed the stick, handle first, down his pant leg, then tied the string to a button Carol had sewed into the top of his slacks, and fastened his clothing back up again. The stick, about eighteen inches long, reached down below his knee. A few minutes later the limousine stopped in front of the Palm Isles Club, the driver jumped out of his seat, came around and opened the door. Cliff put a stiff left leg out of the car, then pulled himself out and up to a standing position.

"Did you pull a muscle or something?" the driver asked.

"I guess it was a case of too much too soon. You get a bit out of shape sometimes at a desk job . . . I don't expect to be in here more than an hour. Just wait for me in front."

The Turk was not downstairs when Cliff walked into the bar, which relieved him—he didn't want to have to explain his peculiar walk. Going over to the bar, he ordered a drink. "Just hold it for me, Joe. I'm going up to the men's room."

"It'll be waiting for you." Cliff walked up the steps, pushed the door open to the men's room and walked in. Nobody inside, just what he had hoped. He walked to the toilet stall he had inspected the night before, pushed the door open and locked it after him, then opening his pants pulled out the dice stick and buttoned himself up again. Then he climbed up on the seat cover. The toilet was an old-fashioned water closet with a water box and a pipe running down from it to the toilet bowl. The box had long ago come loose from the wall and now hung slightly

124

out on its brackets. It took only a moment to conceal the gaffed dice stick behind the box. Perfect.

Cliff stepped down to the tile floor and looked up with a smile of satisfaction, then waited a few moments, flushed the toilet and walked out. The precaution had been unnecessary, no one had entered the men's room.

"Where's that beautiful doll, you should forgive the expression, you were with last night?" the bartender asked, when Cliff had seated himself on a stool.

"She works until four in the morning." Cliff shrugged. "That's the trouble hanging out with show girls." Cliff nursed the drink for ten or fifteen minutes and then, as he had expected, the Turk, constantly making the rounds of his place, came down to the bar to see what was going on. Spotting Cliff he came over and sat down beside him. "Well . . . you came back."

"I told you I would. I figure on winning back my money from last night."

"Maybe your luck will change tonight. I've got a new stick man at the table."

Cliff looked at his empty glass and the Turk motioned to the bartender. "I'll have one too, Joe, the usual."

Cliff sensed that Turk had something else on his mind, something that didn't involve gambling. He decided to help him out. "I guess I won't be able to stay late tonight, Turk . . . a family associate in the oil business came in from Oklahoma today. We've got to go out and look at a few thousand acres of very promising mineral rights—"

"Mineral rights?"

"Umm"—then as though the idea had suddenly struck him —"hey, you've been around here awhile. Have you heard any rumors about oil slicks appearing in the swamps behind Miami?"

"No . . . I don't believe there's oil down in this part of Florida anyway. Why would a guy come all the way in from Oklahoma where there's lots of oil to look for drilling sites here?"

"You never know where you're going to find oil. Personally, Turk, I agree with you. There's an awful lot of oil left in Oklahoma that hasn't been hit yet. As a matter of fact, with the new deep-drilling rigs we've got now, I wouldn't be surprised if we hit oil in places where dry holes were sunk, say, just five years ago."

A glint appeared in the Turk's black eyes. "Now you sound like a professional oilman, Cliff. That's the way I'd look at it too. Did you ever hear of a place called Grove City?"

"Sure. I've been there. They've been getting a lot of production in Grove City . . . 'course the war just about exhausted the reserves there."

"But you just said with the new drilling rigs maybe they'll hit again, right?" Then, almost as an afterthought, "I've got some mineral rights in Grove City. . . ."

"Oh, it's a possibility there's more oil there. As a matter of fact we've talked about giving that area another shot." Cliff turned to Turk, affecting a faintly curious look. "Say, how would you happen to have mineral rights out there?"

"There's a fellow up in Delray Beach, a guy who likes big action, he was involved in Grove City. He paid me off a five grand marker with them. He always said they'd be real valuable some day. . . ." The Turk looked expectantly at Cliff.

"You never know." Cliff picked up the fresh drink and sipped at it as though bored with the conversation. "Tomorrow, after we've done exploring here I'll bring this Oklahoma fellow to the place. He likes his action too."

". . . Would you like to take a look at those leases?" Turk gave Cliff an eager look.

Cliff knew he had him now. Nothing else would have taken Turk's mind off the possibility of enticing another mark into his whack-out joint.

He shrugged. "If you want to show them to me I'll tell you what I think."

"Bring your drink, follow me." Turk was off the barstool

126

and heading for the stairs, Cliff following more slowly. Inside the office Turk pulled a key chain from his pocket, unlocked a desk drawer and pulled it open, taking out a frayed grimy envelope.

"Sit down, Cliff." Turk handed him the envelope and, opening it, Cliff began to shuffle through the documents. "Whoever gave you these must have passed a lot of others around too . . . nobody would start drilling operations on this property," he smacked the papers, "without having the minerals on all the land around it."

"You mean the guy I was telling you about sold a bunch of these things and none of them are any good without the other?"

"That's about it, Turk. Unless somebody seriously wanted to reassemble all the leases that this guy peddled around, there really isn't much value here."

"I should think somebody like you, maybe this Oklahoma guy you say is coming in, would be interested in doing just that. . . ." The Turk's eye gleamed at the chance of a sucker's bail-out.

"It's a possibility I suppose." Cliff put the leases back on Turk's desk and finished off his drink. "Well, I suppose I might just test the action a little before going home."

"Yea . . . look, why don't you ask your friend if he'd be interested in buying up these leases? I'd sell them real reasonable—"

"I'll ask him. I don't know what he'll consider reasonable, though, if he is interested."

"Roy Brian—that's the guy sold them to me—said they were worth at least twenty-five thousand dollars."

"Hey, Turk, I wouldn't even bring it up to my friend when you start talking that kind of money."

"Oh, I'm not trying to get any twenty-five grand. It's just a figure to start from."

"Well, let's forget it . . . I'll go in and play a little now." Cliff stood up and started for the door.

"Wait a minute." The Turk ran from behind his desk. "You think he'd go ten grand?"

"To be honest with you, I doubt he'd go the five grand you gave for them."

"Bring him around tomorrow night, Cliff. Let him have a look. I'd offer you a percentage of what I sell them for, even though I know you don't need it."

"That's right, Turk. Tell you what, I'll talk it over with my friend and if he shows any interest I'll let you know. I might even go in with him myself and try to assemble that block. Never thought of it before but it's probably a decent crap shoot."

"Cliff, for five grand you can walk out of here with those leases right now."

"Okay, we have a price to come down from." Cliff grinned. "I'll get back to you."

"Good, Cliff. I know you won't be sorry."

Inside the casino Turk took him over to the dice table. "That's the new stickman I told you about," nodding toward Pete.

"New shooter coming up," Pete chanted. He rolled a set of dice toward Cliff, and Cliff began rolling them indifferently. An hour later he was four hundred and fifty dollars behind again and turning from the table. The Turk quickly came up to him. "How'd you do?"

"Your new stickman doesn't give me any more luck than the last one." He shook his head. "I guess my mind isn't with it tonight." Cliff started to leave the casino, Turk walking beside him. "You're coming back tomorrow?"

"Turk, I assure you I will be back. I'm now nine hundred and fifty dollars behind and I want to win it back.

"We'll be looking for you . . . and your friend from Oklahoma."

"I'll talk to him while we're out prospecting tomorrow."

128

Turk accompanied Cliff to the door and watched him as he stepped into his sleek black limousine, the door held open by the uniformed chauffeur. As the limo moved southward down Collins Avenue, Turk grinned and nodded in satisfaction. One way or another, he said to himself, he had it made.

15

THE LIMOUSINE DEPOSITED Cliff in regal if lonely splendor in front of the Roney Plaza. It was almost one in the morning but the hotel was alive with activity, lights blazing, people milling about.

Cliff decided to stop in at the Bamboo Lounge to have a drink and run over the events of the day. He didn't really have an appointment the next morning, of course, and there was no big oil operator from Oklahoma coming in to see him, but having so realistically invented his early morning meeting, first for Kathy, then for Turk, he had almost come to believe it himself. He had just sat down at the end of the bar when a very upset young lady left her seat at a cocktail table and pushed her way up to Cliff.

"Hello there, Margo."

"Hello there? Is that all you have to say? I've been waiting for you all evening."

"We didn't have any real set plan for tonight, did we?"

"Set plan? I thought we were going to be together for my whole trip here. That's what you *said.*"

130

"I said I want to see you every chance I can get, Margo, but I'm in Miami primarily on business—"

"I thought you said you were going to put business aside and concentrate on us."

"Well, things came up unexpectedly. How about a drink?"

"Tom Collins . . . speaking of coming up, I'll bet you weren't even going to call my room."

"Look, Margo, it has been a very long day, and early tomorrow morning I have a business meeting with an associate who's come all the way from Oklahoma to see me. He has to catch a ten o'clock train north so we made a breakfast date."

"So?"

"So I ought to get a good night's snooze." He looked at his watch. "Seven o'clock—that gives me about five and a half hours sleep. I've really got to be sharp for this guy."

Margo took a swallow of her Tom Collins. Her voice was low and urgent. "You're telling me we're not going to be together tonight?"

"I told you, Margo, I'm one exhausted fella—"

"Now look *here*, Cliff. You left me alone all evening, I had to eat alone, sit around alone . . . it was very embarrassing. I kept thinking you'd come at any minute, I kept checking my box to see if there were any messages. The desk clerk probably thinks I'm some kind of a call girl. Men kept coming by asking me if I was lonely. Now, after all that, I'm still waiting and you tell me you're too *tired* to be with me tonight, or what's left of it."

Cliff felt guilty about Margo—she was right of course—but the memory of Kathy was still too strong . . . he knew he should tell Margo right now that it was over, but somehow he couldn't bring himself to tell her straight-out that way. . . .

"Margo, I played in a high-stakes eighteen-hole golf game today, then I went to a party that didn't break up until almost midnight, then I had to have a meeting with a business associate. Can't you see? I'm just too damn beat to be any good to you tonight . . . I understand how you feel Margo, and I'm flattered . . . I'm sorry as hell about tonight, I really am, but—"

"Well, what about tomorrow then?" she said, softening some. "We'll be together tomorrow, won't we?"

"I'll leave a message at the desk as soon as my meeting's finished." He tried to let her down gently. When she found no note, she'd realize, and maybe it wouldn't be so embarrassing for her that way.

"Will you at least see me up to my room?"

"Of course. . . ."

Outside her door she tried once again to persuade him to come in, "only for a drink," but finally Cliff took her by both shoulders, pulled her to him, kissed her gently and said, "Good *night,* Margo."

Walking down the hall, he could feel Margo's eyes following him. When he reached the elevators and turned, she was still there, standing outside in the hall. He waved, Margo waved back and the elevator doors opened.

The following day, Thursday, Cliff brought Pete and Carol up-to-date on his activities, including the exact location of the gaffed dice stick, and then quickly went back to the Boca Raton Club to keep his afternoon tennis date with Kathy.

It was a pleasure—although she beat him soundly again—and now, seated on the club veranda, the ubiquitous Count Lazlow was suggesting a reprise of last night's dinner. Cliff and Kathy declined.

"So it's going to be a nice quiet dinner for two tonight?"

"Something like that, Zoltan."

At five o'clock Kathy suggested they drive back to her home for a change and perhaps a swim before dinner, an idea Cliff strongly approved of, and they rode the five miles to Delray Beach in Kathy's robin's-egg-blue Cadillac convertible. Ever since meeting Kathy, Cliff had been curious about how Roy Brian was living on the wealth he had accumulated at Slim

Thompson's expense—but he was hardly prepared for what he saw.

Kathy guided her car between two fieldstone pillars on either side of the driveway . . . and before them was a wide, paved private road culminating in a long, two-story, white stone house surrounded by palm trees, manicured lawns, and neatly clipped hedges. It was the most imposing house he had ever seen, and as they crunched into the white gravel circle in front of the door Kathy, sensing his surprise, laughed and said, "It's modest but we like to call it home."

The interior was just as impressive: a huge living room with windows overlooking what seemed to be half a mile of bright green lawn gently sloping down past a tennis court and swimming pool to the beach and the shimmering blue Atlantic Ocean beyond. Oriental carpeting covered the entire floor and even to Cliff's unprofessional eye it was obvious that everything in the room was expensive.

"Shall we go on out to the pool?" Kathy asked. "I'm in the mood for a swim before cocktails . . . Jackson will have drinks for us when we're ready. . . ."

As Cliff watched her on the diving board a few minutes later, performing flips, jackknives, swan dives, he realized more than ever the enormity of what Roy Brian had done to him and his mother. They might not have lived like this, but at least they could have avoided the semi-poverty they had known ever since Slim's death, her grinding daily struggle to get enough to eat, enough to wear, enough to . . . he had to calm down, he reminded himself. The last thing he wanted now was for Kathy to sense his anger. He had tonight and three more nights before Roy Brian and his wife returned from Cuba. Four days and nights to win her over completely . . .

He reached over to Kathy, took her hand in his and said, "Shall we try that place you were telling me about last night?"

The headwaiter at the Embers restaurant was immediately at their side as soon as Kathy entered and, with much bowing, showed them to a banquette at the far end of the room from the orchestra. As the music wafted around them, they ordered wine and talked and ordered steaks and talked, and the evening floated by.

"You feel like dancing?" he suggested.

"I thought you'd never ask."

His cheek next to hers, her body firmly fitted to his, they danced easily, naturally, for a long time before returning to the table and the cordial they'd ordered. "I'm sorry it's not a Hungarian Flamer," Cliff laughed. . . .

By now it was getting late, and Cliff said quietly, "I suppose I ought to be thinking about getting back. My driver will be waiting for me at the club. . . ."

"Oh?" The disappointment came through clearly. "Another business meeting tomorrow morning?"

Cliff suddenly made up his mind. "No . . . no, nothing really . . . I suppose the driver can wait awhile."

Kathy reached for his hand. "The driver can go home . . . we've got plenty of guest rooms at my house. You can have your choice . . ." Her eyes sparkled.

"You know, Kathy . . . that may just be the best deal I've heard all week."

Forty minutes later they were back at Kathy's house, strolling on the lawn toward the beach. It was a clear night with a bright moon . . . "Just like last night except this time I don't have to leave you—"

Kathy turned to him, silencing him, and they were in each other's arms, and their first tentative kisses became more demanding. Kathy, breathing deeply, took a step backward and reached for his hand. "Come, let's find you a room for the night . . . it's chilly out here . . ."

She led him back through the French doors into the living room and up a wide semicircular staircase to the second floor. "This way is the guest wing . . ." She smiled quickly . . . "Oh I'm not nervous or anything like that." They walked down the hall and Kathy opened a double door, revealing a parlor. "Daddy calls this the presidential suite. We've had the presidents of three oil companies and one steel company here—plus some other questionable characters." She smiled at him and pushed the door open to the bedroom, where an outsize double bed dominated the room. She pointed to another door. "And this is the bathroom."

Cliff stared at the huge tub with the gold fixtures, the luxurious basin, the intricate wallpaper.

"I think I'll pass on this one, a little too much for me."

"I don't blame you. I'll show you the family quarters." She led him down the hall to another room that, from the faintly feminine scent permeating the air, had to be Kathy's. Through the windows he could see out over the lawn, the ocean gently lapping at the beach.

"This is more like it . . ." and once again they were in each other's arms, their kisses beginning this time with such intensity that in a few minutes Kathy said in a small, tight voice, "Cliff, let me go for a minute."

Cliff released her, and she went into the bathroom. "I'll be right out . . . darling."

Cliff took off his clothes, except for his underpants, pulled down the sheet and blanket and lay down, waiting for Kathy . . . for Roy Brian's daughter . . . whom he would soon be making love to in Roy Brian's house. The notion excited him, but it was not an uncomplicated feeling . . . this was a lovely, beautiful, natural girl and, if he wasn't careful, he could damned easily fall in love with her. . . . Kathy opened the door, and the light from the bathroom silhouetted her firm, full figure through the negligee. "I am, as they say, all yours, darling . . ."

Cliff swung his feet over the side of the bed and kissed her. "I'll be right out myself." When, minutes later, he emerged Kathy was sitting up in her bed, smiling expectantly. Laid out along the bottom of the bed was a plum-colored bathrobe. "I thought you might be more comfortable if you had a robe, so I borrowed one of Daddy's."

Cliff looked at the robe. Not only was he going to make love

135

to Roy Brian's daughter in her own bed, but wear Roy Brian's fancy duds between sessions . . . for a moment he hated himself for the vulgarity of the thought . . . and then he stopped thinking and began to do what came naturally. Pulling off his underpants, he slid in beside Kathy. They began to kiss and caress, gently at first, then more and more urgently, and suddenly there was nothing between their bodies, her negligee lay on the floor as, her nipples firm with excitement, Kathy strained her body to his. Slowly, carefully, Cliff entered her and they began to move together, easily, as one, Kathy receiving his thrusts with the same anticipation as when they had danced so close together just an hour earlier at the Embers . . . when they had both known this moment was inevitable.

Gentle movement gave way to the insistent, and suddenly Kathy dug her fingers into the small of Cliff's back, and with a low moan threw herself harshly against him, urging, "Cliff . . . Cliff . . . *now* . . ." Cliff held back, then with a rush felt himself come inside her, her body shuddering against his. For long seconds their bodies were fused in orgasm and then Kathy lay back limply, deep sighs of pleasure coming from her.

Cliff turned to face her, their bodies still in close contact, his fingers tracing the outline of her breasts. "Cliff, you make me feel so incredibly . . . happy . . ."

"And you make me feel delirious, like I've got a hundred and ten degree fever in my brain."

She laughed. "You too? My experienced lover?"

"I'm not so experienced, just inspired."

The quiet period didn't last long. Their languidness soon turned to a new arousal and in a motion so natural and easy it seemed almost rehearsed they once more were part of each other. This time they tried to make it last longer . . . Cliff leading, Kathy following intently, they paused as they approached climax to let the pressure ease off . . . holding each other, feeling their bodies move together, it was finally too much . . . they could hold back no longer . . .

The next thing either of them knew about the world outside

136

was the sun shining through the window of Kathy's room. Kathy turned to Cliff, brushing her lips against his.

"I love you, Cliff. Face it, I'm afraid I'm in love with you . . ."

"Me too, Kathy." His eyes traveled around her room, so feminine and little-girl-like and—then fell to Roy Brian's robe on the floor, thrown from the bed during their lovemaking.

Well . . . round one was over, he had won it . . . and his adversary hadn't even entered the ring, except . . .

"What are you smiling about, Cliff?"

"Us. This has been a beautiful time for me . . . the best ever . . ." And, not according to game plan, he meant it.

"I'm very happy, Cliff. I feel the same way . . . and I feel something else, too, man-eating"—she smiled wickedly—"hunger! I'll get Jackson started on breakfast."

"Aren't you afraid he'll rat on us?"

"I don't care, I'm in love. Everybody around here might just as well get used to the idea."

"Do you think your parents can?"

"They damn well better."

16

THEY SPENT THE rest of the day together. Kathy packed a picnic lunch and they took it out in her boat, discovered a secluded beach where bathing suits were superfluous, finished a bottle of champagne, and made love in the sun. As evening began to fall they drove back toward the house, Cliff at the wheel.

Suddenly he stopped. "Well, I'll be damned." They were at a red light, but what had drawn his attention was a gaudy billboard beside the road, its words tumbled in with pictures of balloons, girls, food. "See that advertisement for the carnival in Lake Worth? It says 'Presented by Bill Stember.' "

"I see it. So?"

"Bill Stember was a friend of my father's. As a matter of fact —" Cliff checked himself. It was too soon to reveal so much.

"As a matter of fact, what?"

"Stember operated in Oklahoma, your dad probably knew him too. Bill's carnival hit all the oil towns."

"My father knew everyone, big and small, and that's a fact."

"I wonder what Bill's doing here in Florida?"

"The population here's growing every day," Kathy said.

"We've got as many customers for that sort of thing as Oklahoma does, and they probably have more money. Do you want to go see your dad's old friend?"

Cliff thought and then shook his head. "No, maybe another time . . . you'd like Bill, though. I'll never forget how he came to see Mother and myself after Dad died. . . ."

The light changed and Cliff drove on, but the poster had made him remember. . . .

"What are you thinking about, Cliff?"

Her question startled him. "Oh, I was thinking about a joke I once pulled at Stember's carnival."

"What was it?" and Cliff told her about the Razzle-Dazzle and the Test-of-Strength and the Hey Rube.

"Man, that carney never knew what hit him." He laughed.

"Served him right, taking advantage of a retarded boy."

"Long time ago . . . I haven't thought of those days since . . . I don't know when."

"Tell me about your family, Cliff. What was your father like? Do you have any brothers and sisters? Come to think of it, I hardly know anything about you."

"I'm sorry you couldn't have met my father and mother, Kathy. They would've loved you," and without taking his eye off the road, he slipped one arm around her shoulders and she snuggled close to him.

It was six o'clock by the time they got back to the house. "I feel delicious, Cliff, delicious-tired." Kathy stifled a yawn, then, giving him a mischievous grin, "Why don't I raid the wine cellar. I'll make us a couple of sandwiches and we'll bring it all up to my room. Okay?"

"Very okay." For a moment Cliff thought about the Turk and his unfinished business at the Palm Isles Club. Well, that could wait.

As they sipped their champagne, Kathy began pressing him again and Cliff decided that maybe now wasn't so bad a time after all to let her in on a bit of his past.

"I still want to know more about you, Cliff," Kathy insisted.

"You want to hear my war stories? I was a lawyer at Fort Devens most of the war—"

"I can't picture you as some old staid army lawyer."

"Actually, I wasn't all that staid. A friend of mine in the army, you'll meet him, Pete White, saw to that."

"Tell me."

"Well, Pete's a con man. You know what that is . . ."

Kathy nodded.

"Pete and I used to take off the odd army mark, just for the fun of it."

"Like I said, I knew you weren't some stodgy lawyer."

"Yeah . . . well, basically Pete ran the gambling games at Fort Devens—craps, cards, you name it. I sort of looked out for his back. It gave me something to think about when I wasn't working on a court-martial."

"What was your biggest score?" Kathy's eyes were full of excitement.

Cliff poured them each a full glass and, wearing Roy Brian's bathrobe tied loosely around his waist, sat back on the bed beside Kathy and began the story of the final golf game. When it was over Kathy put her champagne down on the bedside table and applauded. "Cliff, you're really a bit of a con man too, aren't you?"

Cliff put his glass down to reach out for Kathy, his hands sliding up under the filmy negligee, caressing her breasts. "Maybe, but in your case . . ."

"Right . . . no con for this girl, Cliff. But I admit I love you even more after hearing how you—how did you call it—'took off' those generals and, though I don't know how it's possible, I'll probably love you even more tomorrow morning . . ."

"Well, now that you know I'm not in danger of breaking off my wings if I lean too far back . . . maybe you'd like to come down to Miami with me tomorrow and meet a couple more non-angels—my buddies Pete and Carol. As a matter of fact why don't we do Miami tomorrow night, go to the nightclub

140

where Carol sings . . . and you'll be my guest at the Roney Plaza—"

"Little Miss Kathy stay at a *hotel* in Miami with a man? . . . I accept, sir, though I confess until you it hasn't exactly been my style . . . my God, Cliff, how you've changed me . . ."

He held up a champagne glass. "And that, lady, is just the beginning."

Twenty-four hours later, a radiant, suntanned couple walked through the door of the Roney Plaza Hotel, exciting a stir among the tourists milling in the lobby, and took the elevator to the tenth floor. Unlocking the door of their suite, Cliff ushered Kathy inside and waited while she looked the place over, glanced out the windows at the beach and the ocean beyond, and finally gave her judgment: "Well, it's not as deliciously sordid as I thought it would be. In fact, it's really quite nice for a hotel—"

"True, it's modest, but we call it home." He grinned, then pointed to the bottle of champagne he had ordered ahead. "We might as well drink to our first night in the wicked surroundings of a Miami Beach hotel." Pouring two glasses with great ceremony, "And now, *ta-da,* fanfare . . . the bedroom."

Kathy was delighted by vases of long-stemmed red roses Cliff had had placed about the room. She walked over to one of the vases, took out a flower and smelled it. "No, not so sordid at all . . . I will say for you, Mr. Thompson, when you lure a poor unsuspecting girl into a hotel room, you at least do it with style. How many notches on your belt from this performance? . . . No, damn it, don't tell me."

"Four years as an army lawyer doesn't provide many chances for meaningful conquests."

At least, Kathy thought, he thought it worth denying—"And now, sir, where are your friends?"

"I told Pete we'd meet him down at the Beachcomber Club. We'll have dinner there, watch Carol's act and then, who knows? I'm a poor country boy, can't afford to waste my investment in all these pretty flowers."

"Cool it, country boy," she said, but she didn't mean it.

A little while later, in a new dark suit and four-in-hand tie, Cliff descended to the lobby with Kathy and was escorting her to the door when Kathy stopped. "Wait, as long as we're here let me look around the hotel a little. I've never been here before, you know—"

"Pete and Carol should be waiting for us at the Beachcomber." Cliff's tone betrayed tension.

"I've heard stories about the Bamboo Lounge here." She went on, "You know what I mean."

"I'd guess what you hear is exaggerated," Cliff countered, but Kathy was already walking toward the lounge. Cliff went after her and took her arm, but it was too late. His stomach sinking, he heard Margo's voice: "Cliff . . . where have you been?"

Cliff tried to steer Kathy across the lobby but she held back. "Somebody's calling you, Cliff. Carol?" Cliff turned to face the inevitable.

"Cliff, I've been trying to call you for two days. Where—" Margo cut herself off, seeing Kathy beside him.

With nothing else for it, Cliff mumbled, "Kathy, this is Margo . . . she's staying here, on vacation . . ." The two eyed each other, then turned to stare at Cliff.

"Hey, Margo. I'm a little late for an appointment, I'll—"

"You're a little late for an appointment?" Margo smiled. "Two nights late. I waited until two this morning for you to get through with your last business appointment—"

"I met Kathy—" Cliff replied simply, with unconventional —indeed, shocking—candor.

"*You met Kathy* . . . after what we had together, the best you can say is—"

Margo's voice was rising now and people were beginning to notice. Cliff moved toward her and touched her on the arm.

"Come on, Margo, shape up. You were Margo and you 'didn't know a soul' . . . and I filled in. We got on, and I'm grateful. Period."

Margo looked about the lobby of increasingly beguiled tourists. To hell with it. Them. She turned to Kathy. "Good luck to *you,* kid. I lasted two good nights, count 'em, two," and she turned and walked back to the Bamboo Lounge.

"As you were saying about exaggerated stories . . ." Kathy laughed.

Still awash in truth, Cliff began, "Look Kathy, I met Margo the first night I checked into the hotel . . . in the famous Bamboo Lounge, matter of fact. I didn't know you existed—"

"But now you do. So, as you told your late friend, I suggest, Casanova, that you shape up and get me out on this town, as promised."

Which he did, and which she loved.

It was two A.M. when Cliff and Kathy finally got back to the hotel. Kathy was high on sheer excitement. "I haven't been out on the town in ages, Daddy didn't even like me to come down here to Miami."

Cliff went to the main desk to get the keys to his room and check on messages, and found an envelope in his box which he took along with the keys. "Someone leave you a message?" Kathy asked.

"Looks that way." Up in the suite, as Kathy was in the bathroom getting ready for bed, Cliff opened the note. As he suspected, it was from Margo. When Kathy walked out, she announced, "All ready, sir. By the way, what did Margo have to say?"

Cliff looked up, momentarily startled, then smiled. "She sends her love. Care to have a look? You might as well read it."

"Thank you, no thank you."

Cliff read the note. "Well, reading between the lines, she called some guy in Washington and asked if she should accept the marriage proposal she just received. He told her to get her ass home. Marriage prognosis: one week. Now hear this." Cliff read aloud, "I'm glad I found out the sort of person you really are before it was too late."

Kathy looked at him. "And is there anything I should know before it's too late?"

Cliff put an arm around her and led her into the bedroom. "You could make a pretty good start on it right now . . ." he suggested.

She was agreeable . . . "Nothing, blessedly, coy about this all-American girl."

Latish the following morning Kathy and Cliff were having breakfast in the parlor of their suite when Carol came out of Pete's bedroom and joined them. Cliff was delighted at the near-immediate empathy between them that had started the previous evening at the Beachcomber. Finally he broke into their chitchat, asking about Pete.

"He'll be out in a minute I guess," Carol said. "The Turk kept him working late last night."

Cliff asked Carol to take Kathy down to the shop in the lobby and get her a bathing suit and some casual clothes she could wear around Miami Beach for the weekend, after which on Monday Kathy had to go north to meet her mother and father at the West Palm Beach airport.

Carol liked the idea, and also volunteered to fill Kathy in on the basics of her special betting system on the horses that Pete had taught her in New Orleans. Kathy agreed it would be good fun for her ongoing new education. Her father was known to place a wager, but kept her pretty far from the gambling turf.

When Pete walked in, barefoot and in slacks, he approved. Kathy looked like a find . . . but she could, he thought, also be a serious diversion.

After the ladies had departed, Pete said, "Cliff, the Turk is ripe. He looks for you every night."

"We'll get to him, Pete. The timing on this has to be perfect. Let's wait till Monday, when Kathy's parents come in from

Cuba and I meet them, then we'll have at the Turk."

"So now he's 'Kathy's parent,' not 'that bastard Roy Brian.'"

"Just let me handle this, Pete, it's a very delicate situation."

"I'd say so. Hey, buddy, I've known you a few years and seen you up and down, but I've never seen you like this. That little broad has gotten to you. She's *all* over your mind . . ."

"Only one thing's all over my mind, and don't forget it. I haven't. Now, then, old buddy, how would you feel about a fourth partner in building our paddle for Roy Brian's ass?"

"Who?"

"Roy Brian's daughter."

17

MONDAY AFTERNOON AT three o'clock found Kathy dutifully waiting at the West Palm Beach airport for the plane from Havana, and as she watched the Eastern Airlines DC-3 touch down, then slowly sink back on the tail wheel, Kathy wondered if it showed. Would her mother and father look at her and know what a serious change had happened for her while they were away? Probably, she thought, *anyone* could see how she felt. And why not?

Kathy watched as the door to the plane opened and the steps on the concrete runway rolled over. An assortment of suntanned faces came through the door and then Eleanor and Roy stepped out. Waving, she called their names and, smiling, they waved back, and on the other side of Customs Eleanor Brian threw her arms around her daughter and kissed her. Then she stepped back. "Kathy, honestly, you look positively radiant. I've never seen you look so happy before. What in the world happened?"

Kathy, ignoring her mother's question, quickly threw her arms around her father, kissed his cheek. "Daddy, It's so good to have you all home again—"

146

"Great to be back, darling. Damn, I couldn't have stood another day with all those spics. There isn't a deal going that's worth having to hang around all those greasers." He gave his daughter a kiss and a long happy look. "Looks like you've been out in the sun. Playing a lot of tennis?"

Getting into the car, Eleanor Brian couldn't take her eyes off her daughter. Kathy's face showed a maturity and joyfulness she'd never seen before.

"So—what have you been up to, dear?" Roy said.

"Well, Daddy, I hit the lower depths and went to a Miami nightclub."

Roy Brian turned from the wheel. "A nightclub? . . . You didn't do that alone, did you?"

"Of course not, Cliff took me."

It was suddenly clear to Eleanor, as she'd suspected, what had happened. In the ten days they'd been away, Kathy had met herself a man. More than that, Kathy had apparently fallen in love with the man—that was written all over her.

"And just where did you meet this Cliff?" her father asked.

"At the Boca Raton Club." Eleanor and Roy breathed relief. Anyone Kathy met at the Boca Raton Club would, of course, have to be suitable.

"Is he a member?"

"He's been put up for membership. He has a guest card now."

"Who's putting him up?"

"No less than the Lovells and the Hoyts."

"Really? Well, that's very nice." Roy's jolly good humor was returning.

"Anyone the Hoyts would suggest for membership has to be a fine young man," Eleanor said a little while later as they approached the house. "When are we going to meet this Cliff?"

"Yes, Kathy," Roy boomed, all father and fatherly, as he pulled in the driveway, "we want to get to know your young man. . . . By the way, does he have a last name?"

"Yes. Thompson, Cliff Thompson."

The name prickled under his scalp, but he didn't make the connection . . . he'd been avoiding the memory for years. . . . "Well, we're looking forward to meeting Mr. Thompson soon as possible." Roy got out. "I've got to make a few phone calls before five o'clock."

"Daddy, you're going to meet Cliff *tonight.* We're having dinner at the club. You and Mommy will come, won't you?"

"Tonight? Yes, all right, we'll be there," Roy Brian walked into the house.

"Oh, Mommy, I know it's obvious and awfully fast, but I really am in love with Cliff. I've never known anything like this." Eleanor was a little concerned about Kathy's sudden enthusiasm . . . but, after all, she was almost twenty-four, a mature, sensible girl. And the Lovells and Hoyts were sponsoring him . . .

"It will be nice to have dinner at the club tonight. Veradero Beach was so quiet. Some Americans wanted your father to buy a hotel with them for casino gambling, of all things, and the whole time was just business, business."

Kathy had no interest in Veradero Beach or anything else except Cliff. "Everybody at the club seems to really like him. Something to do with a golf game. I don't really understand it, but everybody says he's a real gentleman. Not that anybody had to tell me. I know the difference."

"Well, we should have an interesting evening, dear. After Veradero Beach, even Zoltan's antics will be a pleasant relief. . . ." She put her hand on her daughter's. "Dearest, I understand perfectly how you feel. I know what it's like to be swept off your feet by the most exciting man in the world . . . but your father may not understand how you feel. So let him get used to the idea slowly. Don't wear your heart on your sleeve . . . if Cliff is everything you think he is, we'll bring your father around. All right, dear?"

"Of course, Mother. We'll let them get to know each other. Man to man."

The Boca Raton Club was buzzing that night. Everyone knew tonight would be Roy Brian's first look at what seemed likely to be his prospective son-in-law.

By prearrangement Kathy met Cliff in the club parking lot and he surprised her by arriving in a new car. "There she is, Kathy, one of the first new Mercurys out of the factory. Still has a wooden bumper—we'll get a metal bumper when the Ford Company gets the steel in. We'll probably be doing a lot of driving in the next couple of months. . . ."

Kathy looked at him. "Where are we going?"

"I'll tell you all about it later, darling. Shall we go in and have them look me over?"

Kathy took his arm and started to lead him toward the clubhouse. "You know everybody in the club thinks you're wonderful, they're already telling my father how lucky he is that I uncovered such a find."

"Let's hope he agrees with them."

"I don't know why he wouldn't."

Cliff paused. Now was the time, he decided. "Kathy, there's something I haven't told you . . . I didn't want you to worry but it will probably have to come out—"

"What is it? Cliff . . . is it something serious?"

"Well, that depends on how your father looks at it. Kathy, I never thought I was a candidate for true love and that sort of thing, and for sure I never thought in less than a week I'd know I'd found the girl I wanted to, as they say, make a life with . . . but, well—feeling all that, we can't live a lie, darling, so . . . you see years ago, your father, my father, and the old carnival owner I told you about a few days ago—"

". . . Stember? Bill Stember?"

"Yeah. Bill Stember got your father and mine together. They were partners for a while."

"What happened?"

"Boils down to your father got rich, mine died . . . that's the short of it and let's leave it at that. . . . Main thing, Kathy, *we've* got to hang in there together. Okay?"

"Cliff I don't care a damn what happened in the past, I love you now . . . hey, that's the first time I said it flat out like that. First time I ever said it to anybody—"

He interrupted. "Okay, then, my love, let's us go in and see how she flies."

As they walked into the main dining room of the Boca Raton Club it was as if everybody had been waiting just for them. To a loud silence, quickly replaced by a swell of murmurs, they walked across the floor, past staring diners, to where her parents sat at their table surrounded by the Hoyts and Lovells and Lazlow. Two places had been left conspicuously open for them between Roy and Eleanor Brian. The jury was assembled.

Although Cliff recognized him instantly, Roy Brian was a far more elegantly turned out man now than the hustler Cliff remembered in Grove City. Tanned, healthy, Brian looked years younger than fifty-four, and had acquired the facade of the very rich. Oh yes, Roy Brian, Cliff thought, it's going to take a *really* big paddle to fit your ass. But Slim Thompson's boy knows how to build it.

Even knowing Cliff's name, though, Brian still didn't seem to recognize him—obviously, and understandably, he'd put his Grove City days as far back in his mind as they could go. Rising from his chair, he shook hands, and, with Kathy looking on happily, began to chat amiably with Cliff. By now, of course, he had heard about the golf game and he was impressed.

"So you're a lawyer, Mr. Thompson?"

"Yes. Maybe Kathy told you, I served in the judge advocate general's office for a few years—"

"Oh, yes, she told us you came out of the army a major. Very impressive. You're a young man. . . ."

"Actually I'm twenty-eight years old, Mrs. Brian. And during the war promotions came pretty fast. Some of the fly-boys were generals before they shaved."

All smiled.

"Kathy says you're a marvelous golfer," Eleanor Brian added.

150

"Well, Kathy's a marvelous tennis player, she makes me look like the hacker I am . . . ."

And so it went, right into coffee and cordials.

"Hoyt tells me you're planning to practice law in Florida," Brian said.

"Well, I'll have to pass the Florida bar exams, but that shouldn't be too big a problem . . . I took the Massachusetts bar exam while I was at Fort Devens just to keep my hand in civilian law. Thought I'd hang up my shingle in West Palm Beach, or Fort Lauderdale, or somewhere around these parts—"

"Good idea," Brian said, and smiles all around confirmed it.

". . . also understand you come from an oil-business background?" Roy Brian said.

"You might say so, sir. Matter of fact, I've been looking into oil rights right around here—"

"Oil? Around here?" Roy Brian laughed, "Son, I've been a wildcatter and I know oil. Believe me, you won't find it in Florida, at least not around the Miami area. Now, maybe in the gulf off Tallahassee . . . but enough about business . . . they tell me you play a great game of golf, Cliff."

Cliff decided there was no point in drawing it out any longer. "Pretty good, Mr. Brian. My father started me off playing when I was ten—in a place called Grove City, Oklahoma?"

Roy Brian almost dropped his brandy snifter, stared hard at Cliff. "Grove City? That where you're from?"

Cliff looked at Kathy with a resigned smile, then turned back to Roy. "I guess you might say so. My father was Slim Thompson . . ."

Roy Brian took the news cool as a burglar—which, of course, he had practice at. He hardly missed a beat, except to take a long sip of his drink. "So you're Slim's boy . . . I should have guessed. You even look a little like him, now I think on it. . . . Yes sir, I remember when your father died . . . a very tragic thing, very tragic. Stroke, as I recall it."

That's right, Mr. Brian. "Funny thing how it happened, too.

He was a sick man, although at the time we didn't know much about high blood pressure. He'd spent years buying up all the oil and gas rights he could lay his hands on . . . and then in two hours he lost everything in a game of skin."

Brian was obviously struggling to remember how much Cliff knew about him and the details of the skin game. He vaguely remembered some kid standing there watching the play. . . . He decided on a hard line. "Don't you think you're getting a little out of your class here, boy?"

"Dad." Kathy stared into his eyes. "Don't talk that way—"

"Please keep out of this, Kathy. You don't know who you've been associating with. I know his background." And with Roy Brian's switch from amiable prospective father-in-law to hard-liner the others at the table suddenly became aware that something was wrong and stopped their talking.

"I'm a lawyer now, Mr. Brian. I'm also in the oil business," Cliff said quietly. "I'm trying to purchase leases and maybe I'll drill myself someday . . . and to answer your question, no I don't think I'm out of my class. You, me—we come from the same place, Mr. Brian . . ."

"That was a long time ago . . . Kathy doesn't even remember Oklahoma. Her life's here in Delray, and so is mine—"

"Kathy and I have been doing some talking, Mr. Brian—"

"I'll bet you have. Did you tell her your father was a gambler and a hustler, and his son is the same?"

"Since you were the one who hustled my father out of his rights, I'd say that puts you way ahead of him. And I'd say that gives you *no* right to tell Kathy I'm not good enough for her—"

"You and Kathy have nothing in common—"

"*Anyone* for the powder room?" Betty Hoyt asked brightly.

Amy Lowell stood up, and Eleanor Brian, embarrassed, joined her. "Kathy?"

"No, I'm staying put right here."

Hoyt, Lovell, and Lazlow were just staring. It was more show than any of them had counted on.

"What I think you're going to do, and right now, Mr. Thompson," Brian said, "is get in your car, drive back to Miami, and never see us, *including* Kathy, again—"

"Well, I guess Kathy will decide that, Mr. Brian."

The whole room was focused in on them now.

"I'm forbidding Kathy ever to see you again. Kathy, I mean it. This hustler here tried to make up to you for your money . . . period. His father was no good; he's no better, for damn sure. . ."

Cliff kept his temper down, his voice even. He couldn't blow it now. "Look, Mr. Brian, I worked very hard all the time you were becoming very rich on my father's oil leases. I helped support my mother, I sent myself through college and law school. I didn't lie to you, Mr. Brian. You never would've remembered who I was unless I'd chosen to tell you."

"That's right, Daddy," Kathy put in, "Cliff told me all about it—he told me just tonight in the parking lot that he had to let you know because he couldn't have a life with me based on a lie."

"That's a hustler's trick, honey. He knows what he is, he's just trying to impress you. He knows I'd have had him checked out . . . if he'd ever so much as played hookey in seventh grade I'd have known about it. Of course he had to tell you—a crook always knows when to come clean. Just before he gets caught." And suddenly he realized he'd maybe gone too far with her and took a new tack. "Look, Thompson, I'm sorry about your father, but he was old and sick and he couldn't take losing. Everybody loses sometimes."

"And also, like they say, dies . . . but my father never had a chance in that skin game you and Bull Larsen rigged against him . . . and I expect you want to forget how you were able to buy your big place in Delray Beach and join this club and be the big millionaire. . . . There's a crook at this table, all right, but it's not me."

Kathy looked miserably from one of her men to the other. "Please, Daddy, Cliff, can't we forget the past? It's our future that's important, Cliff's and mine. We want—"

"What *I* want is for you to get out of here right now, Thompson, and never see Kathy again. If I ever catch you at the Boca Raton Club with my daughter you'll see just how far out of your league you are."

"I'd say you were threatening me, Mr. Brian—"

"I'm not threatening you, Thompson, I'm telling you how it is."

Cliff turned to Kathy and stood up. "I'll say good-bye to you now, Kathy, but you know where to reach me—"

"You'd better make that a damned permanent good-bye, Thompson. No crummy hustler is going to take off my daughter. . ."

"You sure haven't forgotten the lingo, Mr. Brian. . . ." And with members staring, Cliff leaned over and kissed Kathy on the lips. "I'll look forward to hearing from you, darling."

Roy Brian, face red, got to his feet and actually pulled back a ham-fisted right—and then slowly, thinking better of it, lowered it—to fight again, Cliff had no doubt, another day.

"You just made a wise decision, Mr. Brian," Cliff said, and turned to the rest of the table. "I'm sorry the evening didn't turn out more pleasantly. The old saying you know, opposites attract"—he glanced at Kathy, then staring at Roy Brian— "likes repel."

Despite the tenseness of the situation, Lovell and Hoyt laughed, if nervously. Maybe this attractive young man really was something of a con man, but like he'd said, it took one to know one. Anyway, Roy Brian had revealed more of himself this evening than he ever had before, Hoyt thought—and that knowledge might just come in handy someday. He looked at Brian standing there like a wild bull, and mentally awarded Cliff two ears and a tail. Lazlow, too, was thinking . . . what was it about this young man that made people reveal themselves?

"Cliff," Clegg Hoyt said, "you take it easy now—and don't forget you still have a guest card at the club. It takes more than one black ball to keep you out when your name comes up."

"Thanks, Mr. Hoyt"—sounding properly grateful but in a way meaning it—"I guess you'll never know how much I appreciate that. And thanks a lot, all of you." Cliff walked out of the dining room, feeling the eyes of every member on his neck. He stepped out into the fresh night air and looked up at the stars and the moon. Roy Brian had lost another round, maybe. But there were many to go.

18

AS HE DROVE down the highway from Boca Raton to Miami Cliff felt exhausted and exhilarated. He wasn't sure if Kathy would really defy her father and come to him . . . but he felt she would. He needed her, he realized—and *not* just for the paddle, which, he also realized, could be dangerous, but so be it. . . . Well, back to work . . . first step, the Turk.

Cliff pulled his new Mercury up in front of the Palm Isles, gave it over to the doorman and walked into the bar. The bartender waved. "A drink, Mr. Thompson?"

"Sure, why not. Maybe it'll grease the action. Seen the Turk?"

"Sure, he's upstairs. Matter of fact he's been looking for you. He thought you were going to be in for some action a few days ago."

"Well I'm here now." Cliff noticed the bartender pushing a button under the bar, and sure enough, he had hardly taken a sip from his drink when Turk came down the stairs and walked up to him. "Cliff, where you been?" he called out amiably.

"I got lucky, Turk, and I don't mean the dice. I met a girl, had a great three days and then she had to go back north. I

156

figure maybe a little more luck rubbed off on me."

"What about that guy from Oklahoma? You were going to ask about the oil leases, you know, that stuff I got from Grove City?"

"Oh yeah, I talked to him about them. He wasn't interested. He said unless I could acquire the whole of Block II there in Grove City it wouldn't be worth sinking a well. Just what I told you he'd say."

"Okay, so what about it, Cliff, you interested?"

"Maybe."

"Considering the size of the marker I wrote off for them, those deeds should be worth at least ten grand . . ."

"Seems to me I've heard this song before, Turk . . . well, we'll do something together. . . . You know, I feel lucky tonight. For the first time since I walked into this joint of yours I have that good feeling in my bones."

"You're due, Cliff. Ready to go up?"

"Let's go." Inside the casino Pete was busily wielding his stick for the shills standing around the crap table faking a lot of action—as usual there were two, maybe three legitimate players, marks that would be taken off that night.

When Cliff figured Pete had had enough time to plant the dice in the handle of the gaffed stick, he wandered over and the Turk left him, saying, "I'm going back to my office, Cliff. I'll have those leases ready for you."

"Thanks, Turk, I'll probably take them off your hands if we can find a price."

"I'll give you a good price, Cliff—five G's. Fair's fair."

"So I've heard." Cliff then found a place at the head of the table, just to the left of the shooter and looked down at the layout. To his left at the middle of the table was the box man who handled the hard way and field bets. He was also the boss of the craps crew who made all decisions in case of dispute. Directly across from Cliff was Pete, gathering up the dice after each throw with the crook of his stick and returning them to the shooter, or in the event the shooter lost, pulling them home

157

and placing them in a small glass dish about the size of a salad bowl. The dish held five cubes from which the next shooter could select two dice to throw. To the right of the shooter at each end of the table was a dealer who picked up the losers' bets and paid off the winners.

Cliff took his place at the table and Pete slid the dice dish over to the shill who was shooting, who in turn picked up a pair of dice and began going through the shooter's ritual: blowing on them, talking to them, agitating them in his hand. The other shills placed bets, trying to excite the marks into doing likewise. Cliff made no move to his pocket, not yet.

The shooter threw his dice down against the end of the table, and they rolled back toward him—five and four.

"Nine's the point," Pete intoned and, placing a small red cap on the number, he rolled back the dice to the shooter with his stick. Cliff wasn't astonished when the next roll came up seven.

"Seven. The shooter loses," came the chant. Pete scooped in the missout dice he'd thrown into the game with his stick.

"Next shooter." Cliff stepped up now—and because he was expecting it, sensed rather than actually saw Pete press the catch on the handle of his dice stick. A pair of tops rolled into his hand from the hollow handle at the same moment he picked up the missouts, then, imperceptibly, he placed the tops in the dish with his fingers, as with the heel of his hand he pushed the missouts up into the handle of the gaffed stick. Cliff marked the precise position of the two dice Pete had introduced into the dish and when it was slid toward him pulled out the pair of tops. No chance, literally, that he could roll a seven now.

Shaking the tops in his right hand, spieling the shooter's chant for luck, he reached into his left pocket and pulled out two one-hundred-dollar bills and threw them on the line, betting that he would "come"—hit a seven or make his point. The dice rolled out across the table and bounced back, a three and two spot shining up at the players. "The point is five," Pete called out.

While Pete hooked in the dice with his stick, Cliff placed

158

another two hundred dollars on the come line. A point of five gave him three-to-two odds; he stood to win five hundred dollars if he threw a five before the seven. Then, surprising the box man, Cliff bought all the front numbers, laying two one-hundred-dollar bills each on numbers four, five, six, eight, nine, and ten. On numbers four and ten he would be paid two-to-one odds if he didn't seven before he fived, on numbers five and nine the payoff was three to two, and numbers six and eight paid six to five. To lay down this type of massive bet the shooter had to pay a five percent commission to the house for the privilege of getting the correct odds on all the numbers he bought, and the six numbers, at two hundred dollars each, totaled sixty dollars. Cliff casually tossed the money at the box man.

Even the shills were caught up now by the excitement of this outside mark coming in and betting so heavily against the house —of course, they all knew, the Turk wouldn't permit such a win. The box man had thought he'd seen everything, but this topped them all . . . obviously the mark was begging to be taken off, maybe he got his jollies that way.

Cliff picked up the dice, said a few kind words to them, and threw them down the table. They came up four. The dealer next to him paid off two to one, four hundred dollars, and Cliff took a ten-dollar bill out of his jacket pocket, tossed it to the box man as the commission on a new two-hundred-dollar bet on number four, and dragged the four-hundred-dollar win back in front of him. The next roll came up eight. Two hundred and forty dollars were added to the pile stacked in front of him. "Box man," he called "run a tab for me on the commissions I owe."

"Yes, sir," the box man said, giving Pete a glance that clearly said, *get those missouts into his hand!*

Cliff threw a ten for another two-to-one and four hundred dollars, then two sixes for two hundred and forty dollars each, two nines for three hundred dollars each, and finally he hit with his five. He was standing with five thousand dollars in front of him, twelve hundred dollars on the line, and ready to shoot again. Pete glanced at the box man and gave him the office, a grim sort of nod that said, I don't know what the hell's up, hit the buzzer for the Turk. . . .

The box man reached for the buzzer, looking down to find it, and just as he did Cliff made a sudden victory gesture with his right arm, distracting the two dealers, while Pete scooped up the tops. By the time the Turk came through the door to see what was wrong, Pete had slickly opened the hollow in the handle of the dice stick, released the Turk's standard missouts, and put the tops safely back in the handle.

The Turk took in the situation quickly. Cliff, a beatific grin on his face, was standing behind a pile of bills and preparing to throw again, every number on the line covered with two hundred dollars. The son-of-a-bitch rolled tops, the Turk thought. "What's up, Mack?" The box man shrugged, and the Turk grabbed the dice Pete had just put into the dish. They were the house dice all right. He jammed his hands into Pete's pockets and belt to see if an apron might be hanging there, but Pete was clean.

"Hey boss," the box man said under his breath, "it was Pete here gave me the office, he couldn't figure what was going on either."

"Off on all bets!" Cliff called out, pulling his money, his face tight.

The Turk realized he'd panicked and made a fool of himself in front of a prize mark.

"Hey, Cliff, come on, it's nothing. This is a new man, I just thought he might be playing games on me—"

"Just because I won on my first roll? After all the rolls I lost my first two nights here?"

"I'm sorry, Cliff, I didn't mean nothin' by it, keep shooting . . ."

Cliff shook his head. "Not after that little performance, Turk. I'm getting out of here—"

"You got five G's of my money, you walking out after one roll?"

"Yeah. But let's have a look at those leases before I go."

160

The Turk brightened again. "Okay, fella, come on into my office. . . ."

Across the hall, Cliff thumbed through the documents. "Like I said, Turk, they're not much good unless you get together all the other rights in the area. Nobody sinks a well to make his neighbor rich . . . if I take the risk—"

An angry Pete White strode in. Paying no attention to Cliff, he threw his stick down on the Turk's desk.

"I quit. If you haven't got any faith in me, if you gotta frisk me right in front of the players, if you gotta rob me of my dignity . . . well, mister, there's just no way I can work for you."

"Let's talk later, Pete—"

"Forget it, Turk. We're square," and he stalked out of the office. The stick he had just slammed down in front of the Turk was the legit stick, Cliff's gaffed version was now safely returned behind the toilet water box.

"Your stickman seems kind of pissed off," Cliff observed.

"Fuck him, he's the temperamental type. . . . Now let's get back to the deal. Five G's for the leases, okay?"

"Okay,"—Cliff reached into his pocket, pulled out the wad he'd just won and counted out four thousand fifty dollars— "and now sign each one of those leases over to Clifford Thompson of Grove City, Oklahoma."

"You're short nine hundred and fifty dollars."

"That's for the five hundred you beat me my first night and the four-fifty you took off the second."

"But that was a straight-up loss—"

"Not so straight . . . so forget it then. I'll keep the five G's and be on my way." He started to get up.

"Okay, okay, I'll take the four G's and the fifty." Grumbling, the Turk signed the leases and put them on the table.

Cliff placed the money beside them, releasing his hold on the bills only when the mineral rights were firmly in his jacket pocket. "So long, Turk. Nice to meet you."

He walked to the door of the office, pushed it open and, with Turk's eyes on him all the way, walked down the stairs and out.

161

With a roar, Turk stalked into the casino and yelled at the box men, there being nothing but shills in the room now. "Did I get taken off?"

"No way, Turk, couldn't have happened. I watched everything."

"You mean to tell me that son-of-a-bitch beat one-hundred-to-one odds?"

"I tell you, Turk, there was no way he could have rolled tops, it just had to be some kind of blind, shit luck—"

"Blind shit luck, huh? Well, I don't believe in luck. It's bad business. If I ever get my hands . . ." A grim smile spread over his face. "Well, I took him off anyway. Four G's for those lousy leases. Mr. Thompson thinks he's real smart, but let me tell you something, Mack—nobody's smarter than the Turk."

Unless, the box man thought, they turned out to be not so worthless as the Turk thought. He kept his thoughts to himself, his mouth shut.

19

KATHY'S EYES STUNG as her car sped along the highway. The atmosphere in the dining room of the Boca Raton Club had been hushed and embarrassed after Cliff's rather dramatic exit and, unable and unwilling to take the stares, she had said a quick good-bye and run out.

Now she was driving north, she didn't know where, but she had to have time to think . . . about Cliff, her father . . .

It wasn't until she reached Lake Worth that she realized where she had been heading all along. In the distance she could see a brilliantly lighted Ferris wheel, its gondolas leisurely working their way to the top of the wheel then sliding down the other side, and all around it more lights, more rides. It was Bill Stember's carnival. Parking her car in a dusty field, she walked up to the red-white-and-blue-striped entrance gate and told the bowler-hatted barker taking tickets that she would like to see Mr. Stember.

"Certainly, young lady, and I'm sure he'd like to see you, too. Just go down to the end of the midway past the booths, and you'll see his van right next to the Test-of-Strength, you can't miss it, it's the red one. Give my best, and tell him he's a lucky man."

Kathy walked by the geek show and the girlie show, and through an army of barkers urging her to try your hand, little lady, they've been winning tonight, but it was all a blur to her, a whirling confusion of lights and sounds.

At the end of the midway she saw a red van that seemed to match the ticket taker's description. She went up the steps and knocked on the door. It opened and a stout, bald man wearing a string tie and candy-striped shirt looked out.

"Mr. Stember?"

"Yes?"

"Mr. Stember, you don't know me but I really need to talk to you . . . my name is Kathy Brian, my father is Roy Brian—"

"Roy Brian . . . haven't heard that name in a long time . . . well, come in, come in—sit down. What can I do for you?"

"Mr. Stember . . . I . . . I just want to know something about my father and a Slim Thompson. You see his son, Cliff Thompson, and I are—"

"Cliff Thompson? Well, there's another name from out of the past. I haven't laid eyes on Cliff since he was fifteen, sixteen. . . . You mean, Slim Thompson's son and Roy Brian's daughter are . . . how do I know you're who you say you are?"

"Well . . . Cliff told me about a Hey Rube . . . I think that's what he called it . . . that he once caused at your carnival in Oklahoma."

"We get lots of Hey Rubes."

"Not like this one, apparently. Somebody thought the Razzle-Dazzle operator had stolen his jacket—"

"By God! I remember that now—you mean Cliff did that?" Stember began to laugh. "I'll be damned, that sure sounds like Cliff. And his dad . . . he never was one to let anyone take advantage of him—"

"But I guess someone did do that. My father . . .?"

"Your—uh, yes, can I get you a drink or a cup of coffee, miss—"

"No, thanks, I've had everything I need, everything except a little truth. . . . Mr. Stember, please. I want you to tell me what really happened. Did my father do something awful to Slim Thompson?"

"Well . . . Slim needed someone to finance his oil wells and I knew Roy Brian was interested, so I introduced them in this very van, as a matter of fact. While I was out taking care of Cliff's Hey Rube, they struck up a deal and I guess it was Brian's idea to get a driller named Bull Larsen into a game of skin. Slim thought he and Brian could finagle Larsen into contributing his services, then cut him into the profits later, but it didn't turn out that way. Instead, Larsen and Brian brought in a mechanic and whacked-out Slim for all those mineral rights. Slim had a stroke and died. . . . That's about it, as I recollect it, Miss Brian."

"So my father did cheat Slim?"

"I guess you might say so . . . then again, some others might disagree—"

"And Slim's family?"

"They scraped along best they could. This is the first I've heard of them in a long while. . . ."

"So Cliff was telling the truth . . . to say the least. . ."

"Yes . . . well, look here, Miss Brian . . . don't be too hard on old Roy. Back in those days a man did what he was big enough to do, lot of men got rich on the bones of others . . . it was the Depression, after all. And you gotta remember Slim, much as I liked him, was out to take Bull Larsen the same way Bull and Roy took him. Even Slim's widow told young Cliff, I remember it very well now, I was sitting there, 'Cliff, I don't want you to think what you're thinking. Your father lived by the hustle, he died by the hustle. That's over with. Now we've got to make something out of you.' "

Kathy stood up.

"Where are you going?"

"To talk to the two most important men in my life. You've been a real help, Mr. Stember. . . ."

Roy Brian was waiting in his study when Kathy got back. "Kathy? Honey? I'm in the den."

Kathy walked down the hall to her father's office and stood in the doorway.

"Did the drive . . . uh, clear your mind, sweetheart? You know all I want is what's best for you, and that's the God's truth. . . . I want you to be happy, but I have to help you spot the phonies when they come along—that's something a rich girl always has to think about."

"How did we get so rich, Dad?"

"In oil, sweetheart, you know that. I got lucky with some wells back in Oklahoma."

"After you and Bull Larsen cheated Cliff's father—"

"That what that cheap young hustler told you?"

"No, Dad, that's what Bill Stember told me. Cliff never told me the half of it."

For a moment Roy Brian looked stunned. Then, finally, "Bill Stember? How the hell do you know Bill Stember?"

"Cliff told me about him—and his carnival happens to be playing in Lake Worth. He told me the whole story tonight . . . about you and Bull Larsen—"

"Kathy, darling, listen, it's a lie, I *know* Stember. He's just another crook and he's in with Thompson on this whole phony deal, don't you see it?" Then, as Kathy remained silent, "Goddamn it, Kathy, if I tell you it's a lie, it's a goddamn *lie*. Are you going to believe these two-bit con artists over your own father?"

Kathy looked at her father, then slowly turned from the room. "Who's conning who, Father?"

Brian got to his feet and started to go after her, but Eleanor, who had heard the whole thing, stopped him.

"Roy! Leave her alone, let me talk to her. Roy . . . I don't

166

know what this is all about or what may have happened between you and Cliff's father a long time ago . . . but I've got to say . . . Cliff Thompson seems a decent young man and I don't see what he's done wrong. No, Roy"—she lifted her hand —"don't try to explain it now. Let me go and talk to Kathy. But later . . . you and I've got a lot to talk about. . . ."

Roy Brian beat what he figured was a strategic retreat to the big chair behind his desk. He never could really handle Eleanor.

20

THE NEXT MORNING Pete, Cliff, and Carol sat in their room in the Roney Plaza Hotel making plans. "It does worry me," Cliff said, "I don't know what connections Roy Brian may still have with the Turk, but if Brian gets wind of what we're doing he could sure foul us up with the others. Still, from everything I've heard, the two of them haven't spoken for years . . . let's just hope it stays that way."

"So," Pete said, "what's our next stop? Pittsburgh?"

"Pittsburgh. Right. The Ganoff brothers."

Pete and Carol couldn't help noticing, though, that Cliff kept looking back and forth from his wristwatch to the telephone. Obviously he had the fair Kathy on his mind. . . . Suddenly, the door buzzer sounded and Cliff nearly jumped to his feet to get to the door and open it. Room service. Cliff turned from the door to be met by knowing looks and clucking noises. And then he heard the tinkling laugh and, "I hope there's enough chow for this hungry girl too."

Cliff whirled around. "Kathy!" In three long strides he was holding her in his arms. "You did come—"

"So it seems," and she waved over Cliff's shoulder to Carol and Pete.

"Good to see you, baby," Carol said, "I told Cliff you'd be along."

"And you were right. I just had some unfinished business of my own to take care of."

Cliff hugged her again. "Would you two excuse us for a few minutes? We've a little business of our own to catch up on. . . ." He took Kathy into his room and closed the door behind them.

"What happened, Kathy?"

"Well, my father ordered me not to leave and my mother started to cry and then both of them said they would reconsider letting me see you, but I know Dad. . . . No matter what he says he'll never back down. It's not his style . . . so I told them I was coming to you—okay?

"Very much okay . . . but I realize it was a big decision to make, Kathy. . ."

"I know," and she told him about Bill Stember and what he'd told her and about her father's final accusations. "Somehow I don't feel so bitter about it now," she said. "I guess I know my father did what he thought he had to do, and now you're doing what you have to do. And *I'm* with *you*, Mr. Cliff Thompson. . . . Now let me hear all about it from you."

And she did. He told her about Grove City I and Grove City II and Roy Brian's palming off what he thought were worthless leases to Block II onto five of his associates. He talked about the seismic and geological surveys and the new drilling techniques that maybe could draw oil out of Block II. And he outlined how he planned to get the oil leases back—starting last night with the Turk.

"I want to help, Cliff, any way I can."

"Sweetheart, that's all I wanted to hear. . . ." He opened the door to the parlor and bowed her through. "Ladies and gentle-men, may I present the fourth member of the team." Pete and Carol applauded. "On to Pittsburgh and—you should forgive the expression—the Ganoff brothers.

21

THE DRIVE TO Pittsburgh took four days, and each night brought Kathy further out of her old protected shell. Sometimes in ways Cliff had all he could do to cope with. She assured him he'd improve with practice.

It was a sunny, bright afternoon when Cliff's Mercury swept up to the front of the huge William Penn Hotel, which dominated an entire block in the heart of the Steel City.

"That's got to be the largest hotel I've ever seen," Kathy said, staring up at the sprawling red-brick pile. "Maybe we ought to find something smaller and cozier."

"It's the best place in town," Pete said, "and that's exactly what we need. Lesson One, Kathy—when you do a job, do it in style."

As Cliff and Kathy registered, Pete struck up a conversation with the bell captain.

"Hi ya, Eddie," glancing quickly at the name tag, "sure been a long time since I been in Pittsburgh, not since before the war. Things pretty much the same here?"

"Sure, maybe a little dirtier. Steel mills went twenty-four hours a day during the war."

"Say, where's a good restaurant these days? I can't remember where I used to go."

"Depends what you're looking for."

"You know, where the ballplayers hang out, the fight game guys . . . like where I'd find someone to take my action."

"Oh, you mean Sammy's Steak House. . . ."

"Yeah, that sounds like the place." Pete's eyes followed a bellman. "You know, I used to hop bells myself back in New Orleans, the Monteleone Hotel. You ever been in New Orleans?"

"No, but I sure heard of the Monteleone, you'll be right at home at Sammy's."

"I used to know a couple of guys from Pittsburgh always stayed at the Monteleone, the Ganoff brothers. You ever hear of them?"

"Sure I know them. Abe and Benny? Everybody at Sammy's knows the Ganoffs."

"Yeah, well it would be good to see them again, cut up some jackpots with them, if you know what I mean."

"Sure, you can't miss Sammy's Steak House. It's only about four blocks from the hotel, right in the Golden Triangle. You checking in here?"

"Yeah, that's my man over there. He and his wife come all the way up from Florida."

"Yeah? How come somebody'd leave Florida in the middle of winter to come up here?"

"I'm asking myself the same question," which was the opening Pete had been hoping for. "All the dough he's got, and you should see his mansion in Boca Raton, why does he have to come up here?" He leaned closer. "I'll tell you something, keep it under your hat, seems like someone in Pittsburgh's got a new kind of rig, drills the deepest oil wells in the whole world. . . ." He jerked a thumb at Cliff. "He's from one of the big oil families in Oklahoma."

Eddie looked impressed, as Cliff motioned from across the lobby.

172

"Well, see you later, Eddie. Looks like the boss needs me."

That evening they were greeted at the door of Sammy's Steak House by a tall, heavyset man whose broken nose and scarred face went with a few too many years in the ring.

"Reservations for four . . . Thompson . . . is Sammy around tonight?"

"Sure, he's here."

"Could you ask him to drop by our table?" Pete asked. "I have some friends here I think Sammy would know."

Sammy himself showed up a few minutes later. "Mr. Thompson, is everything all right?"

"Just fine."

"Sammy, I wonder if you could help us," Pete put in. "I got a couple of friends in town here, we used to spend a lot of time together in New Orleans before the war. You ever see Abe and Benny Ganoff?"

"Sure, you'd been here yesterday you'd have seen both of them. They were with their fighter, the China Kid."

"What the hell kind of a name is that? Is he a Chinaman?"

Sammy laughed. "No, he's a big Swede, he got that name 'cause he worked for them in their pottery plant in China, Ohio."

"China, Ohio, where the hell's that? I thought they lived here in Pittsburgh."

"This is their town, but this joint they've got—the plant— is only about forty-five miles from here."

"We ought to go out and say hello," Pete turned to the others, "you really got to meet Abe and Benny. Sammy, just how the hell do you get to China, Ohio?"

"Easy. Take Route 22 west to Steubenville, turn right when you cross the Fort Steuben Bridge, then go six miles up the road to Toronto. Ask anyone, they'll tell you where the pottery plant is. Hell, they all know the Ganoffs, their plant's the only action in town."

"Thank you, Sammy."

Sammy bowed slightly. "Enjoy your dinner, folks."

173

The next day Pete drove out to China alone. As he drove he thought back to the days when he was a bellhop and then the night manager of the Monteleone Hotel. Pete always knew where to find a friendly girl, a deck of cards, or a bottle of whisky after hours back then and the sporting crowd among the hotel's clientele appreciated it. That was when he'd first heard of Steubenville. The sharpest hustlers in the business came from Steubenville; in fact fifteen years ago it had had the only school in America that actually taught gambling. Pete had even considered enrolling, but he'd ended up learning his trade the hard way . . . and, come to think on it, the results hadn't been all that bad.

He drove through a mill town and saw the workers in their hard hats, their expressions full of weariness and despair, their faces covered with soot. He could have been like that, a working stiff. . .

Twenty minutes later, he came to a gate in a high fence with a sign: "China Pottery Co., Private Property, Trespassers Will Be Prosecuted. Keep Out."

Ignoring the warning Pete drove through and up to a dingy-looking three-story building with windows opaque from decades of accumulated filth. Parking directly in front of an "Absolutely No Parking" sign, Pete got out of the car, pulled on the tarnished brass handle of what looked to be the main entrance and walked inside. He was in a dingy office; behind a wooden gate to his left sat a huge lump of a woman vigorously pounding on a typewriter. "Where would I find the Ganoffs?" No answer. The typewriter clacked. "Ma'am, I said where would I find the Ganoffs?"

"Which one?" she said without looking up.

"Benny, Abe, either one."

Raising one hand from the typewriter, she pointed to a door. "That's Abe's office over there."

"Thanks." Pete pushed through the swinging gate in the barrier, then opened the door. At a desk piled high with papers, catalogs, and crockery sat Abe Ganoff. He hadn't changed much since Pete had last seen him; perhaps more stooped over, his massive face a little heavier. His stringy black hair, obviously dyed, hung lankly about his head, framing sad eyes and a bulbous nose. As Pete walked in, the sagging shoulders straightened slightly and a slow smile of recognition spread wide.

"Hi ya, Abe. Been a long time since you and Benny was laying lumpics on thc tourists down in New Orleans." Pete first met the Ganoffs when they were selling watches guaranteed to break in a matter of days to guests at the Monteleone Hotel.

"Jeez-ziss! If it isn't the gambler man from the Crescent City hisself. You look like ready money, Pete, you must have made a good score to buy them sharp threads you're wearing." Abe turned toward an open door at the side of his office and shouted, "Hey Benny, come in here. Look what just blew in." Benny Ganoff, shorter than his brother, bald, wearing bottle-bottom glasses, appeared in the doorway, and did a double take. "He looks like he just came out of a Hollywood movic picture. Some outfit, eh, Ben?"

"Pete White . . . damn, you look grcat, Pete," Benny said, "where you been?"

"Well, I just come from Oklahoma inspecting some oil fields—"

"Don't tell me you struck oil, Pete," Abe said.

"Not yct, but I'm on my way." Pete flashed an appropriately sly grin. "I'm traveling with an Oklahoma millionaire who made it big in oil. He's one helluva guy, I'll tell you, makes bets for me on ball games and fights, cuts me in with the wins and I don't have to come up if he loses."

"You can't beat that," Benny said.

"Yeah, the guy is queer for betting fights, that's why I came here. I know you guys always was dead sharp when it comes to fighters."

"Yeah? Well, we'll see if we can help you out." Abe stood

up. "Let me show you around the plant."

"How come you guys are so far out in the sticks? I thought you liked to stay close to the action."

"We found this plant out here and named the town China," Benny said proudly, "so we can stamp on all of our pottery 'Made in China' and still be on the square. Folks pay more, and like it."

"Come on, Pete. Let's show you the layout, we really got a nice setup here." Benny led Pete through a maze of corridors, kilns, and loading docks, then up to the second floor where nearly a hundred young women sat at pottery wheels turning, wetting, and molding clay into cups and dishes.

"You got a hell of a setup here," Pete said in frank admiration.

"Yeah, we're doing okay . . . you came at a good time. It's just about time for lunch—come on up to the third floor," Benny invited.

When Pete stepped off the elevator, he had a surprise waiting for him. In front of him was a lunch hall, ordinary in most respects, except that instead of being ranked in straight rows, the tables formed a hollow square, in the center of which was a regulation boxing ring. There, being cheered on by an audience of enthusiastic factory girls, was a tall blond young man in black trunks grunting, jabbing, feinting, and otherwise destroying an imaginary opponent.

"That your boy?" Pete asked, wondering how the fighter would look against a real opponent.

"That's him." Abe stared almost reverently at the young boxer.

"The China Kid," Benny intoned. "We're going to make him the top heavyweight in the country, I guarantee you. . . . Now what were you saying about your millionaire buddy that likes to bet on fights?"

"You got the China Kid lined up for a fight?"

"Sure. Two nights from now. Friday. In Pittsburgh."

"Is he any good?"

"Is he any good? Look at him. Listen to the girls, they love him."

"You come to the fight, bring your friend, we'll figure how to score big."

Pete pretended disinterest and, looking around the room, he spotted a food stand in the corner manned, if that was the word, by a sallow, acned youth wearing a white overseas cap and stained apron.

"Who's that?"

Abe stared across the floor and grunted. "That? Oh, that's some jag-off my kid married, I put him in business for himself. It beats havin' to give him money outta my own kick." He laughed. "After all, Pete, half the money goes to my daughter anyway. Ain't that right?"

Benny turned the conversation back to the subject at hand. "Pete, what are you doing up here anyway? There ain't no suckers around these parts. If you think you spotted a mark in this town, take my advice, don't bet against him. If he says the sun's gonna come up in the west tomorrow morning, come daylight you better be facing China—the real one."

"No, it's nothing like that. It's like I told you, I'm with this guy from Oklahoma, see, and he's interested in oil, so he's seeing some big engineering and geologist company in Pittsburgh to get reports on the mineral leases he owns. Something to do with the new deep-drilling rigs that were developed during the war . . . look, I don't know what the fuck he's talking about when it comes to oil. All I know is after working hours he spends money like it's goin' out of style—he loves to gamble, especially on fights. Tell you the truth, though, I can't get lucky with him. Every damned thing I tout him on goes the other way. I just can't seem to make a buck with him." Pete shrugged. "You know where he's having lunch right now? . . . the Duquesne Club, with all them oil tycoons he came up here to see."

Abe and Benny, apparently impressed, exchanged glances. After a moment of serious thought, Benny presented his considered judgment. "Fuck him, take him off yourself. Put him on

a loser and you book it. That way you keep all the money
. . . or if ya can't do that, steer him into a bookmaker and take
half the action. You can't lose either way, you know?"

"Naw, I can't do that. The guy's been too nice to me and
besides, he's a millionaire, maybe he can do something for me."

"Let me tell you something about millionaires," Abe said,
"there ain't one son-of-a-bitch millionaire will do anything for
you. They just keep you around for a little while till they get
hip to the outside, then when you quit gettin' 'em broads, or
they get tired of lookin' at your kisser, they blow you off, just
like they would a broad."

"Yeah," Benny said, "that's why they're millionaires. So take
some advice, take your shot while you got one because, baby,
you'll kick yourself when it's too late."

Pete nodded slowly. "Yeah, maybe that's the reason I came
over here after all. Small stuff I can handle, but this is a big one
and I don't want to make any mistakes. Like you said, I only
got one shot."

Abe and Benny actually beamed at each other, eyes shining
with larcenous intent they could no longer camouflage. Abe
placed a hairy hand on Pete's shoulder. "Pete, listen to me,
would I steer you wrong? I treat you like my family. After all,
we all three come up the same way, from the streets."

"That's right," his brother put in, "remember when we were
all together in New Orleans, Pete, back in the thirties?"

Pete grinned, nodded. Actually he hadn't ever particularly
cottoned to the Ganoffs even then.

"When you weren't working nights at the Monteleone you
was out at the track—remember how you hung around the Fair
Grounds all day? When the hell did you ever sleep?"

"Well, I was a young stud then, didn't need any sleep unless
it was with a broad." All smiled, like old conspirators.

"That's right," Abe said, "what times. Best whores in the
U.S. of A. for twenty-five a throw. And stay with you as long
as you wanted to go. Them old sporting houses had carpets so

thick you couldn't see your shoelaces, and gold and crystal chandeliers come from the Palace of Versailles, I heard. Really . . ."

Benny's thick glasses seemed to steam up as he reminisced. "And if you was about broke, even the one-dollar girls in the cribs wasn't bad. You wanted to change your luck you could get a high yellow for fifty cents. Those really were the good old days."

Benny sighed and Abe, thinking he had Pete, kept working him. "And now just because we got lucky and opened up this plant, don't mean you can't get lucky too. Just let me meet your man and I'll figure a way to get a score, and you get one third. Like I said, it's family."

Pete appeared hesitant, and Abe patted his shoulder. "Hey, what's the matter with us, I'll bet Pete's hungry. Come on over, we'll see what Irving's got to offer . . . that's my jag-off son-in-law over there."

They were sitting at a table eating sandwiches and reminiscing about New Orleans, when the China Kid, his workout finished, came by.

"Kid, meet Pete White," Abe said.

The China Kid's name turned out to be Jon Petersen, and after a passing nod asked Abe to loan him ten dollars until the fight on Friday.

"What ya *doin'*? Pissing away all the money you make?"

"You should learn to save," Benny admonished.

"I'd save, Mr. Ganoff, if I had anything left to save."

Pete, pushing back a smile at this devastating logic, and noting the Ganoffs' resistance to the bite, reached into his pocket, pulled out a ten and slipped it into the China Kid's hand.

"Here you go, big Jon," Pete said quietly. "I'll be at the fight Friday. Good luck."

"Hey, thanks, Mr. White," said the Kid, and pushed the bill into his pocket.

"You shouldna done that, Pete"—Abe was obviously chagrined—"he's our boy, it's our responsibility to take care of him—"

"So why argue for a lousy ten bucks?"

"Good-bye, Mr. Ganoff," the China Kid said hurriedly, "I'll see you here tomorrow," and before either of the Ganoffs could say anything he was already on his way down the stairs.

"I still say you didn't hafta do that, Pete," Benny said. "That kid's always chasing money, always putting the bite on us."

"Like I said, I'll be at the fight. I'll get it back there."

Benny let it go. "Let's discuss this friend of yours . . . from Oklahoma. If we come back to Pittsburgh now, can you knock us down to him? We'll take it from there."

"I can't just up and introduce you right off, Abe, I gotta have a reason. He's a businessman and I know sure as hell he ain't interested in dishes even if they're *really* from China."

"Got any ideas?"

"We got to find a gimmick that will interest him. He likes fighters, sure, but that's not strong enough. Now if it was something to do with oil . . ."

"Hey, Benny, wait a minute, hold it. Ya remember those deeds or leases or whatever the hell they was Roy Brian sold us, told us we'd make millions on? The ones Irving found in that old safe he was cleaning out and asked you what they was? You know, the bullshit papers Brian laid on us about oil in Oklahoma?"

"Yeah, I remember . . ."

"Jesus Christ, don't you see, we could use them for our meet with Pete's moneybags, especially him being from Oklahoma and all."

Benny looked at his bigger not overbright brother. "Abe, that's the first good one you've come up with since you spotted the China Kid." He turned to Pete. "Now listen, I'll tell you what. Tomorrow me and Benny'll drive into Pittsburgh. You tell this Thompson a couple of old pals of yours, important

180

businessmen you tell him, have made a big investment in Oklahoma oil and they'd like his advice on what they bought. Then we'll get talking about our fighter, see. We ain't too confident in China Kid, we'll say, because he's fighting the Battling Irishman, Paddy Kilbane."

"Hey, Kilbane was moving up fast before the war. You putting the Kid up against him?" Pete said.

"There you go," Benny crowed, "your man will figure the same way. We'll get him to bet some big dough on the fight against the China Kid, maybe we can even get him to put up cash against our mineral rights."

"But he knows all about oil, especially Oklahoma oil. You aren't going to get him to put up big dough against worthless rights."

Benny shrugged. "Maybe they ain't worthless, or at least maybe he'll think they're good . . . anyway, we'll get him betting money on the fight. And, like I said, whatever we take him off for, you get a third."

"Suppose your boy loses?" Pete asked. "All I've seen him fight is air. Kilbane is a top-notch fighter, he was almost a champ when the war started. If he wins I'm out my share and I still can't say he'll put up cash against your papers."

"Pete . . . if your man figures the leases have any value why would we want to sell them to him anyway? We use them to bait him into betting on the fight. This way instead of just getting his money for the leases we take him down for a few thousand bucks more."

"And if he bets any money against the leases, we know from an expert they're really worth something."

"My brother, he's brilliant," Benny said sarcastically.

"But Kilbane—"

"Kilbane goes into the tank in the sixth. It's all set."

"Why the hell would he do that?"

"It's been five years since Kilbane fought any competition. The army slowed him down, he's in his thirties now."

"Yeah, Pete," Benny said, "Kilbane's broke, he needs money, and while his name's still good he's using it to build a bankroll. You understand?"

"Sixth round, huh? Hey, you guys are pretty cute."

"You picked the right time to move your man," Abe laughed. "Now you play the outside to get him betting heavy. Right?"

"You bet your ass." Pete laughed.

An hour later, Pete had left the Ganoff brothers and was starting back to Pittsburgh when he saw a tall, well-built young man wearing a sheepskin-lined leather jacket standing beside the road at a bus stop. . . . Well, well, this was sooner than he'd expected. Pete pulled quickly to a halt. "Can I give you a ride, Jon?"

The China Kid leaned over and, recognizing his recent benefactor, pulled open the door and jumped in. "Thanks again, Mr. White."

"Glad to help you, Kid, and call me Pete. Okay?"

"Sure. Say, you don't know how much I appreciated that ten-spot, Pete. Those Ganoffs make me beg for every penny . . . the sons-of-bitches—sorry, I shouldn't have said that, they're your friends—"

"Forget it, Jon. You're dead right."

The Kid smiled, and as they drove toward Pittsburgh he began to relax and open up.

"You know, Jon, if the Ganoffs are so tight, maybe you should get a new manager," Pete suggested at one point.

"I wouldn't know how. I'm just hoping that I'll start winning some big fights and then a real manager will take me on . . . and I hate that 'China Kid' stuff. Why couldn't they let me call myself the Fighting Swede or something like that?"

"You know, I might have an idea for you. Did you have lunch?" Jon shook his head. "Yeah, I couldn't eat that shit they gave me either. How about we stop and get a steak—on me, Jon."

182

"A steak? I haven't had nothing but hamburgers and hot dogs since the Ganoffs took me on."

"So you're going on a new diet now—how can you fight without eating right? Right?"

As they sat in a restaurant outside Steubenville chewing on the biggest sirloins the place could find—Pete's special order—Pete casually mentioned, "What do you think about the fight coming up on Friday with Kilbane?"

". . . What do you mean, Pete?"

"Can you take him?"

"Sure as hell I can. He's an old man, in his thirties. He's all out of shape from the army."

"Yeah? How about you?" Pete moved in, "do you want to be like that six, seven years from now, washed-up in your thirties with scrambled brains, flat-out broke, on the street . . .?"

"No, sir, what I want is to make enough money to buy me a small spread back home in Oregon—"

"How much you figure that spread will cost you, Jon?"

"My uncle said he could fix it so I could buy a nice place, maybe three hundred acres, for two thousand down, say another thousand to make the house livable and another thousand, fifteen hundred for capital."

"How much do the Ganoffs let you keep out of each fight?"

"Shit, maybe a hundred bucks. They take everything off the top—percentages, training expenses, even the cost of heating the top floor of the factory, for Christ's sake. By the time they're finished, I'm lucky if I got enough left to last two weeks."

"Jon"—Pete's voice was especially warm now, like a father talking to his son—"I want you to come over to the William Penn tonight and meet my boss . . . I think he might have some mighty fine ideas for you. . . ."

22

PETE WHITE STRODE down the corridor of the William Penn Hotel and stopped in front of the double doors with the brass letters proclaiming "The Governor's Suite." Grinning, he unlocked the door and walked into the spacious living room. He sure hoped the con worked, he thought gazing around—he was beginning to get used to living like a millionaire. The room service waiter had set up an impressive array of bottles, glasses, and mixers and he was just building himself a bourbon and ginger ale when a key clicked in the lock. Carol and Kathy walked in, a pile of packages in their arms; with a graceful swoop, Carol put her boxes down, took off her coat and swirled around for Pete's inspection.

Pete whistled, "Well, hello there, fine lady. What happened to you?"

"Don't you like it?"

"Like it? I love it. The kid's got a whole new class. What'd you do to yourself, honey?"

"Kathy did it. She took me shopping and then to the hairdresser and told them how to do my hair. Oh, Pete, isn't it gorgeous?"

"I'll tell ya, kid, you could go down to Boca Raton or Delray or any of those joints and out-class every broad in the place. . . ."

Kathy looked Pete up and down. "Maybe we can take care of you next—"

"I wonder what's taking Cliff so long," Pete said. "Must be with those engineers and geologists still . . ."

While they waited Carol told Pete about her Pittsburgh cultural tour, courtesy of Kathy . . . including such high-water marks as the Carnegie Museum fronted by the statue of Stephen C. Foster playing his banjo, and such instant information as that the first movie theater and radio station in the United States were in Pittsburgh. It was touch and go there for a while, Carol said, whether they'd end up that night at the Syria Mosque seeing Fritz Reiner conduct the famed Pittsburgh Symphony Orchestra . . . but that much culture she figured she couldn't handle in one day.

The top of the day, Carol said, was Max Azen's, "the most scrumptious store I ever saw, nothing like it in Miami. That's where we got this dress." She twirled around, the skirt rising above her knees.

"It must have cost a bundle," was Pete's only remark.

"Yeah . . . and wait 'til you see what's in these boxes . . ."

"Uh, Carol . . . baby . . . I love you but we've got a big job to do in the next few months and we're going to need all the cash we've got."

"Don't worry, Pete," Kathy said, "it's on Mr. Roy Brian of Delray Beach, Florida. I paid Azen's by check on an account opened by my father. He'd never allow a check on his account with his name on it to be returned for insufficient funds. We'll pay him back later."

Pete brightened considerably. "Sure we will . . ." And just then the door swung open and Cliff walked in wearing a Chesterfield, a gray felt hat, and toting a very businesslike attaché case. He looked the perfect picture of a proper young corporation president.

"Ladies and gentlemen, I've had a most productive day. The engineers at Hammer and Stone are doing a complete geological and seismic report on Grove City Block II . . . and in their estimable opinion, we could have ourselves one hell of an oil field. . . ." He grinned. "Now, first things first. How'd it go, Pete?"

"Not bad. . . . We were right about the Ganoffs, Cliff, they'd never have gone for a straight deal . . . but what we got going now, we should get those leases—and maybe a few thou for a chaser. . . . Now, in about fifteen minutes a fighter, the China Kid, if you can stand it, is coming up to talk. . . ." And he filled in Cliff on his day. "Oh, and Cliff, be sure to call him Jon and not Kid or the China Kid, he's a sensitive fellow. Then tomorrow around five the Ganoffs will be here with their mineral leases I told them you'd 'evaluate' for them. It gets sort of complicated, doesn't it?"

"Yeah, it'd be a lot easier to do a straight buy . . . but with the Ganoffs, forget it. Anyway, each score just sharpens us up for the big one, right?"

"Right, partner. Now remember, when the Kid gets here, he's fighting a tanker on Friday, Kilbane dives in the sixth. I'm not even sure Jon knows it . . . Abe and Benny were very cute with me when I asked about it. . . ."

The telephone rang and Pete answered. "Send him up . . . Jon Petersen is on his way up now."

"Good." Cliff knocked on Kathy's door. "Kathy, we'll need to work this one ourselves for a while. Let the Kid get a good look at you, then you and Carol go down to the lounge for a drink and we'll join you later, okay?"

Kathy kissed him.

Better and better.

The doorbell rang and Pete opened the door to an awed Jon Petersen. It was obvious the China Kid had never seen digs like the Governor's Suite before.

"Jon," Pete said, "I want you to meet my boss, Mr. Cliff Thompson . . . Cliff, this is Jon Petersen from just outside

186

Portland, Oregon, he's the rancher and prizefighter I told you about."

Cliff took the Kid's large hand and shook it warmly. "It's a pleasure to meet you, Jon, Pete's been telling me a lot about you."

"Jon, would you like a Coke, ginger ale, anything?"

"Nothing, Mr. White . . . Pete."

"That's better, Jon. Come on, let's sit down over here."

At which moment Kathy and Carol walked through and Jon's eyes boggled further. The two girls showed it off for a few minutes, then Carol said, "Good-bye, Jon, I'm really sorry we can't spend more time with you now," she leaned closer, "but we'll be rooting for you on Friday. 'Bye now. . . ."

Petersen mumbled something, and Kathy and Carol left the boys to their business.

"Well, where do we go from here?" Kathy asked when they reached the lobby, "that boring-looking lounge?"

"Never!" Carol hailed a cab. "The Copa Club, please. . . ."

"Carol LaRue!" A beaming character introduced by Carol as Lenny Litman, owner, embraced her. "Haven't seen you in years . . . I still say you were the classiest act this club ever had. . . ."

The drinkers rubbernecked the ladies who had just arrived. It was obvious these girls were more than a few cuts above the usual brand in the club.

". . . For you, the best table in the joint . . . and the drinks are on the house. Hell, two lovely ladies are always good for business."

"Come on Lenny, sit with us for a few minutes."

"I could refuse? . . . You know, Carol I'll never forget the last time you were here . . . remember the guy, Ginsberg it was, who said you had an identical twin in Cleveland?"

"Oh, Jesus, you should forgive the expression, Gins-berg . . ."

Lenny picked it up for Kathy. "It was like this . . . Ginsberg

187

sees Carol, who's singing here, and after her first set, he calls her to the table and says, 'Dollink'—that's the way he talked —'Dollink, do you know you have a twin in Cleveland?' 'A twin?' asks Carol, batting her eyes, 'No, why ever do you ask?' Then Ginsberg tells us about how this girl in Cleveland advertised these oriental rugs, she says she got them from an uncle who died broke and all he had left were these rugs he'd spent a lifetime collecting. She really laid it on, and by the time she'd finished, Ginsberg was too. He bought every one. At this point Ginsberg shakes his head and says, 'And vould you believe it, they vas all phonies—and when I check, the girl is gone! . . . You sure you don't have no twin?' "

As Lenny and Kathy laughed, Carol shrugged, "Well, what's a girl to do between gigs? Especially in Cleveland. I learned the oriental carpet dodge when I was seventeen . . . from my aunt." She sighed. "I hope I never have to do that again."

Lenny looked at her appraisingly, "Say, Carol, Kathy, you doing anything now? . . . How about dinner with me and a friend of mine . . . very rich man, this friend . . ."

"Kathy and I are both engaged, Lenny . . . our fiancés are with us."

"Oh, fiancés, uh huh . . . well," he stood up, "great to see you again, Carol. And don't forget, anytime you want to play the Copa just let me know. There'll always be an opening for my favorite twins." And he hugged her again before he left.

"You've really been around, haven't you, Carol?" Kathy chuckled when Lenny had left.

Carol laughed. "Around and around, I guess you might say, honey, and there's more than a few high old times I'd just as soon have skipped . . . still, though, without those the good ones wouldn't have been so sweet. . . ."

"Tell me more," Kathy's tone was sincere. "I'm not the little angel my father and mother seem to think, but I've hardly gotten much beyond the college-country club circuit. This business about my father and Cliff's has made me start thinking

188

about myself, taking stock some, so I guess I'm curious about a lot of things that passed me by up to now. . . ."

"Okay, honey, pull up a chair and listen to how the other half lives. I come from a big family in Haines City, that's smack in the middle of Florida. My old man and old lady and aunts and uncles worked the citrus groves there, and I got a shot of real life myself at . . . let's see . . . I was just fourteen, I think, when an oversized, underwitted lunk of a cousin got me behind an orange tree and raped me. I didn't put out a broadcast, exactly, but when my aunt, who wasn't much older than I was, suggested the two of us take off for Miami and get shet of our orange-pickin' family, I was right on that bus with her. . . . By the time I hit a ripe old seventeen, I knew my way around Miami, Memphis, and New Orleans, where Aunt May and I ended up. She got me some gigs in third-, fourth-rate joints where the customers figured the talent was for after-hours too."

"How about you and Pete? How did you meet?"

"Don't tell him, but Pete was the first decent guy that ever happened to me. He was the night manager of the Monteleone Hotel in New Orleans. He was good to me from the start, got me singing jobs. I didn't know him really all that well until one morning when he took me out after my last set. He'd just quit the hotel and was going into full-time hustling . . . he loved the track, they call it the Fair Grounds in New Orleans, and we used to see each other after that quite a bit. Of course, he ran crap games most of the night and I worked for Turk, the guy Cliff and Pete took off in Miami before we came up here. Then the war came and Pete was off. He was always telling me he loved me and we kept in touch, saw each other sometimes when he got a furlough . . ."

"Pete wasn't your only lover, was he?"

"Kathy, in the business I was in, you couldn't afford an only lover. A girl had to live off men . . . it was men who got you the work, but then again you wouldn't know too much about

189

that, I guess, which you will please not apologize for. . . . And now you've got Cliff, and I've got Pete. . . ." She grinned. "And God willin', a *whole* lot of money. . . . Not so bad for a couple of southern ladies, hmm?"

23

AT FIVE O'CLOCK the next day Pete White was standing in the
lobby of the William Penn Hotel when Abe Ganoff came shuffling through the door, followed by his shorter brother Bennie,
peering through his thick glasses.

"You're right on time," Pete greeted them.

"Everything set up?"

"Even better than we'd planned . . . I told him you were
important businessmen and were interested in oil . . . and
boxers. Cliff liked that—and then we got a real break. He spent
all morning with the engineers and geologists, then had nothing
to do for the afternoon. You know what I did? . . . I got him
to go with me down to the gym and watch Kilbane work out.
He likes Kilbane . . . he's still a helluva fighter, you know."

"Sure, we know. That's why we're paying him so good to dive
in the sixth."

As they took the elevator up, Pete said, "Now look, I may
not get a chance to talk to you alone again before the fight, so
just make sure Kilbane puts on one hell of a show for five
rounds. The Irishman looks like he's creaming the Kid, my
boss'll up his bets each round. Got it?"

"Yeah, yeah Pete, that's good thinking. We'll take care of it."

Pete knocked on the door and a moment later Carol opened up, dressed in her sexiest, and with a lingering smile escorted the Ganoffs across the parlor to where Cliff and Kathy sat, wearing a look of warm, but distant attention.

"Cliff, this is Abe Ganoff and his brother Bennie."

"Mr. Ganoff, a pleasure to meet you . . . and you, Mr. Ganoff. May I present Kathy Brian?"

Kathy extended her hand and smiled graciously. "I'm so glad to meet you. Pete has been telling us so much about your marvelous plant . . . you know, pottery has always been one of my great hobbies, and everytime I go to England, I make certain to visit the Wedgwood plant, and the same with the Delft factory in Holland. I'm just sorry we don't have time to visit *your* China . . . what an appropriate name for a town whose chief industry is making chinaware." She bestowed friendly smiles on the two brothers, who were properly impressed by this regal presence.

"Aw, Miss Brian, I'm afraid our little plant in China isn't up to those ones you was talking about." Abe obviously couldn't take his eyes from the large emerald-cut diamond on Kathy's left hand. That was Kathy's touch—Pete had purchased it at a costume jewelers that morning.

"We were all about to have a drink," Cliff said. "Would you join us?"

"Yeah, Mr. Thompson. Good idea there."

"Pete, see what our guests would like. Why don't we all sit down over there in the corner. . . . I understand you're both interested in the fight game. . . ."

"That's right, Mr. Thompson, we've got a great boy, the China Kid . . . uh, he's young and inexperienced, though, needs some work, but we're trying to build him up."

"Those things take time, of course," Bennie added, "you know how it is, you win a few, you lose a few . . . Our boy, the China Kid, he's going to lose a few before he's a winner but we're sticking with him."

192

"He's fighting tomorrow night, I understand, Mr. Ganoff. Pete told me about him . . . well, maybe we should try to get some tickets—"

"Oh we'll have ringside seats for you, Mr. Thompson, right in the first row . . . that is, of course, if Miss Brian doesn't mind being so close to the action."

"I've never seen a fight before, Mr. Ganoff. I certainly want to be right there, as you put it, close to the action . . . right up there where you can hear every blow and see the beads of perspiration on the gladiators' faces. . . ."

Abe and Bennie exchanged glances.

"Yeah, that's where you'll be, Miss Brian. You can see the perspiration real good from there."

"I believe I remember something about your fighter's opponent, Kilbane," Cliff said. "He was almost a champion before the war, wasn't he?"

"He's still great. Naturally, we're supporting our boy completely, but he's going to have a hard time beating the Battling Irishman or even winning a draw . . . but that's how kids learn the game, don't they? They take their lumps and learn . . . should be a good fight though."

"Well my money's on Kilbane but it'll be interesting to see how your China Kid makes out. Who knows, maybe five years from now we'll all be able to say we once saw the future world champion get knocked out. . . ."

Bennie's and Abe's noses twitched with the scent of sucker, and it took all their willpower to restrain themselves from asking Cliff how much money he wanted to bet. Instead, Benny switched over to the other subject at hand. "Mr. Thompson, when Pete came out to the plant yesterday he mentioned you were in the oil business. . . ."

"That's right. I buy up mineral rights and then I drill. It's a matter of luck of the hole, you might say. Still, I do fairly well. . . ." He laughed modestly.

"Well, it so happens, Mr. Thompson, that we have some mineral rights out in Oklahoma we believe are very valuable—

Pete may have mentioned them to you. You see, my brother and I were associated for a while with this multimillionaire oil developer, see, and the gentleman gave us a chance to buy these mineral rights . . . now we don't know much about oil, but the chance looked too good to pass up, and you being an expert and all . . ."

"I'll be glad to look at them for you."

"Well, we'd sure appreciate it, Mr. Thompson." Bennie bobbed his head at Abe who quickly opened a briefcase and pulled out five folded blue-backed documents which he handed to Cliff. "With all the new oil technology being developed we figure they should be worth something. . . ."

Cliff took the deeds and one by one unfolded and studied them, allowing the suspense to build. The Ganoff brothers watching anxiously.

"Isn't this interesting . . . Grove City . . . you know, the reason I'm here in Pittsburgh is to see a geological firm doing studies around Grove City. Perhaps you know them . . . Hammer and Stone?"

"Uh, Hammer and Stone, sure . . . so what do they say?"

"Well, I'm afraid they say mineral rights like these are probably worthless . . . but they *could* be valuable if one of the majors drilled a couple of deep wells."

"So what are the chances for that?"

"Not too good. It's going to take some very special hardware to pump oil out of that area . . . some of the dry holes have been as deep as eight thousand feet. Still I'm tempted . . . my grandfather and my father would never have approved, I'm afraid. If they had one firm policy it was always—never wildcat."

"You mean you might drill a deep well yourself?"

"It's a possibility, a remote one of course. It would cost better than a hundred thousand dollars to try for oil at twelve thousand feet. . . ."

Abe couldn't hold it in any longer. "Look, Mr. Thompson, would you like to buy these mineral rights off of us?" Benny gave his brother a look for popping off, but it was too late.

194

"Well . . . I suppose I might if the price were right . . . chances are of course I'd never do anything with the rights . . . your leases are at least a mile and a half from anyplace I'd want to sink a well. . . ."

Now that the question had been asked by Abe, Bennie was forced into what he still considered premature negotiations. "What would the leases be worth to you, Mr. Thompson?"

Cliff shrugged. "Oh I suppose a couple thousand dollars maybe. As I say, the chances are I'd never be able to use them . . . but it is curious, a coincidence like this—"

"We felt fifteen grand would be a steal."

"No . . . look, I pay for what I get. If you want mineral rights these days, you've got to pay for them . . . but these just aren't worth that much. I suppose if you really want to sell them to me I'd go as high as five . . . I'll probably lose five grand anyway the next trip I make to a casino."

"If they're worth five they're worth fifteen," Bennie pressed.

Cliff shook his head and smiled. "No, doing business is one thing, gambling is something else."

"I got an idea, Mr. Thompson." Bennie's eyes gleamed through his glasses, "You like to bet on fights, I understand . . . how 'bout a bet tomorrow? You take Kilbane against our boy, the China Kid. You say the leases are at least worth five thousand—if the China Kid wins you pay us five thousand, if Kilbane wins, you get the leases."

"Gentlemen, I accept. A perfectly sporting proposition."

"Well, you're a real sportsman, Mr. Thompson."

"How would you like the stakes to be held?"

"We trust you, Mr. Thompson, we trust you all the way . . . why don't we have your man Pete White here hold them?"

"Fine by me . . . these deeds are made out to you, Mr. Ganoff. If you sign your name right there." Cliff pointed to the line on the deeds that made it a negotiable lease, "then give them to Pete to hold and I'll give him my five thousand."

"I'll tell you, Mr. Thompson, we'd rather sign the leases after the fight if we lose . . ."

195

"Fair enough, then I'll hold on to my five thousand until after the fight too."

"But that's different—"

"Come, come, Mr. Ganoff, you have to sign the deeds sometime . . . it's just like signing a check. . . ."

"What's the difference, Benny?" Abe said, *"sign* them."

Benny shrugged. "Okay. I never argue with a gentleman." He took a pen, scribbled his name on the bottom and put the leases in his briefcase. "We'll give them to Pete before the fight tomorrow."

"Can I offer you another drink?"

Benny and Abe looked at the girls and settled back to enjoy the high-class company, secure in the knowledge that they were about to become five thousand dollars richer. "Well now . . . don't mind if we do. . . ."

Cliff and Kathy arrived at the Civic Arena just as the last rounds of the final preliminary were being fought. Pete and Carol were already there, and Abe and Benny stood up as they approached ringside.

"Mr. Thompson, Miss Brian, good to see ya," Benny said, pumping their hands, "our fight's next . . . and Pete's got our leases." Pete nodded and Cliff reached into his jacket pocket, pulling out a thick wallet.

"Well then, Mr. Ganoff, I have here ten William McKinleys to match them," handing the five-hundred-dollar bills to Pete. "Pot's right?"

"Pot's right," Pete answered as a loud chorus of boos rolled from the stands behind them, signifying displeasure with the referee's decision.

"Lousy fight," Abe grumbled.

Five minutes later a feminine scream rose from the general admission seats at the back of the arena—the girls from the China Pottery Company were there in full force, and their cheers were for himself . . . the China Kid, now entering the ring.

196

"Cost us fifty bucks for the bus to bring 'em in and two hundred bucks for their deuce-and-a-half seats," Benny complained.

"Yeah, but it's good employee relations," Abe said, "and good for the Kid's morale, you know?"

". . . one hundred ninety-eight pounds, from China, Ohio . . . and at two hundred and twelve pounds . . . from Boston, Massachusetts . . . the Battling Irishman—Paddy Kilbane!"

A throaty roar of approval from the Kilbane fans. "Hey, you got a fourteen pound advantage over the Kid," Pete said loudly. Cliff turned to Abe. "I'll take five hundred more on Kilbane— if you believe that much in your boy."

"Ya got it." Abe peeled five hundred-dollar bills off a fat bankroll. "I see you're a percentage man."

"Only when it's in my favor."

"Well then," Abe nudged Bennie, "let's make it an even G."

"Like the man said, 'Ya got it.' "

The bell for the first round sounded and the China Kid charged to the center of the ring. Kilbane advanced on him and threw a left hook that missed by a foot as the Kid danced backward and answered with a succession of flicking left jabs. The blows glanced off Kilbane's gloves, though, and he let go with a right cross that missed the Kid's chin by an inch.

"If that shot had connected your boy would have been on his back for the count," Cliff laughed.

"Yeah . . . well if that's what you think, you want to press your bet?"

"Another grand?" The Ganoffs nodded. More money in Pete's pocket.

The first round was dull, the two fighters mostly feeling each other out, but in the second Kilbane came out shuffling flat-footed and reached the Kid on the forehead, cheekbone, and chin with a series of lightning left jabs that seemed to confuse him. The Kid managed a right to the solar plexus, but Kilbane shook it off, his left jab continuing to connect.

197

"I don't think your boy could break an eggshell," Cliff laughed.

"Is that so? You want to press your bet again?"

"I think I will, thanks. I have here a Grover Cleveland." Cliff handed a thousand-dollar bill to Pete.

"Hey, no Clevelands, we gotta discount one of them a hunnert when we let loose of it . . . too many of them in the black market."

Cliff tossed in another hundred dollars and Benny, satisfied at the payment of the vigorish, passed two five-hundreds over.

The rest of the second round was almost as dull as the first —even though the girls shrieked every time the Kid stirred a little air with a glove—but again, when the bell rang for the third, Kilbane charged into the ring, swinging now at the Kid with lefts and right crosses. "You know, if he could come within half an inch of the Kid's chin just once, the breeze would knock him down," Cliff said.

That set Benny and Abe off again, and two thousand more was added to Pete's by now overstuffed pocket as the crowd hooted for some action, "Whatsamatter, Kid, you got a hole in your ass?" The boos mounted until suddenly, in the fourth, the Kid seemed to come alive, dancing, reaching Kilbane first with a left and then a right cross. Kilbane looked momentarily shaken, but answered with several left jabs, and was about to land a right to the side of the Kid's head when the Kid went into a clinch, blocking the shot. Kilbane shoved him away and threw a wicked right cross that missed the Kid's jaw by half an inch. "That's the way, Kid, keep dancing," Abe hollered.

"Each time he swings, Kilbane comes closer," Cliff replied. "Before this fight's over the Irishman's got to nail him."

Just then Kilbane landed a solid left to the nose, followed by a hard right to the chin, which rocked the China Kid back against the ropes. Kilbane came after him with one vicious chop after another, to the body, the head, doubling the Kid over and then straightening him up, as the crowd howled for his blood.

198

Only the clang of the bell seemed to save him from being counted out right then and there.

Abe winked at Pete, who nodded back. Despite the beating he had absorbed, the Kid walked back to his corner, a spring in his step, as though Kilbane'd never laid a glove on him.

"You see, Thompson . . . my boy took a helluva lot of punches and they didn't do nothing to him. He's in great shape, the Kid can take it."

"Yeah, Thompson, whaddaya say now? Ya wanna go another G?"

"Certainly, gentlemen, another thousand on the Irishman. . . ." The pot was now five thousand and the mineral rights against ten thousand dollars in cash. . . .

The Kid charged out of his corner in the fifth, dancing around the Irishman, pushing him into a corner with a flurry of lefts and rights to his shoulders, arms and chest, but Kilbane, his powerful body absorbing the blows, counterpunched his way back to the middle of the ring. The shouts were deafening now, the screams from the China Pottery girls seeming to rise several decibels above the rest.

Now, in the center of the ring, the Irishman was set to throw one of his famous right-hand misses—but then something strange happened. Though the punch was telegraphed to every eye in the Civic Arena, the Kid seemed to . . . dance right into it. He landed on the canvas with a crash that could be felt throughout the stands, and as the referee slowly, deliberately began to count the Kid out, long, high-pitched groans could be heard coming from the general admission seats. Twenty seconds later, the Kid was still out cold.

Pete was one of the first spectators to recover from the shock —clutching the money and deeds he jumped into the ring and knelt for a moment beside the Kid before he was hustled out of the ring by the referee and a cop.

"I think he's dead," Pete said into the stunned crowd and the word "Dead! Dead!" reverberated through the arena. "Jesus, he's killed the Kid!" a woman screamed.

Cliff turned to the shocked Ganoffs. "If he's dead, you'd better watch out, they could investigate you for mismatching him . . . and I hope you're ready to take care of his hospital and maintenance expenses if he survives. He could be a vegetable the rest of his life, I've seen it happen—"

"Oh, Jesus Christ!" from Abe.

Benny stood up, his face ashen, as two attendants carried a stretcher into the ring. "Come on, Abe, let's get outa here. . . ." The boxing commissioner had entered the ring and was looking out beyond the ropes as though searching for someone.

"His managers are over there," Pete called out, but even as the commissioner shifted his gaze, the Ganoffs were pushing, shoving and kicking their way to the exit.

"You and your big ideas . . . a dive in the sixth you said . . . easy money, you said . . . why the hell couldn't you keep your toilet shut . . . and that goofball son-in-law, happened to dig out those leases . . . why the fuck. . . . Goes to show you, a jag-off is a jag-off . . . you two should go in business together . . . Jag-Offs Incorporated."

As the Ganoffs beat it for the state border, Pete and Cliff, declaring themselves the Kid's acting managers, were being admitted to the Kid's dressing room. Pete walked sorrowfully to the Kid's comatose body and, stooping, whispered something into his ear.

"Jon . . . the Ganoffs just took the fastest lam since Tojo heard about Hiroshima . . . the next bus leaves for Portland, Oregon, in an hour and you're going to be on it . . . with five grand in your pocket."

As in a miracle, the China Kid suddenly sat upright, eyes open and alert, a smile on his face. "He seems to be all right now," Pete commented to the assembled, and in a half hour they were all gone.

It was a happy Jon Petersen who boarded the first Greyhound bus heading west. "Mr. Thompson, I'll never forget what you've done for me, and I swear, if you'll give me an

200

address I'll pay every penny of that five grand back as soon as I can."

"Forget it, Jon—consider it a gift from the brothers Ganoff . . . two old China hands deeply interested in your welfare and future. . . ." Jon laughed, waved, and the doors shut.

They watched until the bus disappeared, then as they started back to the hotel. "I think," Cliff said, "that discretion being the better part of valor, we would do well to check out tonight and stay in a motel. . . ."

"You bet your ass," Pete agreed. "The Ganoffs start thinking, they just might decide to send some muscle to call on us at the Governor's Suite. . . ."

"Well, *we're* all packed. . . ." Carol said, her arm linked in Kathy's.

"Then what are we waiting for? Next stop—New Orleans!"

24

THREE DAYS AND two nights later—Cliff had decided to make it a leisurely drive, "no sense getting ourselves so tired we can't out-hustle the hustlers"—they arrived in the Crescent City . . . New Orleans. They checked in, of course, at the Monteleone Hotel.

"Pete White!" the night manager said, "Well, I'll be a son-of-a—where the hell you been?"

"Oh, been pretty busy, Bert, working with my friend Cliff Thompson here . . . he's in oil, you know."

"Yeah? You in oil now too, Pete?"

"I'm learning the game. . . ." They signed the register as Mr. and Mrs. White and Mr. and Mrs. Thompson.

"You all go on upstairs," Pete said. "I need to talk to Bert a little more. . . . Now Bert, tell me, is George the Greek still around?"

"I guaran-damn-tee he is . . . matter of fact, he's half-owner of the Athens Olympia now, you know that Greek restaurant on Decatur Street some of us used to hang out at?"

"Sure, but what's a bookmaker like George doing in the restaurant business?"

202

"The owner of the Athens owed George so much betting horses he had to take him in as a partner, only way he could pay off. It works out pretty good, though, George is the best customer the place has. He's there every afternoon after the last race . . . you wanta see him, that's where he'll be."

"Thanks a lot, old buddy . . . see you later."

That evening, Pete went to see George the Greek. The Athens Olympia was only two and a half blocks from the Montclcone Hotel, one of those narrow, jammed places with a picture of the Acropolis on the wall. Pete walked down the booth-crowded aisle, turned right, and there in an alcove in the back was George the Greek's table—and, without question, George the Greek himself.

He sat surrounded by cohorts, his olive complexion set off by a thick mane of gray hair combed straight back from his forehead, his almond eyes set above a long aquiline nose. As Pete approached, he blinked once, shook his head, then with a roar pushed his chair back and stood up.

"Pete White? That you after all these years? Damn, where you been?"

"Well, it's like there was this war and they needed me—"

"Yah, yah, I heard all about it. So you decided to come home, do you need a job, anything? What happened to that doll, what was her name?"

"Carol? She's with me."

"Yeah? So what you doing now, Pete? Come on, sit down, sit down."

"Well, I'm working for a sharp young guy who's in the oil business, George . . . matter of fact, he's also a high-roller, likes to bet the horses . . . maybe I can steer him into you. He pays me pretty good, but I can always use a little more, you know?"

"You bet I do, Pete. Steer him here . . . he can bet me with both fists . . . and I'll see you get something."

"Great, the only thing though, George, is he doesn't know you like I do. He's been around gambling all his life . . . matter of fact his father was a big hustler out west, Oklahoma I think

. . . anyway Cliff always says when it comes to bookies he doesn't want to have to win twice."

"What's he mean by that?" Knowing damn well what he meant.

"He means, George, that when he picks the right horse, he wants to make sure he's got someone who's gonna pay off. . . ."

"Hell, he ain't got nothing to worry about with me. I lay off action out of Miami, Chicago, Boston, New York—you name it."

"Oh I know you ain't no candy store bookie, you ain't about to walk him . . . that's why I okayed you—"

George nodded. "You know, Pete, a lot of assholes call themselves bookies but they're really players . . . they go up against craps, sports, broads—the whole thing. But not me—this Greek don't bet on nothing . . . not even the sun coming up tomorrow. They can bet me, I don't bet them. That's why I got property"—he gestured around him—"this restaurant, cash, a good reputation . . ."

"George, that's what I figured. That's why you're the only bookie I trust with Cliff . . . because I can't afford to lose a guy like that."

"His name's Cliff?"

"Right, Cliff Thompson."

"Thompson? His father wasn't Slim Thompson from Grove City, Oklahoma?"

"Yeah, that's him . . . but Cliff's legit. He's a law graduate, specializes in petroleum law . . . that's oil."

"I know, I know . . . you don't think I know oil is petroleum?"

"*I* didn't."

"You say he's got money now?"

"Yeah, a lot of people pay him to give them the straight dope on oil."

"Who?"

"People who got oil problems, that's who."

"Well, if he's got the money to gamble, bring him to me . . . why don't you all come over here for dinner tomorrow night after the last race?"

"I'm sure he'd love to, George. He's got this girl with him."

"So he'll bring his girl, and you bring Carol . . . Slim Thompson's boy, eh? What was it that happened to Slim anyway . . . he got whacked-out somewhere, right?"

"Yeah, fella named Roy Brian got him in a skin game—"

"Yeah, yeah, I remember now . . . something about oil . . . what are you and Thompson really doing here?"

"Like I told you, George, New Orleans is home for me, I wanted to show it to Cliff, and the Fair Grounds are open."

"He wouldn't be trying to buy up oil rights?"

"I don't know, you'll have to talk to him about it . . . I do know that he likes to bet horses. . . ."

The Greek got back to business. "How does he bet?"

"He's a bookie's dream. He loves to beat the races."

George the Greek smiled to himself. "You can beat a race, but you can't beat the races. A good horse, he don't feel good, he gets bunched in, a cheap speed horse throws him off stride, he gets hooked on another horse, his jockey don't pace him right . . . he's out of the money. Too many things can happen in a race, that's why bookies that stick to their business get all the money—and nobody can overcome the seventeen percent put on by the track."

"Cliff thinks he's got a system for betting the horses . . . I don't understand it, but I've seen him score big."

"Well, there's hot horses and smart money bets, but that's only occasional. I deal with the wise guys too, as long as they bet regular with me, but if they only bet occasional I tell them to take their business to Walgreens."

"I don't know how long we're going to be here, George, but I'm sure you can get Cliff betting regular . . . how much of his action do I get?"

"I'll be fair with you, Pete. Haven't I always? You bring Thompson and his lady over tomorrow evening . . . we'll see what we can do."

The next morning over breakfast, Cliff said, "Are you sure there's no way I can help you with the setup, Pete? I feel kind of guilty taking the day off. . . ."

"No, Cliff, you just show up tonight. We're on my turf now and this is something only I can do . . . sorry, *we* can do," placing a hand on Carol's arm.

Late that day, Carol sitting beside him, he drove down the Esplanade, the wide boulevard running the entire length of the city. "It's good to get home," he sighed, "everybody's got to have some place where they can go back to . . ."

"Yeah, terrific, I've got Haines City, Florida . . . and those damn orange trees."

"Baby," patting her hand, "we do everything right we're going to get us a home and put down some *real* roots."

"I hope so, Pete."

"We will, baby, we will. This is what we've been waiting for, no more hustle, no more club dates for you, we'll have us a nice little place somewhere and stay home nights and listen to the radio—"

"That's really what I want, Pete."

"And that's really what you're going to have, doll." They were leaving the commercial district of the city. "I never told you where I was brought up, did I?"

"Just New Orleans, is all I know."

"Well, today I'm going to show you where I lived 'til I was fifteen."

A few minutes later Pete pulled up beside the Saint Louis Cemetery; beyond it Carol could see the Fair Grounds track.

"You're not going to tell me you grew up in the cemetery?"

"No." Pete helped her out of the car. "If you'll look across the street you'll see where my childhood, such as it was, was misspent."

206

"In that church?"

"No, right next to it . . . Mother Cabrini's Orphanage."

"Pete . . . you never told me you were an orphan . . ."

"Strictly speaking, I wasn't. I knew my mother . . . but she was dirt poor and she got pregnant and her family threw her out . . . my mother was very close to the sisters, so that's how I came here . . . to the Mother Cabrini Orphanage for Girls. They made an exception in my case."

Carol laughed. "You really started young, didn't you? One boy and all those girls. It must have been a ball."

"No . . . no it was no damn ball. The girls all picked on me, and when I was old enough to find out what boys and girls were all about, the sisters watched me so close life wasn't worth living. But I shouldn't complain . . . they fed me, gave me clothing, sent me to school, and best of all"—he pointed—"I could run right through the cemetery, climb up on that tombstone over there and jump over the fence into the Fair Grounds.

"The sports got used to seeing me around and gave me odd jobs around the stables, then one day when I was fifteen a guy from the Monteleone said he could get me a job as a bellhop. That's how I started working there."

Pete took Carol's hand and led her into the cemetery. "Everybody's buried above the ground here. They have to . . . you dig down four feet and you hit water." They looked at the banks of white marble shelves thirty squares long, five high, standing like rows of dirty-white filing cabinets. "My mother's in one of those drawers."

"Which one, Pete?" Carol asked softly.

Pete led her down the rows of crypts to one marked "White," chiseled in stone in the front of the small vault. "She never was married, so they put her family name on the grave . . . my name now."

They walked on in silence until they reached the far end of the cemetery, where they could look over at the racetrack, the stands filling up with people for the first race, the grooms and trainers working on their horses, an air of excitement seeming to hang over the place. "I loved it over here . . . I bet I knew the Fair Grounds better than anybody." He pointed to a two-story house just the other side of the cemetery fence but off the Fair Grounds' property line. "Look at that house! I used to see gamblers past-post there all the time."

"Past-post?"

"Sure. A bookie will bet with you on a race that's already been run if he thinks there's no way you could know who the winner was . . . so guys would go up to the second floor, watch the races through binoculars, spot the winner and send the information out with a runner who'd phone it in. A partner would take it from there. The only thing is, the bookies got so hip to it, the sharpies couldn't work it anymore and stopped trying. I doubt anybody's pulled it in years now. . . ."

"Is that what we're going to do?"

"You'll see . . . hey look at that big crypt right next to the iron fence, see the one I mean with the angel on top of it? That's the one I used to jump on to get into the Fair Grounds."

"Pete White . . . taught by the sisters, educated by the touts . . . some sweet child you were."

"I guess I came out about as well as could be expected . . . let's go back."

"Pete, I feel like I just found out about a whole new side of you. I feel . . . Pete, do you really love me?"

"Sure, baby . . . you know I do, I always have."

"I hope so, Pete, because if you're conning me, I'll kill you." She looked up at the entrance to the orphanage—the high arched doors, the figure of Christ, his hands outstretched on the second-floor balcony above the main door.

"Pete White," she said, "I'm no angel, you know. Now come here and kiss me."

"I know," he said, and did.

Kathy and Cliff were enjoying their day off. Cliff took Kathy down to Bucktown on the riverfront, where the beers were five cents and soft-shell crabs two for a quarter. They wandered about the city hand in hand, soaking up the atmosphere along the Mississippi River banks and watching the ferries and boats ply their way up and down the river.

At seven that evening they joined Carol and Pete, who led the little group to George the Greek's table and were greeted with open arms. "Pete, my friend, Mr. Thompson, ladies . . . welcome to the Athens Olympia. Tonight we're going to have a real Greek supper—a feast!" He gazed at Kathy appreciatively. "Miss Brian, I'm so happy you joined us tonight."

"Oh thank you, George—may I call you George?—it's going to be a real treat for me . . . we don't have any restaurants like this in Delray Beach."

"You're from Delray?"

"Sure she is, George," Cliff said. "As a matter of fact you might even know her father . . . Roy Brian."

"Brian?" There was no hiding George's look of surprise. "Yes . . . yes of course I know your father, Miss Brian—"

"Please call me Kathy."

"All right, Kathy. Uh—"

"She knows all about it George," Cliff said.

"Yes? Well, good . . . good!" George grinned broadly, but there was a speculative look in his eyes. "That's a new one on me . . . the son and daughter of . . . well, sit down, sit down, for Christ's sake, have a drink!"

The evening passed smoothly, everyone eating, drinking, enjoying each other's company, Cliff and George discreetly sounding each other out on oil, mineral rights, and horse betting. Cliff gave George his by-now-standard assessment of the value of the Grove City oil leases that George had gotten from Roy Brian, his possible use for them, even though it was more romantic than businesslike . . . in memory of his father, and all . . . and George touted Cliff on the great action to be found at the Fair Grounds. By midnight, when the party broke up, George had promised to pick Cliff up the next morning to take him to the races. . . .

"I'll bring a scratch sheet with the morning line."

"Right, and while you're at it, bring along those mineral deeds," Cliff added, as they stood up to leave. "Maybe we'll do a little business."

Back at the hotel, the four of them gathered for a strategy session.

"You think you can handle everything in the morning in time? If you need another day, we can stall the Greek off," Cliff offered.

"Nah, Carol and I have it all staked out. Don't worry about us, *Major* Thompson." He threw a mock salute.

Cliff smiled. "The girl at the switchboard all taken care of?"

"Bert, the night manager, 's got it all worked out—he doesn't know what we're doing but he's with us . . . I'll slip the girl another twenty bucks, though, just before Carol and I go out to the Fair Grounds."

"Great . . . by the way, Kathy, you did quite a beautiful job on the Greek tonight. George fell in love with you."

Kathy gave Cliff a teasing look. "Secretly I've always had it for older men."

Cliff went over to the double bed, turned Kathy over and spanked her a shot.

"Hey! . . ."

Pete stood up, grinning. "Well, kids, don't want to spoil your fun . . ." He turned to Carol. "And how do you feel about older men?"

"Come along and find out, grandpa."

210

25

THE FIRST RACE was due to be run at 1:15, so Pete and Carol arrived at the Fair Grounds by noon, pulling up in front of an ancient two-story frame building housing a bar on the first floor. Pete looked at the house. "I don't know how that place stands up. If they didn't slap a coat of paint on it every year, I swear it'd come unstuck."

As they entered, the bartender gave them a nod and the proprietor, an old friend of Pete's known as Jack Leggs, came through a door at the end of the bar to greet them. "Everything's set up for you, Pete, now for God's sake be careful and don't let yourself get spotted. If I hadn't known you since you was a kid trying to get a drink at fifteen, I'd never do this for you—"

"I appreciate it, Jack."

"Well I hope it helps you out, Pete, but just remember, if I get caught aiding and abetting past-posting I'm gonna have my ass in hock with the track authorities."

"Ah, you been in trouble with the track authorities for twenty years, Jack, but don't worry, we'll be careful—and like I said, I'll make it worth your while."

"Oh I know that, Pete." He looked approvingly at Carol. "It was smart to bring the lady. No guy could hold onto that phone booth, he'd get hisself thrown out in two minutes, particularly just after the race, but a lady . . ." he grinned. "Well, good luck."

Cliff stood in his pajamas and robe, ruefully fingering the stubble of beard on his chin. "I hate looking this raunchy at twelve noon."

"You look absolutely perfect, Cliff," Kathy said. "Anyone would think you'd just got up ten minutes ago."

"Yeah . . ." he turned to her, "honey, you're the key now . . . if we pull this off today, that's three down, only two left."

Kathy moved to him and kissed him on the lips. "Don't worry about me, Cliff. This lady is learning."

The telephone's sharp ring interrupted them, and Cliff waited until it had sounded four times before picking it up.

"You have a visitor coming up, Mr. Thompson . . . and this is the way I'll ring when Mr. White calls me."

"Thanks, Sophie." Cliff hung up. "Okay, Kathy, into the next room with you. You know what to do."

"Got you." Kathy slipped out the door and a few moments later there was a knock. Cliff pulled it open and confronted a surprised George the Greek.

"Come on in, George."

"Hey, post time for the first is one fifteen. I thought you were going to be ready."

"Sorry, George, I overslept. I had a little beef with Kathy last night after we left. . . . She went and got herself another room and I couldn't sleep, so I went and had a few drinks until the bars closed."

"Roy Brian really came up with a gorgeous daughter."

"Yeah, but a spoiled little rich bitch . . . she wanted adventure, forbidden fun, you know the drill . . . and when her father told her she couldn't see me, that made it all the more exciting

212

for her. I've got to admit she's the best young stuff I ever had—"

"I don't make bets, I take 'em . . . but if I was a betting man I'd give three to one odds you ain't gonna lose her. . . ."

"Nah, she won't really leave me—she loves what she gets from me too much. That bunch of pansies around Delray Beach wouldn't know what to do with it if they saw it. . . ." He laughed. "Old Roy Brian fucked my folks and me when I was a kid . . . well, I'm getting a little of it back now."

"Yeah . . . look, Cliff—" George pulled out a racing form and scratch sheet from his pocket.

"Don't worry, George, I'll be with you in a few minutes, it won't take me long. How 'bout some coffee?"

Cliff picked up the phone and ordered coffee and Danish, then, hanging up, turned to George, palms up, "I swear, George, I just don't understand women. I used to think I did, now . . ."

George laughed. "If you did, pal, you'd be the only one. . . ." He looked down at the scratch sheet. "Maybe you'd like to look over the morning line. You can bet the first race with me right here."

"Thanks, George. I'll get myself fixed up and then maybe I'll be able to concentrate on the horses."

"By the way, Cliff, I brought those mineral deeds with me . . . right here . . . see what you really think they're worth."

Cliff took the deeds, studied them, then dropped them on the bed. "I leveled with you when I said maybe they are and maybe they aren't of some value. It's going to take a lot of money to explore Block II. Mostly, I just want what was my father's own, even, like I say, if it's worthless, and then maybe, just maybe I can do something with Block II someday."

"You still burned about Slim being taken off by Roy Brian?"

"You might say."

"But Slim was a pro. When a pro takes off a pro, nobody should get sore—"

"That's about what my mother always said. And that's why I never really went after Roy Brian."

"Until now?"

"Not even now. Unless of course you call taking away his daughter taking him off. . . . What do you want for those rights?" Cliff asked abruptly.

"What did you have in mind?"

"Not much. A few thousand, I guess."

"A few thousand? Seems to me the deeds ought to be worth at least ten grand. . . ."

"Look, I told you, those leases are probably worthless to anybody but me—" A knock at the door. "There's our coffee."

When Cliff came back, George said, "Tell you what we'll do . . . you're looking to make a score at the track, right?"

"I suppose so."

"Okay. I'll use the mineral deeds as part of my bankroll to take any action you want to put down. Okay?"

"You're on . . . help yourself to the Danish."

"Thanks . . . here's the scratch sheet, see if there's anything to your taste." Cliff took the scratch sheet and leisurely looked down the post positions. "Better hurry, though. The first race starts in about twenty minutes, maybe less."

As Cliff read, the telephone rang five times. Finally Cliff picked it up. "Hello . . . I told you, Kathy, I'm not putting up with any more of your hysterics . . . so *go* back to daddy and mommy. When you're ready to act like a grown-up, let me know." He hung up.

Cliff shrugged. "Sorry you have to be in on our little domestic problem, George. Let me take a shower and shave and we'll get after those deeds on the first race. Okay?"

"Sure." George kept his eyes on Cliff as he went into the bathroom and took off his robe. As Cliff turned on the shower, he called out, "Hey George, do me a favor . . . don't answer the phone if it rings again. It'll be my little broad. I don't want to talk to her yet," and he stepped into the shower.

Half an hour earlier, armed with a handful of nickels, Carol had placed herself in a phone booth across the street half a block down from the bar where she and Pete had been talking with Jack Leggs. Pete, meanwhile, had climbed a ladder into the cupola of the building, where from between the slats he could easily see the finish line at the Fair Grounds. He was careful not to let his binoculars protrude as he checked out the racetrack, then turned to where Carol was standing in the phone booth pretending to be in a long conversation. She turned from the phone, took her binoculars and focused them on the cupola. Pete reached one hand out, holding up five fingers. Through his glasses he saw Carol do the same.

With everything in order, Pete took out his scratch sheet and looked at the numbers. Nine horses running in the first race . . . he hoped a horse with a low number won. The idea of the phone in Cliff's room jangling as many as nine times made him nervous. If George the Greek ever suspected . . .

But if all went right, he wouldn't. Pete was also counting on a built-in edge. From long experience, he'd noted that the wisest guys were often the best marks, providing they were set up right. Being pros, they mostly were convinced that they knew it all, that there was only one sucker—the other guy. And not looking for the take-off, they were sometimes the most suscepti-ble to it. Once again, providing you set them up right. It took one to take one off, and that was at least partly why things had worked out with the Ganoffs and the Turk. George the Greek was even surer of himself, which made him that much more open for the take-off . . . Pete hoped—because if something went wrong, well, Pete knew a couple of guys who had crossed the Greek and had never showed up or been heard of again.

Pete watched the horses being led to the starting gate, then the gate spring open. "They're off," he muttered to himself. Through the binoculars Pete saw the favorite, Gulf Pride at six to five, get off to a slow start. Just as George the Greek had said, a couple of cheap speed horses—both with high numbers—had got in front of the betting choice. Then another horse seemed to be catching up coming around on the outside. It was horse number four.

"God," Pete mumbled to himself, "let number four win." Horses numbers one, two, and three were running well in the rear and only number four seemed to be clear. He glanced at the scratch sheet and saw the horse's name was Tasha, a filly who had run only two races before. At eight-to-one odds, her winning could cinch the deeds on the first race alone.

"Come on Tasha, Tasha, keep moving Tasha, you're moving great, baby . . ." Coming into the stretch Tasha was still ahead, running flat out. "Come on, sweetheart, you're beautiful, go Tasha, go . . . you've got it, baby!" as Tasha made it across the finish line two lengths ahead. Immediately, Pete whirled around and stuck his hand out between the slats of the cupola, holding up four fingers. Through the binoculars he could see Carol indignantly berating a horse player who obviously wanted to get into the booth himself.

"Come on, Carol," he said, jiggling up and down, "look up *here*," and as the disgruntled player moved away from the booth, Carol lifted her binoculars, nodded, and held up four fingers. Pete clenched his fist and shook it, the signal she was correct, then watched as Carol dropped a nickel into the pay phone and put through a call to the switchboard at the Monteleone Hotel.

As George the Greek impatiently sat and watched, Cliff slowly lathered his chin in the windowless bathroom and stared at the scratch sheet. The Greek kept glancing at his watch and as it came time for the first race, he stood up, walked over to the only window in the bedroom and pulled down the shade. Cliff glanced up at the sudden decrease of light, allowed himself a smile, said nothing.

Showered and shaved, Cliff was just slipping into a clean shirt when the telephone began to ring. "Don't answer it, George, it's that crazy broad."

The phone rang again. "If I let her think she can just pick

216

up the phone and call me and get me back that easy, there'll be no living with her. That was the trouble with Roy Brian"— the phone rang a third time—"he's a tough son-of-a-bitch, but he lets his daughter walk all over him. It's going to take a hard man to make an easy-to-live-with lady out of her." Cliff, scratch sheet in hand, walked to the middle of the room. "Let me borrow a pencil, huh?"

Cliff sat down on the edge of the bed and ran down the post-position column as he added one to the number of phone rings and stopped at the number four. "Yep, here's the horse I like in the first, I picked her out while I was shaving. Her form looks good." He drew a circle around a filly named Tasha and tossed the form back at George the Greek. George looked down, noted the eight-to-one shot, and smiled to himself. A real sucker bet.

"What'ya betting on this horse?"

"What are you asking for the leases?"

"What'ya think they're worth, Cliff?"

"I told you a couple, three thousand dollars. No more . . . ah, what the hell, you'll probably end up beating me for them anyway."

"Okay, Cliff, how's this? Five thousand dollars . . . I'll put up the leases for five large, what do you say?"

"It's too damn much, but okay, what the hell. So I got to make sure I have five thousand dollars at the end of the day, huh?"

"That's right, Cliff," George said, finding it difficult to mask his pleasure at this bargain.

Cliff nodded and poured himself another cup of coffee, then began to talk, seemingly at random.

"Like I said, George, those leases probably don't mean much to anyone but me . . . but I don't know . . . I've had the top geological survey company in the Southwest and the best in Pittsburgh make new studies for me and they both said the same thing . . . the dry hole Roy Brian sank, the hole that turned him off Block II, wasn't deep enough. If he'd gone down another eight thousand feet he should have hit oil—but that would have been damn deep drilling in the thirties . . . and of course there wasn't any reason to go that deep for oil when he had all he could market in Block I.

"Now here we are, 1946, the war's over. The automobile companies are making more cars every year, the country's burning more oil, it's going to be economical to go down eighteen thousand feet for oil . . . what I want to do is put all these deeds together, incorporate them just like Brian did, and then talk a major into sinking a deep well. . . ." Cliff was pacing about the hotel room now, his excitement tangible, George could feel it coming off him. "But George . . . what I'd really . . . if I could afford to I'd wildcat and put the well down myself. I know how deep I have to go . . . it might cost me a quarter-million dollars, but then it'd be all mine and George . . . the studies say Block II might have maybe four or five times the reserves of Block I."

"Hey, Cliff, you know something, I believe you. If I was a player I'd take a piece of that wildcat action myself."

Cliff shook his head. "It's a long shot. You're better off playing pick-outs like I'm doing—no bull, the odds are better."

George looked down at the scratch sheet and smiled, remembering Cliff's sucker bet.

"And the majors," Cliff went on, "they don't put up money easily. And if they do they want it all for themselves. . . . No . . . I'm being square with you, George, when I say the mineral rights have some value to me, but I have to put them all together and spend at least a couple of years of my life doing something with them. They're a dry hole, I'd say, for anyone else—"

The telephone rang again, and Cliff looked at it wearily. He shook his head. "Oh, hell, I guess I'd better talk to her for a minute."

"Yes, Kathy . . . no, I couldn't answer before, I was in the bathroom. Look, I'm talking business now, why don't we just let it alone for the rest of the day? When I get back from the track we'll talk things out . . . *no,* goddamn it, I told you, not now."

Cliff looked over at George and shook his head, then into the phone: "No. Where are you, anyway? The cocktail lounge? Why don't you lay off the sauce and take a little walk for yourself?" He hung up. "Broads, they'll drive you crazy . . . tell you what, George, let me finish getting dressed, then we'll drive out to the track. I'd like to watch the tote board and see them in the paddock. Maybe I can pick a winner better out there than here."

"Sure, Cliff, whatever you want. We won't be able to make it for the second race, but I'll take your action on it right here if you want." Cliff walked back to the bathroom, closely followed by the Greek who checked out the bathroom, assuring himself there were no windows, only a ventilator in the ceiling.

It was almost 1:40, post time for the second race.

"George, let me have that scratch sheet again . . ." George handed him the daily racing form and the Harvey A. Junior scratch sheet. Cliff walked back into the bedroom and laid them on the bed, carefully knotting his tie. Then he walked to the closet, took his time selecting a sports jacket, went back to the bed, picked up the racing form and studied it some more. It was just after 1:40. "Let me have that pencil back again, George."

Cliff began marking up the sheet . . . then stopped and walked over to the bureau where he had a bottle of Scotch. "Would you like a touch?" The Greek shook his head. "Mind if I have one? Maybe I'll get a little inspiration for the second race."

He poured a shot as George the Greek glanced at his watch, realizing the horses in the second race were probably coming across the finish line by now. Finally Cliff turned, "Okay, George, I think I've got my horse for the second."

He was raising the pencil—when a shout came from the hall. "Cliff Thompson, you let me in, you let me in right now!" and a furious Kathy began banging on the door. Seven times. Cliff circled the number eight post position on the sheet and said,

"Okay, it's Shaikh in the second race. Sorry about this disturbance, I'll quiet her down. Let's get ourselves out to the track."

"I'm ready." The Greek looked down and saw that Shaikh was running at ten-to-one odds. Jesus, another sucker bet. Cliff was a bookmaker's dream.

Cliff angrily jerked the door open and Kathy almost fell into the room. "Please Cliff, I've got to talk to you. I'm sorry about last night. You know I didn't mean it . . . it's just that I'm scared. I've never been away like this before, I can't help worrying about my father and mother and what they're thinking—"

"Take it easy, Kathy. Why don't you go back to your room and get a little sleep, huh? I think that would do you good—"

"But I want to see you *now,* Cliff." She looked at the Greek. "George, I'm sorry to make a scene like this, forgive me—"

"Sure, kid."

"Look, Kathy, I told you I'd see you later. Now go on back to your room and wait until I finish at the track. . . . Okay, George, let's get going, I want to get out there at least in time for the third race."

"Is that all you can think of, Cliff, betting on horses? Gambling? What about *me?*"

Cliff brushed past her and moved down the hall. "Don't you think you're being a little rough on the kid?" George asked.

"I told you, George, once you let these broads walk all over you, you've had it with them for the rest of your life."

George looked at him, nodded solemnly. A car was waiting at the front of the hotel for them. Cliff and George climbed into the backseat, two of George's henchmen rode up front.

"That's some horse you picked in the second, that ten-to-one shot," George said.

"I like that horse . . . Shaikh could steal the race. Hey, let me have a look at the form. I'll start picking a winner for the third." George happily handed it over.

The car pulled up in front of the Fair Grounds. They walked

in and immediately went over to the bulletin board, where the results of the first two races were posted. There it was: Tasha, $18.60 to win. Shaikh, $28.40 to win. Then underneath the two results, Daily Double—$340.00.

Cliff let out a groan and slapped his forehead. "Look at that will you? That fight with Kathy last night cost me, let's see how much did it cost me?—goddamn it, cost me eight and a half G's. If I'd been here at the track early like we planned, I would have bet the double, at least fifty . . . fifty would have got me eight-five hundred . . . it just goes to show, you shouldn't argue with broads . . . hell . . . all right, George, how do we stand?"

But George the Greek was still staring at the bulletin board. It was impossible. This sucker had hit two pick-outs, two long-shot pick-outs in the first and second races. It just didn't happen —he'd checked out the room, pulled the shades . . . it didn't happen, but it did, and he was a professional. "I owe you four thousand one hundred fifty on the first race and six thousand six hundred on the second. A total of ten thousand seven hundred fifty. And we ain't even into the third race yet . . . who do you like in the third?"

"I don't know . . . let's go down and look at them in the paddock."

George led Cliff out of the clubhouse and underneath the stands to the indoor paddock where on the benches lining either side of the tunnellike hallway sat bookies, touts, players, and spectators, all hustling a day at the races. There was hushed, respectful silence for the Greek as he passed.

As Cliff and the Greek watched the horses that would be running in the third race, their grooms leading them around the dirt circle for inspection, one of the horses suddenly stopped and, with great dignity, defecated.

"That's my horse, number seven. He just took a crap," Cliff announced triumphantly. "He'll be lighter and run faster."

George the Greek looked at Cliff. Could this character be for real?

"Will you take a grand on number seven, Cajun?"

221

For a moment, the Greek hesitated. Was it possible this sucker did know something? He'd certainly hit on those first— but, no, impossible, he couldn't do it again. "That's what I'm here for, Cliff. One grand on Cajun at, lets see . . . four to one."

"It's a good thing I'm betting with you, George. I go and put that grand in at the windows and the price would drop to three, maybe even two and a half to one."

"That's what gets me the action." It would probably take him the rest of the day, but the way Thompson was betting, the Greek figured he had to get his money back, and then some.

They went back to the clubhouse for the third race, and despite the fact that Cajun had thoroughly relieved herself, she got off to a slow start and came in next to last. For the next half hour, Cliff sat morosely sipping Scotch.

"Cliff, don't you want to go down to the paddock before the fourth race?" the Greek asked.

"Nah . . . I'll pick a name."

George couldn't believe it, this sucker was getting crazier all the time. A few minutes before the fourth race, Cliff downed his Scotch, drew a circle around a number and looked up at the Greek, a crooked smile on his face. "Hey, George, how you like this one? A beautiful little filly named Daddy's Girl. Isn't that something? Daddy's Girl . . . Daddy's little girl Kathy and her beef last night cost me the daily double." Cliff took another shot of Scotch. "One grand on Daddy's Girl, George. Do you want to handle it?"

George looked at the tote board. Daddy's Girl was ten to one. Another long shot, but if it hit . . . "Of course I'll take that action, Cliff."

By the middle of the fourth race, Daddy's Girl was so far behind Cliff didn't even bother to watch the finish. He walked over to the bar, ordered another drink and glumly began to study the scratch sheet again. George the Greek was beginning to feel better. The world wasn't so crazy after all. A sucker was a sucker.

"Let's see George, how do we stand now? . . . You owe me ten thousand seven hundred fifty after the end of the second race, then you beat me for two grand on the next two. That leaves me eight thousand seven hundred fifty, right?"

"Yeah, we figured the leases at five thousand so I owe you the leases plus three thousand seven-fifty cash."

"Right . . . you know, George, I've been thinking . . . what you said back there at the hotel, I shouldn't be so tough on Kathy. She's sitting back there alone in a strange hotel room and here I am out at the track . . . I'm going to take your suggestion. I'm going to give the kid a break and go back."

"But there's five more races, Cliff."

"Ah, my heart's just not in it, you can see that, George. Tomorrow's another day—I'll bring Kathy with me and the two of us will have a ball. You think my system's crazy, wait till you see the way Kathy bets. She *always* plays the long shot —she figures if she wins just one race a day she's ahead." Cliff laughed. "Even *my* pick-outs aren't that crazy."

"Yeah . . . well, okay Cliff, whatever you say."

"Great, let's settle up and we'll start all over again tomorrow."

The Greek took the leases out of his pocket and laid them on the table. "Okay, the leases are five grand . . ."

"Five grand when you've signed them over to me."

The Greek endorsed them and Cliff tucked them away in the inside pocket of his jacket. "Three thousand seven hundred and fifty to go."

"I don't have that much cash with me, Cliff . . ."

"No problem, George. Just give me what you've got. I'll come over to the restaurant and get the rest after I've given Kathy a break."

George looked at his bankroll. "I've got about fifteen hundred here . . ."

"Tell you what, George, just give me seven hundred and fifty

now, that'll leave an even three grand for me to pick up tonight."

"Yeah . . . fine . . . say, Cliff, you sure you don't want to pick
one more race? . . ."

"Now, George, you wouldn't want me to keep the little lady
waiting, would you?"

Forty-five minutes later Cliff, Pete, and the girls were congratulating themselves on their successful score and George the
Greek who had driven back with Cliff was seating himself at his
usual table in the Athens Olympia.

"What did you do with the oilman, George?"

"Would you believe it, Bernie? This kid Thompson beat me
on the first two races today, Tasha in the first and Shaikh in the
second—longest shots you ever saw—then we get out to the
track and the first thing he does is start crying because he didn't
make it there in time for the daily double."

"Yeah? . . . Where were you when you took that action?"

"Up in his hotel room."

"I dunno, George, there's something feels wrong here . . . I
think he had something going for him."

"Ya mean he past-posted me? How could he? I checked the
place out just in case—"

"I don't know, George, but I'm bettin' somebody must have
given him the office from outside—"

"I was with him every minute, I tell ya. Besides, this guy isn't
that kind of horseplayer, he's in the oil business. And you know
who his girlfriend is? Roy Brian's daughter!"

Bernie shrugged. "Maybe you oughta call Brian up and get
a rundown on him."

"Yeah . . . maybe you got yourself a good idea there." He
reached for the telephone. "I'll call Nate Burger in Miami. He'll
know where to reach Brian."

In five minutes George reached the card room in Miami.
"Nate? This is the Greek in New Orleans. . . . Yeah, just fine.
Look, Nate, I want you to get hold of Roy Brian, will you do
that? . . . Yeah, tell him to call me right away, it's very impor-

224

tant. Right away, Nate. Okay? . . . Great." George hung up and turned to Bernie. "I still don't see any way this Thompson coulda past-posted me. . . ." But by the time the phone rang some twenty minutes later, Bernie had him in such a state that the Greek was nearly convinced Cliff had taken him off. Roy Brian's call did nothing to alter that impression—it took only the mention of Cliff's name to set Brian off on a tirade that lasted ten minutes.

By the time Brian had calmed down, George knew for certain he'd been taken off by a professional con man, and a sickening thought came to him. . . . "Roy, those leases . . . the ones you sold me back in thirty-nine? Are they really worth anything?"

From Brian's voice, George could tell Roy thought they were indeed worthless, and that eased him a little. Oil leases were something Brian should know about.

"Well, then, this Thompson kid ain't so smart," the Greek said, pleased again. "All he got from me were those useless deeds and seven hundred and fifty dollars . . . just let him try to collect the other three grand. When he comes over tonight I'll take care of him good . . . what? . . . Yeah, Roy, your daughter, I'll hold on to her until you get here . . . and don't worry about Thompson . . . he won't be in any shape to bother her anymore. We try to keep things nice and orderly here in New Orleans. . . ."

The Greek hung up and nodded to Bernie. "You were right, that son-of-a-bitch took me off. Nobody takes the Greek off in New Orleans. We'll explain that little fact of life to him when he comes back—"

"What makes you think he's going to come back?"

"For three grand? Why not?"

Bernie shrugged. "Maybe he's already got what he wants—"

"Yeah, you're right. . . . I better reach out for him right now." He raised his hand and signaled one of his men. "Hey, Piko, get over here . . . I got a job for you."

26

CLIFF AND PETE were working at the remnants of a steak when a worried-looking Bert Lawrence came up to their table. "What's up?"

Bert looked at the girls, then said in a low voice, "Can I talk to you a minute, Pete?"

A few minutes later Pete came back, the same look on *his* face. "We've got to beat it. Just follow me, we'll walk through the kitchen and then out to the garage. *Now.*"

There was no mistaking the anxiety in his voice, and the three of them stood up immediately and followed Pete into the kitchen. When they reached the garage, Cliff asked, "What happened?"

"Two of George's people are in the lobby asking questions about us. We're lucky Bert heard them and told them we'd gone out for an hour. They're sitting in the lobby right now."

Cliff whistled. "It didn't take George long, did it?"

"What are we going to do?" Kathy was more curious than frightened.

"Beat it," Pete said. "Bert's sending a bellhop to the room to get our bags—it's a good thing we had them packed already.

Then we'll drive from here right down to the waterfront and take the Algiers Ferry across the river to Belle Chasse. Bert overheard one of George's men say the Greek already has people watching the roads out of town, but nobody goes to Belle Chasse. The town's owned by Leander Perez, he's got his own little empire there and none of the regular New Orleans mob even sets foot in the place. Bert'll call the Belle Chasse Inn for us. He said we'd better stay four or five days before trying to drive out of New Orleans. The Greek is pretty mad—and I mean killing mad—"

"For seven hundred and fifty dollars?" Kathy asked.

"It isn't the money, it's the fact we took him off. He's got to do something about it or they'll be saying he was made with a finger."

Cliff agreed. "They'll laugh him out of the clubhouse at the Fair Grounds when the story gets out—especially if I blow town with all my parts intact. . . . Belle Chasse, huh? I hope there's a golf course, Pete. I've got to keep in practice for that Willy Bishop thing we got planned next in Hot Springs."

"Look, Cliff, we can worry about Willy Bishop when—"

Just then their car arrived, and at the same moment Bert Lawrence appeared with a bellhop and their suitcases.

"Here you go, Pete, take care now and remember to lie low . . . this oil business you're in sure is a strange one. . . ." They all piled in and Pete took off, guiding the car through alleys and little-used streets, zigzagging toward the waterfront and the Algiers Ferry terminal on Canal Street.

Cliff and Kathy huddled in the backseat making sure their heads were down. It seemed forever, but they finally got there and then, for ten agonizing minutes, they waited until, with three other cars, they could drive aboard the ferry. It was not until they were safely in the middle of the river that any of them were able to relax.

The sun was just setting when the ferry pulled into the slip on the other side of the Mississippi River and let the cars off. It was country here—Belle Chasse could have been a hundred miles off for all it resembled New Orleans. The small Belle Chasse Inn was hardly more than a guesthouse, but it looked like it would do fine for their purposes, and when they walked in, the manager-owner came over and introduced himself as Bill Perez, a cousin of Leander. A heavyset, ruddy-faced man in his forties, he had a wide toothy smile, which he turned on his visitors.

"Ol' Bert Lawrence, he tol' me to expect you-all. We don't get many guests here, particularly this time of year. Summer's a different story. . . . Which of you two gentlemen is the golfer?"

"That's me," Cliff said, surprised. Pete looked at him and winked.

"I've got it all set for you here at the golf club. Joe Buck, he's the pro, says to come over tomorrow morning and he'll have a game for you. He was pretty happy to hear another golfer'd come into the town . . . like I say, this time of year things are pretty slow."

They were shown to cheerful bedrooms and enjoyed the rare luxury of unpacking all their clothes in anticipation of staying several days.

"This," smiled Kathy, "is going to be lovely. Between hustling out of Pittsburgh and beating it out of New Orleans, I could use a bit of a rest."

"Just think," said Carol, "whole days without planning a con or putting on an act , . . just rest and relaxation for us good folk."

But Cliff was already thinking ahead . . . to Hot Springs, Arkansas . . . and Willy Bishop.

The next morning, right after sunup, Cliff was out at the Belle Chasse Country Club introducing himself to Joe Buck, the resident pro. "I'd just like to come out here for the next few days and try to get my game tuned up," he told Joe.

"I'll try to find you some competition. What's your handicap?"

"Scratch."

Joe Buck grinned. "An honest man has found his way to the Belle Chasse Country Club. You know Mr. Thompson, there's a gentleman, a member of the club since he was ten years old, you might enjoy playing with, a real good guy. Teddy Linden. He comes over here every day in the morning and usually plays the course alone. He used to be a scratch golfer, then he lost his right arm at Bastogne—but don't let that fool you. He plays a pretty good game with just that left arm. I think he'd appreciate a chance to play with someone like yourself."

"By all means, let me know when gets here." Cliff then took his bag out to the driving range and began hitting balls. Fifteen minutes later Joe Buck came back with a tall, lean, handsome young man. The empty right sleeve of his sport shirt was tied in a knot.

"Nice of you to play with me, Mr. Thompson," Linden said. "Until I get good again, I kind of hate to put myself onto somebody."

"Cliff's the name, Ted, and it's a privilege to play with you."

They shook hands—their left—and went out to the first tee, while Pete sat in the clubhouse sipping ginger ale with Carol. Kathy elected to walk the round with them.

Ted teed up, swung—and Cliff was amazed by the two-hundred-yard drive Linden got off with only his muscular whip of a left arm. He followed it with a solid three-wood and was on the first green in two, Cliff right beside him. They both parred out.

"Not so bad, Ted. I don't know many two-armed golfers who could play with you."

"Yeah, well I've been out of the army six months and over here practicing every morning. When I first started I couldn't do much, but bit by bit I'm working up."

Cliff finished the eighteen holes with a one-over-par seventy-three. "Looks like I'm going to need some more practice myself."

Ted shot an eighty. "Yesterday I was eighty-one. Maybe I'll do even better tomorrow."

"Eighty's hardly anything to be ashamed of now."

"Ted, you were great, really wonderful," Kathy praised.

Ted smiled at her. "I think I could play over my head every day if you walked around with me." They went back to the veranda where Pete and Carol were still sitting and talking, and the rest of the afternoon passed effortlessly, as the bayou breezes blew through the trees.

At the end of the afternoon Ted reluctantly left. "My parents will be looking for me. See you-all tomorrow . . . I enjoyed our game, Cliff."

"Same here, Ted. See you tomorrow."

On the way back, Kathy stretched, enjoying the leisure of having nothing to do, then leaned over and kissed Cliff. "Cliff, thank you, this is so *good.*"

"It wouldn't be so good if the Greek's execution squad had caught up with us."

"Cliff . . . do you think he called my father?"

"I'm sure he did—and your old man probably put a bounty on my head . . . and a premium for your return home."

She turned away from him—her father was, after all, still her father, even if the evidence against him was pretty devastating. . . ."

For a week Cliff played eighteen holes every day with Ted Linden and the four, sometimes the five of them, had dinner together and laughed and relaxed, but finally Pete and Cliff began talking seriously about Hot Springs, Arkansas. The next batch of deeds was there in the possession of one Willy Bishop, a known golf hustler, but to take him off required the assistance of one other person. . . .

"Count me in," Ted said, "it sounds like a ball . . . as long as Pete doesn't mind that part about Carol and me being husband and wife for a few days."

"Just as long as it's strictly play-acting . . ."

"But Pete, darling," Carol said, wide-eyed, "we have to make it look good, otherwise Cliff's whole plan goes down the tube—"

230

"Yeah, but—"

Cliff stepped in. "Okay, okay—Carol, Ted, you know what to do. . . . Pete, I want you to find Saint Louis Dutch right away, then beat it to Miami. If we make it through this scam we've got just one more in front of us—but it's going to be the most dangerous. We'll need the best readers Dutch has . . . I remember my father was one of the best customers for Dutch's gaffed decks. Okay? Everyone clear? Then let's go. . . ."

The new foursome made the overnight drive to Texarkana, Arkansas. Then on the outskirts of Hot Springs, they stopped in a small town named Malvern, where Cliff and Kathy checked into Mrs. Burns's guesthouse.

"Ted, Carol, you two take the car," Cliff instructed. "Kathy and I will stay here at Mrs. Burns's for a couple of days before we check into the Hot Springs Spa and Golf Club. You play it cool and ask the locals for the best spot to stay that's close to a golf course. They'll tell you the same place, so we'll end up together. Without arriving together."

Hot Springs, Arkansas, the safety valve of the dry, God-fearing Bible Belt of the Southwest, a wide-open town where liquor and gambling flowed twenty-four hours a day. For this privilege, naturally, various members of the state government received a piece of the action.

It was late afternoon when Carol and Ted drove into the middle of the town of Hot Springs and pulled up in front of the Chamber of Commerce building. Beneath a sign reading "Tourist Information," a cadaverous-looking middle-aged man wearing steel-rimmed spectacles looked up at them. "Can I help you?"

"Yes, my husband was recently discharged from the service and we're looking for a place to spend a week's vacation. We were wondering if you could recommend a nice hotel with good food and a golf course . . . my husband used to love golfing . . , before the war."

The clerk glanced at the empty sleeve of Ted's jacket but kept his thoughts to himself. "Golf, ma'am? Best place is the Hot Springs Spa and Golf Club, no doubt about it. And the golf pro is a tournament player." He took a pad of paper and scribbled some words on it. "Just take this to the assistant manager there, Mike Starr, and he'll take good care of you, I guarantee it. Place is run by a fine gentleman, Mr. Willy Bishop."

"Really? Well, maybe we'll get a chance to meet him."

"What's your name?"

"Carol Linden . . . we're Mr. and Mrs. Ted Linden."

"Well, Mr. and Mrs. Linden, I'll give Willy a call personally and tell him to look you up and make sure everything is the way you want it. He'll do anything he can for veterans, particularly veterans who have given what you have for your country, Mr. Linden. I can promise you'll both have a fine vacation."

At the desk of the Hot Springs Spa, Mike Starr greeted them warmly. "Oh yes, Johnny down at the Chamber of Commerce called and told us you were coming. Welcome to Hot Springs Spa, folks. I hope you enjoy your stay."

Starr hit the bell and a bellhop took their suitcases and golf clubs, and escorted them to a comfortable corner room.

"What a lovely place," Carol said after he'd gone.

"Nice place for a honeymoon . . . everything a fellow could ask for except for one little point." Ted gave a wry smile. "Well, I'll do my best to live up to the trust Pete has put in me . . ."

"Don't worry so much about Pete. The important thing is to make our marriage look for-real." She even smiled when she said it.

"I feel like it's real already," Ted said. "Look we're supposed to be on a sort of second honeymoon, right?"

"That's right, Ted . . ."

"Well, it wouldn't do for the hubby to look all tense and frustrated, would it?"

"No, Ted, it wouldn't," she patted his cheek. "So try to look satisfied, hmm?"

232

Ted sighed. "Well, you can't say I didn't try . . . let's go down and have a drink. Maybe it'll take my mind off more important things."

In the cocktail lounge, Mike Starr came up to them. "Everything all right?"

"Everything is just fine." Carol gave the manager a bright smile. "I know we're going to love it here—and maybe Ted will learn to play golf again. You know, he used to be a scratch golfer before the war."

"Well if anybody can help to get his game back it'll be Ben Snead, our pro here."

"If I could just shoot in the nineties, if I could play to a handicap of twenty, I'd be happy," Ted said.

"Mr. Linden, I'll personally introduce you to our pro tomorrow morning and ask him to work with you. What time do you want to start?

"I'm an early riser . . . no point in sacking out all morning—" He glanced at Carol.

"About nine o'clock then?"

"Nine o'clock would be just fine."

27

TWO DAYS LATER, with Ben Snead's lessons and encouragement, it seemed that even with his terrible physical handicap Ted Linden might actually soon break one hundred. Each morning at eight o'clock Ted met the pro at the practice tee for a lesson, then the two of them went nine holes, with Ted dutifully trying to apply what he'd been shown during the lesson. Afterward Ben would go off to his duties and Ted would go around the second nine by himself, without a caddy—he said he felt freer and less inhibited that way to experiment—and in the process spray his shots left and right, into the rough, into the traps, testing, observing, pacing off distances to the flag from various positions, getting the feel of the greens, their grain and breaks. All this he would then report back at night to Cliff by telephone.

The morning of the third day Ted and Ben set out as usual at nine o'clock, except this time they were joined by Willy Bishop. This one-armed veteran interested him. On the first nine—Willy had to leave after that for an appointment—Willy shot a par thirty-six, Ben a one-under thirty-five and—a real accomplishment, both men agreed—Ted a forty-eight. On the back nine, which Ben played this time with Ted, Ted managed a fifty, and was appropriately ecstatic over drinks at the "nineteenth hole."

"You really are a magician," he told Ben. "I honestly never thought I'd ever break a hundred again."

"If you can break a hundred you can break ninety . . . if you break ninety you can break eighty." Ben turned to Carol. "Your husband's doing real good, Mrs. Linden."

"I'm very glad to hear you say so. . . . Golf meant so much to him . . . before the war."

"It means a lot to him now . . . well, I'm off. See you tomorrow, Ted."

"Right. . . ." He watched Ben go, then, staring morosely into his drink, said, "This has got to be the most frustrating vacation-honeymoon anyone ever had . . . I can't let myself out and really play golf and, of course"—he looked up at Carol—"it gets harder every day to play happy-husband-on-second-honeymoon-with-gorgeous-wife. Louses up my digestion too. . . ."

"Come on, Ted," Carol said, laying her hand on his, "it isn't exactly a ball—in more ways than one—for me either."

Ted looked up brightly. "Is that a fact?"

"Yes, that's a fact . . . damn it, you are a very attractive guy, and just because I go for Pete doesn't make me immune to our kind of close quarters . . . hell, I'm no saint . . ."

"Then why fight it, Carol? After this is all over you'll never see me again, Pete'll never know the difference—and we'll sure be able to put on a better act the next two days."

Carol slowly finished her cocktail. "I'm not saying you don't have a point. . . ."

That night after dinner Willy Bishop dropped by the table to congratulate Ted on breaking a hundred and ended up staying for an hour, regaling them with stories of high jinks at Hot Springs.

"Do you by any chance like to gamble?" he asked finally.

"We've got the finest casino east of Reno, you know."

"Afraid not much, Willy," Ted told him.

"I like to play red and black on the roulette wheel," Carol said.

"Well, you really ought to try our place, I bet you'll have some luck." He looked at the two of them and winked. "But then I can see you two don't need to waste your nights gambling . . . have a good time, kids. Ted, maybe we'll have at it again in the morning," and he went off toward the casino.

"Like Willy Bishop says, why waste time gambling?"

Carol nodded and rose, and together they went upstairs. In the bedroom they began the usual routine—Carol going into the bathroom to undress, while Ted poured himself a drink.

Carol came out of the bathroom, but instead of the usual old flannel nightgown, tonight she was wearing an opaque lace and silk negligee. Ted, hoping, looked from Carol to the big double bed.

"They could at least have given us twin beds, might have made it a little easier—"

"Pour me a drink, Ted?"

"Sure . . ." hoping even more Ted poured Carol a Scotch, added ice and splashed in some soda. He handed it to her, then went into the bathroom himself, emerging a few minutes later. Carol was in the large bed, sitting up, sipping her drink. She looked up at him, and there was no artifice.

"Well, tomorrow should be the big day," she said, which clearly wasn't what was most on her mind. "Are you all set for it?"

"I suppose so. I just hope they don't break off my other arm—"

"Ted, you're great—really great. I don't know how Cliff would have had a chance to pull this one off without you—"

"One more day playing happy honeymooner, happy to break a hundred—"

"Ted?"

"Yes." He sat down on the bed beside her.

"I wasn't kidding, Ted. It's hard for me too, this deal isn't exactly natural." She leaned toward him, her breasts visible, and kissed him on the cheek.

Ted reached out and pulled her to him. At first she resisted the urgent kiss but soon couldn't help herself and gave in to his demanding, passionate embrace. Finally she pulled slightly away from him. "You're right, Ted." Her voice was low. "Ships that pass in the night and all that. It will all be over tomorrow. . . ."

Hope was reality. He needed no further invitation. He switched off the lights and slid into bed beside her. Only tonight, unlike the others, he wouldn't lie miserably facing the wall away from her, his back to hers, his rear end making contact with hers occasionally, increasing the biting desire he felt for her.

Carol let him slide the flimsy gown over her head as he threw off his own pajama top, and then they were together. "I did want it, Ted, as much as you . . . see how ready for you I am. It's been like this every night—" She gasped and cried out softly as he gently entered her. Moments later he groaned. "Oh, God, Carol, I'm sorry I couldn't hold back better."

Carol stroked his head. "I did the same thing; accept and enjoy."

"God, I wish that golf game wasn't tomorrow," Ted whispered, "why in hell did we waste the last two nights?"

"I was trying to be good, we both were . . . I'm supposed to be kind of engaged, you know—*Ted*, not again. . . . You won't break a hundred, much less eighty."

Still later . . . "Carol, I will never play a better game of golf in my life than I will today."

"Feel better, do you, lover?"

"God, do I. Except . . . never again?"

"I don't really see how, baby."

"What a memory of Hot Springs. . . ." It seemed only a minute later that a fresh, fully dressed, smiling Carol stood over him.

"Time to move, lover, rise and shine. Today's your day."

28

ABOUT AN HOUR and a half later, Cliff and Kathy arrived at
the Hot Springs Spa and Golf Club and asked for Willy Bishop.
The receptionist announced the presence of Mr. Cliff Thompson and said, "You can go right in, Mr. Thompson. Mr. Bishop
is expecting you."

"Thank you, miss . . . it's what I figured, Kathy, your father
got to Bishop ahead of us. You wait out here, love, okay?"

"Sure, Cliff, good luck!"

"Look, Thompson, I know all about you," Bishop said as
Cliff came through the door. "You're traveling with Roy
Brian's daughter. I can tell you he wants her back and—"

"So you talked to Roy Brian?"

"There isn't anything I don't know about you, Thompson. I
heard how you took off the Turk, then the Ganoff brothers.
Brian told me you even past-posted George the Greek down in
New Orleans—you were a lucky rat to get out of that town in
one piece—and I know exactly why you're here . . . you want
those mineral rights deeds I bought from Roy Brian . . . well,
he told me not to sell them to you."

"I won't comment on the other things you said, Mr. Bishop

238

". . . but I should think you'd be glad to unload some worthless paper for cash—"

"Maybe they aren't so worthless."

"They're sure as hell worth nothing to you. I'll give you five thousand dollars for them."

"Sure you will. You want those deeds? The price is twenty-five thousand . . . take it or leave it."

"But all of them put together aren't worth twenty-five thousand dollars—"

"That's my price."

"Mr. Bishop it's a matter of simple business. I'll pay you a reasonable amount of money for them outright, say seven thousand dollars . . . or I'll gamble with you, I'll go either way you say . . . that is if you're not too chicken to bet on yourself."

"Listen kid, when I was a punk in knee pants the one thing my old man told me was 'Never be afraid to be scared.' I told you Roy Brian gave me the wire on you. You're a cutie, a hustler just looking for some way to take me off—"

"All I know is what I said before . . . I'm not afraid to bet on myself. Anything . . . pool, checkers, chess, cards, golf . . . name it. . . ."

"Golf, huh? Cut the bullshit, I know you're a scratch golfer. You think I've got mud on my shoes? Follow me, I want to show you something." Bishop led him out a side door onto the wide lawn that separated the spa from the golf course.

"Look at this. One hundred bedrooms . . . best hotel in Hot Springs, and the best gambling casino in the East . . . see that golf course, it's a championship layout. We have a tournament here every year . . . and look over there, see that swimming pool, it's Olympic size. I'm a millionaire ten times over. How do you think I got all this? By letting some hustler like you come in and take me down."

"I'm not trying to take you down, Mr. Bishop. Yes, you do have a beautiful place here. I don't blame you for being proud of what you've accomplished, I'm trying to accomplish something too. I want to make a fair deal with you to buy those oil leases, and I'll go as high as ten thousand. I can't go any higher than that, I don't have it . . . unless of course you want to take a note from me to be paid when I get my operation going."

"Take your marker?" Willy Bishop laughed aloud.

"Well, what do you want to do then? Put a price on the deeds and play golf for them?"

Willy Bishop laughed again. "You just don't quit, do you? You think you can come here to my hotel and hustle me?" Bishop looked out over the driving range and suddenly saw Ted Linden with his one arm struggling through some practice shots. An idea began to come to him. . . . "Tell you what I'll do, Thompson. I *will* play golf with you for those leases, and cash too. You give me a stroke a hole and you're on."

"A stroke a hole!"

"That's right, a stroke a hole and you've got me for whatever you want."

"You must think I came in here on a load of watermelons." They were nearing the driving range. "Hell, there isn't a son-of-a-bitch ever played golf that could overcome that. I'd rather play the numbers at a thousand to one. Now I see how you got this layout."

"You heard my deal, Thompson. Twenty thousand for the deeds or I'll play you for them. A stroke a hole."

"Man, I can't believe it!" He noticed Linden. "Hell . . . you give that one-armed golfer a stroke a hole and I'll bet on him. . . ."

Willy Bishop sprang the trap. "All right, Thompson, I'll *give* that one-armed golfer a stroke a hole and you bet on him. Put up your twenty thousand cash, I'll put up the leases."

"Now . . . wait, Mr. Bishop, I was just trying to make a point. I didn't really mean—"

"You made your bet, I took it. It takes two to make, two to break." He looked over at Ben Snead. "You heard the wager Mr. Thompson just made with me?"

"Yes, Mr. Bishop, I surely did." The other golfers who'd

240

been standing nearby nodded too. Linden looked at Bishop, then at the newcomer. "Mister, I couldn't let you lose your money on me, I'm not—"

"Hey, Ted, come on, take him up on it. You've been playing real *good,* " Bishop urged.

Carol walked up and put an arm around her "husband's" shoulder. "You know, Ted, maybe it *would* be good for you to try . . . think what it would mean if you even came close to winning . . ."

Snead, seeing that his boss had a sucker on the hook, went on. "Sure Ted, give it a try . . . I saw you hitting some good ones just now."

Ted looked at him dubiously, then back to Cliff. "It would be fun to play . . . but I'd just lose your money for you."

"You see, Mr. Bishop," Cliff said, "the man doesn't want to play."

"Ah, come on, kid," Bishop cajoled, "give it your best shot, why not? Look, how about this . . . you and your wife can be my guests at the hotel as long as you want to stay—win or lose. How 'bout it?"

"Go on, Ted,"—from Carol—"we could stay five more days."

"Stay a week, stay ten days, whatever you want." Bishop grinned in triumph as Ted finally, reluctantly nodded.

"Bishop, I . . . okay, Bishop, but I get to coach him, I can talk to him and tell him what his best shot will be, how to play his ball . . ."

"Sure, Thompson, sure, you can do that . . . if you think it will help."

A lovely young woman approached them just then, and Cliff smiled ruefully. "Sorry Kathy, I just let myself get mouse-trapped . . ."

Bishop looked closely at her. "Are you Kathy Brian?"
"Yes."
"I'm Willy Bishop, I talked to your father just a few days ago.

241

If you don't mind me saying so, he's pretty broken up about you. He told me when I saw you to be sure and have you call him. Will you do that?"

"How did he know I was coming here?"

Willy Bishop looked over at Cliff and grinned. "Your friend, Mr. Thompson, can answer that question."

"Kathy, dig in your pocketbook for our bankroll. I just made a bet—twenty thousand dollars against those mineral deeds your father sold Mr. Bishop."

"But Cliff, that's just about all we've got—"

"It isn't all that tough, Miss Brian," Bishop said soothingly, "Linden's actually a pretty fair golfer."

"Come on, get your deeds, sign them, and let's get started," Cliff said grimly. While Bishop hustled back to his office, the one-armed golfer walked over to Cliff. "Hi, I'm Ted Linden . . . I'm really sorry about your getting into this position."

"Cliff Thompson. Hell, don't worry about it, Ted. Who knows . . . between the two of us maybe we can beat the odds. We do have a stroke a hole after all—even if we are up against one of the best golf hustlers in the country."

"Hey, he's not a hustler," Snead said. "He just plays good, everybody knows that."

"He's also the owner of this place," Cliff said. "Take it easy, pro . . ."

A minute later, Bishop returned with the blue-wrapped mineral deeds. Cliff studied them a few minutes, nodded. "Yep, these are the ones. Who's going to hold the stakes?"

"How about Mr. Linden's wife. I suppose she's as neutral as anyone," Kathy suggested.

"Good idea, Miss Brian." Bishop signed and handed the deeds to Carol, then Cliff handed her twenty thousand dollars in five-hundred- and thousand-dollar bills.

"My God," Carol said, "I never saw so much money in one place in my life. I'm scared to hold it."

"Maybe Kathy could hold the stakes—" Cliff suggested.

"No," Bishop put in, "Mrs. Linden will hold them . . . I'm

sure she'll get used to that much money before we're through."

They decided to play a threesome, Ben Snead joining Bishop and Ted Linden, Cliff permitted to walk beside Linden and coach him. On the first tee Ben and Willy each knocked out drives of two hundred and twenty yards and Ted hit one two hundred and ten. Willy and Ben congratulated him, but Ted's second shot didn't make the green, while both of the others got theirs within a birdie putt of the cup. Ted hit his third shot onto the green but far from the cup and bogeyed the hole while Willy Bishop and Ben Snead each sank their putts for birdies. Even being spotted the stroke, Ted had lost that hole.

"Your man's doing pretty good today," Bishop said. "You want to make it more interesting? Like to go a thousand dollars a hole for the next seventeen?"

"On top of the bet we already have? My twenty grand against your leases?"

"Yeah, if you got the money."

"Kathy, come here . . . will you take a check from Miss Brian on the joint account she has with her father if I lose?"

Bishop nodded emphatically. "You're damned right I will."

"Okay, you got it. A thousand dollars a hole on top of the bet we've already made."

Bishop laughed and turned. "You heard that, didn't you, Ben?"

"I sure did."

"Don't worry, Willy . . . you may be hustling me but I always pay my bets. Now excuse me while I do some coaching."

On the second tee, a long par-five, Bishop hit first, a satisfactory two hundred and twenty yards down the fairway, the pro hit his two hundred and forty yards and then it was Ted's turn. He stepped up to the tee, Cliff beside him, whispering advice, even stopping to adjust Ted's club-head position. Bishop couldn't restrain a laugh, but it quickly turned into a choke as Cliff stepped back and Ted whacked out a two-hundred-and-fifty-yard bullet right down the middle of the fairway.

As the gallery applauded, Snead grudgingly congratulated

Ted, with a sidelong look at Cliff, and Bishop thoughtfully addressed his ball with a three-wood. The shot popped cleanly through the air and landed in good lay-up position thirty yards short of the green. Snead's went a little farther, onto the fringe of the green. Another conference between Cliff and Ted . . . "No, use more club than that . . ." and then in disbelief Willy Bishop watched as Ted's second shot sailed into the air and landed neatly on the green, thirty feet from the pin—a routine two-putt for a birdie. Bishop, away, selected a short iron and managed to land his shot twenty feet from the pin, but Snead's ball was stymied by Ted's and as Cliff started to pick it up and mark it, Bishop shouted, "Hey, Thompson, don't touch that ball. Only the player picks up his ball."

Cliff grinned to himself—Willy was getting rattled already. Ted and Willy marked their balls, and when the pro putted-out for a one-under-par four and Ted two-putted for the same, all Bishop could do was two-putt for a par five.

"Well, we're even now," Cliff remarked as the three golfers walked over to the third tee. "Maybe I'll give up the oil business and become a teaching pro. What do you think?" Willy Bishop looked away.

It was Snead's honor now, but as he stepped up to the two-hundred-yard par-three tee, Cliff turned to Bishop and said loud enough so no one could miss it, "Are you big enough to make that another thousand dollars a hole, Willy?"

Bishop gave Ted a long, speculative stare. Linden was shaking his head at Carol, obviously amazed at his performance ". . . nah," he decided, "last hole was a fluke . . . wasn't it?"

"How about it, Willy?" someone called out from the gallery that had collected.

"Tell you what, Thompson . . . I'll take the extra thousand —but no more coaching from you."

"What are you talking about, Bishop? Coaching was part of the original bet."

"Not if we push it another grand a hole."

244

"... all right, I don't want to argue. How about I coach him on one shot a hole only? Fair enough?"

Willy looked as though he were about to refuse but the gallery heard it and he knew he couldn't afford to back off in front of his own people.

"Okay, Thompson, you got a bet."

With that, Snead stepped up again, selected a two-iron and hit his ball neatly onto the third green, and then it was Ted's turn. Ted approached the tee alone—Bishop was surprised Cliff hadn't picked this shot as the one to coach him on—gripped a *three*-iron in his powerful left hand, swung . . . and landed his ball short of the green in a shallow sand bunker. The crowd, most of them for the underdog, let out a sigh and Willy, wearing a broad grin, stepped up and used a five-wood to belt his ball onto the corner of the green.

Cliff walked over to where Ted stood in the bunker, apparently studying a poor lie, and earnestly began sighting on the pin and studying the edge of the trap. "Okay," he whispered after a couple of minutes, "let's give them something to think about," and pulled out Ted's three iron. Ted promptly hit a lovely touch shot with the low-lofted club carrying the ball up and over the lip and then rolling down the slightly inclined green to stop ten feet from the hole. Bishop gave Cliff a look to kill as the gallery applauded.

Unfortunately, Ted followed it with a two-putt for a one-over-par four to Willy's three and Ben Snead's remarkable long putt for a birdie two, but with his stroke a hole Ted was still even with Bishop. . . .

Going to the tenth hole, Bishop had won the first, lost the second, tied the third, and then lost the next six to Ted at two thousand dollars a hole, putting *him* in the hole for thirteen thousand dollars, and the by-now-swollen gallery was openly and loudly on the side of the one-armed war hero. Ted had won each of the holes with a single spectacular shot planned and directed by Cliff and accompanied each time by loud and unavailing protests from the mouth of Willy Bishop.

As they finished a Coke before starting the back nine, Cliff moved over to a thoroughly disgruntled Willy Bishop.

"So, Mr. Bishop," Cliff said as they rested, "you in the market for a teaching pro?"

"Thompson, why don't you take a Duffy, huh? Get lost."

"Right after you pay off on the eighteenth hole," Cliff replied cheerfully.

"Damn it, Ben, what is it with this guy's coaching makes the kid play so good? What does he say?"

"Beats me—I seen it happen before maybe once, twice at the most. The guy just seems to play over his head, that's all."

"Nah, I'm just a born coach, Willy, admit it. Sure hope you have the cash, though. The whole town seems to be here . . . you wouldn't want to welsh in front of them, would you? Two days it would be all over the United States."

"Goddamn it, Thompson, shut up. Nobody ever welshed at my place and nobody's ever going to—and that includes you. Hell, I'm not even warmed up yet."

"Well, I guess it's about time you did then, wouldn't you say, Willy? You got to win seven out the next nine to break even."

"All right, Thompson, you so damn sure of yourself, how about we double the bet on the next nine—and *no* coaching."

"Four thousand dollars a hole and I can't help the kid?"

"I'd say he's doing all right."

Cliff sprang the trap. "Okay, Willy. You got yourself a bet. Four grand a hole on the next nine."

The crowd whooped, and Bishop now realized, with an icy, nerve-clutching certainty, that he'd been taken off. It all fell into place . . . Thompson was a golf hustler, *Linden* was a golf hustler . . . and he was up the proverbial creek at his *own* club.

Grimly he approached the tenth hole.

Cliff, now in the gallery with Carol and Kathy, watched as Ted stepped up to the tee, the muscles rippling in his left arm, and whipped the ball straight down the middle of the fairway for two hundred and thirty yards. His second shot landed in the

246

middle of the tenth green, a par-four hole, and instead of two-putting he sank a twelve-footer for a par three.

And now Willy Bishop truly began to sweat. Hole after embarrassing hole passed in progression as the most disastrous game of golf ever played by Willy Bishop at the Hot Springs Spa and Golf Club became history, the gallery applauding every stroke. Finally, on the seventeenth hole, Ted Linden's magnificent performance showed signs of weakening as he double-bogeyed to Willy Bishop's par and went on to lose the eighteenth, but he had still won seven out of nine holes, a decisive victory and, ironically, precisely what Bishop would have needed to do to break even.

"Sorry about the seventeenth and eighteenth, Mr. Thompson," Linden said as he came off the last green. "I guess I had to come down some time."

"Are you kidding, Ted? You were spectacular, absolutely spectacular . . . wouldn't you agree, Bishop?"

It took all of Willy Bishop's willpower, but he nodded—a short, sharp motion that contained within it all the frustration and anger of the afternoon. With a flourish, Carol handed Cliff the mineral deeds and cash, then put her arms around Ted and kissed him. "Darling you were just great, I can't believe how well your game has come back—"

"You can cut that out, Mrs. Linden, or whatever your name is," Bishop snapped, "you can all cut out the bullshit. Thompson, I'd be pleased if you were off the premises within an hour."

"I thought you said I should call my father," Kathy said sweetly.

"If you never call your old man again, he's ahead of the game."

"There is one last little detail, Willy . . . a matter of twenty-eight grand for the second nine, thirteen for the first, making forty-one thousand dollars, right?" Cliff said.

"You wait here, Thompson, and I'll write you a check . . . I wouldn't want to keep you from your *next* scam."

Cliff looked at his watch. "Thank you, Bishop, that's very

considerate. We'll just have time to take it to the bank . . . your check *will* be on the *local* bank, won't it?"

Willy glowered and walked off, and within five minutes returned, wordlessly handed Cliff the check, and stalked away. Two of Willy's security men went for Cliff to start him on his way, but he and Kathy were already headed for the taxi stand where a cab waited to take them to the bank.

Later, they sat on the porch of the guesthouse in Malvern, poring over the deeds and luxuriating in their success. "Only one more set of deeds to go . . . but that one is going to be the hardest to come by," Cliff said. "Each time it gets tougher than the last . . ." He turned to Carol and Ted. "You two didn't accept Willy Bishop's invitation for a week on the house, I see."

"To be honest with you, Cliff, I was tempted," Ted said, "but I kept feeling this hostility . . . I can't understand it."

"Well, maybe this will make up for any ill will I helped you acquire in Hot Springs . . . ten thousand big ones—you earned it, buddy."

"Hey, Cliff, I wasn't in this thing for the money. I just wanted to do it with you—"

"My friend, you made it possible for me to take off Willy Bishop for some rights I wanted in the worst way, in addition to stinging him for forty-one large in cash. Believe me, the ten is yours—in this game everybody gets his share or it's no good."

"Well, if you twist my arm . . ." He said it deadpan. "Hell, this buys me a whole year before I have to go to work . . . wait'll you see my golf game *then.*"

"I just might take you up on that . . . well, boys and girls," and Cliff started to wrestle the suitcases off the porch and put them in the car, "it's been my experience that the sooner you get out of town after a take-off the better. I suggest, since it's still early, that we drive down to Texarkana and spend the night there, then Ted can get a train for New Orleans and we can head on down to Miami and link up with Pete."

Ted and Carol exchanged a glance. "No, no problems at all."

248

Then, under his breath, "At least the ships are taking their time passing . . ." Carol nodded.

"Miami . . ." Kathy murmured. Cliff looked at her quickly. There was something in her tone he didn't like.

29

ON THE ROAD from Texarkana to Miami, Kathy couldn't help asking Carol, when they were out of Cliff's earshot, about her fake honeymoon and finally Carol allowed as how it hadn't been quite so fake the final two nights.

"But it was for the cause, right? We had to get those deeds from Bishop and Ted could only do it for us if he was happy and up to form, right? . . . then . . . afterwards . . . well we both felt we deserved a little reward. Look, Kathy, you say *one* word of this to Pete *or* Cliff . . ." But Kathy had her own thoughts.

It was nightfall two days later when the odyssey finally ended right where it had started, at the Roney Plaza Hotel. As soon as the car came to a halt, Carol jumped out and ran into the lobby to phone Pete, only to find he wasn't in his suite; her disappointment was short-lived, however—turning from the phone, she found herself in his arms.

"Jeez, have I missed you baby."

"Oh, me too, Pete, I missed you so much. I don't think you should leave me again, Pete—"

"Never again, babe."

250

"Hey Pete," Cliff said, "did you get the package from Saint Louis Dutch?"

"You bet I did, old buddy . . . twenty-five decks. I had to wait around while the Dutchman made up the last ten. Best work I've ever seen . . . the guy's a wizard for sure, Cliff."

The bellman carried the suitcases up to their old suite, and as they relaxed in the familiar surroundings, Cliff ambled over to the window and looked out over the beach and the ocean. "It's nice to be home again. . . . And now for the big one."

"They've all been big ones, Cliff."

"Yeah, but nothing like this, Pete. By now I guess Roy knows how valuable those mineral rights really are and getting the last of them from old Nate Burger is going to require very special planning . . . let's see, with that last forty-one grand we took off Willy Bishop minus the ten to Ted Linden . . . I figure our bankroll's about one hundred thousand dollars. That's not any too much to get into the kind of game I've got in mind."

"Look, Cliff, will you tell me what the game is? You've been making this big mysterious deal about it—what's the paddle for Nate's ass? You know Nate plays the way Roy does. He won't bet on nothing unless it's a sure thing."

"Exactly. And *that's* the paddle—we'll nail them both at the same time! Roy Brian is going to be—"

"Haven't you done enough to my father?"

Cliff and Pete stared in astonishment as Kathy suddenly stood in the doorway, her face strained.

"Kathy . . . what—?"

"Cliff . . . I've been with you all this time, right? You've humiliated my father in public . . . and now you're on the verge of finally getting back the last of those deeds he stole from you. But you're still looking for the 'paddle to his ass' as you put it. I know he did wrong, but isn't this *enough?* Can't you forget the rest of this revenge?"

"Kathy, listen, honey, I *can't* forget. . . . Slim Thompson was my *father—*"

"And Roy Brian's *mine*. Cliff . . . I still love him. He's always been good to me. Cliff, please . . . leave my father alone now."

"Kathy, I can't . . . for Slim, don't you see. That's who this whole thing was for. I thought you agreed with us."

"I did, and for a long time, but the last few days I've been thinking and he's . . . he needs me . . . look, Cliff, can't you please be satisfied getting your deeds back from Nate Burger and leave it at that?"

Cliff shook his head. "No, darling. I'm sorry—"

"I'm sorry too." She turned away and walked back into the bedroom, coming back a few moments later with her suitcase. "Cliff, I'm going home, I feel like it, I want to touch base . . . yes, yes . . . if you change your mind, you've got a girl waiting for you. If you care . . ."

There was nothing to say, nothing more. Not now.

She left, and Pete started after her but Cliff stopped him. "No, damn it, let her get some breathing room. She needs some time to think. I've seen it coming ever since Hot Springs but I hoped . . . well, she's got to do what she has to do, I guess . . . for Christ's sake, Pete, don't look so down. She'll be okay, I give odds"—whistling in the dark—"and anyway right now, old buddy, we got to get back to work."

Good speech, he thought, feeling rottener than he ever had in his life, since the day his father died.

That evening Cliff was led immediately into Nate Burger's office at the back of the card room. "You might as well know Roy Brian called," Nate began. "Wanted to know if I'd sold the deeds to you yet. Brian told me how you took off the Turk, then the Ganoffs, George the Greek, Bishop . . . my God! Willy Bishop's never been taken like that in his life." Nate stared at Cliff and shook his head. "You're in the big leagues now, kid. You better watch your ass."

"All I want to do is buy those mineral rights you got from Brian."

"No problem, kid. Twenty-five thousand dollars."

"Nate, you know they're not worth half that."

"Maybe, but that's my price. Willy Bishop asked you twenty grand."

"Yes, and that's how much I bet against him for the leases."

"Twenty-five thousand dollars."

"All right Nate, I'll play you some cards for them . . . and there's hardly any reason for you to get nervous over that . . . you got my money from my last trip here, I didn't wind up with a cent of yours. . . . You're way ahead. As for Roy Brian, his nose is out of joint because I happen to love his daughter and she loves me, and if he thinks he can stop me from what I aim to do, why he can get his red ass down here and do whatever he's big enough to do—"

"Okay, okay, big shot . . . what did you have in mind?"

"Low ball. Big stakes."

"How big?"

"Twenty-five thousand dollar freeze-out. That's the price you put on your leases, correct?"

Nate looked at him, then: "I'll get back to you."

"Sure, Nate. I'll sit in on one of the games here and get me a little practice."

After Cliff left, Nate telephoned Roy Brian . . .

Roy and Eleanor Brian had just finished a highly emotional reunion with their daughter, welcoming her home and begging her not to go back to Cliff Thompson, who by now even she must agree had proved he was just a hustler.

"But you're wrong . . . Cliff's going to drill for oil once he gets those rights together. That's his real business—"

Roy laughed. "Kathy, darling, you don't go drilling wildcat wells anymore. Costs too much. Besides, I drilled on that section, there's no oil there."

"But there *is.* I've seen the seismic studies Cliff had made by Hammer and Stone in Pittsburgh. They say Cliff will find oil all right, between twelve thousand and fourteen thousand feet. Why do you think he went to so much trouble to get back his father's oil rights?"

253

"Hammer and Stone. . .?" Roy Brian became abruptly silent. He'd heard of them, all right . . . good outfit . . . the Turk, Abe and Benny Ganoff, George the Greek, Willy Bishop—and now Nate Burger. Maybe Thompson did know something and maybe Roy Brian should never have let those damn deeds go . . .

The ringing telephone intruded. It was Nate Burger.

"Roy, I've got Cliff Thompson here. The wise-ass wants a low-ball game with a twenty-five thousand dollar freeze-out. This looks like your chance. You want to put it together?"

Brian glanced at his daughter a moment and then looked away. This was no time to back off. "Sure, Nate, lock it in for ten o'clock tonight . . . Excuse me for a moment, Kathy, I've got to make a call." When she'd left he dialed an unlisted number. "Hello, Toby . . . I want you to deal a game at Nate Burger's tonight. There's a punk down there I want straightened out, name's Thompson . . . you bet, I'll leave it to you . . ."

At the Roney Plaza, Cliff outlined his plan to Pete. "Let's reach out for your friend Karl Eddy. Didn't he say he was staying at the Biscayne down in South Beach?"

"Yeah . . ."

"Then let's go look for him . . . I have a job I think he can do."

They found the safecracker in South Beach. Cliff's instructions were short, to the point. "Stay by your telephone," he said as he handed over a hundred-dollar bill. "Don't move from it. There'll be four more of these when I need you. The worst that happens is you don't leave this place for twenty-four hours and you're a hundred ahead. Okay, Karl?"

"I've been doing this since before you are born, Mr. Thompson . . . don't worry."

By ten o'clock that night the word was out: heavy action down at Nate's—but only a few of Nate's highest-rated blue-chip customers were allowed in to witness the spectacle of Nate Burger, Cliff Thompson, Roy Brian, and two of Brian's shills

254

cash in twenty-five thousand dollars each for chips. It was an impressive sight, but even more impressive was the way Toby, Brian's dealer, stacked, shuffled, and dealt seconds. Cliff noted every move. "Watch how good that Toby is," he said to Pete after taking him aside. "One of the best mechanics I've ever seen."

"Call him on it. Cliff, they're playing you five against one and hitting you with seconds besides. How're you going to top that? They'll grind you into the ground—"

"And I'm going to let them." Cliff was well aware that all the money in the game, except Burger's twenty-five thousand, was strictly Roy Brian's. He watched Roy's smug smile and listened to his needling and allowed himself to appear agitated by them, deliberately making a few bad plays.

Cliff was playing his own outside now and doing it to perfection, moving carefully, making sure he lost while appearing to be trying to win. The most important thing to Cliff was that Brian had put up one hundred thousand dollars just to take off twenty-five thousand of his money. Brian's need to score off him was very personal now, tied up with his desire to destroy him so he'd never be a threat to his daughter. That, Cliff figured, ought to be a plus for our side. . . . After losing a large pot, Cliff said, "Goddamn it, I should have Kathy by me, she always brings me luck—"

The muscles tightened in Brian's jaw, Cliff was pleased to note. The question now was, if Brian was willing to put up one hundred thousand dollars to take him off for twenty-five, would he risk double that for fifty? It was time to find out. Maybe one more stinger in Brian's hide would do it. Cliff put the last of his chips behind a losing hand and watched as they were raked away. "Okay Nate, I guess I'm through. You guys were too good for me tonight—"

"Well, Thompson, looks like bad cards run in your family," Brian sneered. "Maybe you need to take some lessons."

"What I need is my Miss Lady Luck. Tell you what, Brian, if you think I need lessons, how about you giving me one?"

"Tuition's twenty-five grand."

"Double it."

"You're on," Brian said without missing a beat.

At an almost imperceptible signal from Brian, the others at the table immediately agreed. The time would be ten o'clock the next night. As Cliff and Pete left the cardroom, Brian's laughter could be heard in the background as he took the money from his shills and paid off Toby the dealer, as well as cutting in Nate Burger for his share of the winnings.

"Now this is what I call a sure thing," Burger said as he pocketed the money. A half hour later, the last man to leave his cardroom, Nate gave his usual admonition to the night watchman—a cousin of his wife—to stay awake for a change, locked up and drove off.

Ten minutes later Cliff, Pete and Karl Eddy left their car parked across the street from Burger's. It was four-thirty in the morning, almost pitch-black out, and Cliff, carrying an attaché case, followed Eddy with his satchel of tools, and Pete with Eddy's set of master keys held firmly in his right hand. Together they moved up to the side door of Nate Burger's cardroom. Karl Eddy took the keys from Pete like a doctor being handed a scalpel, and quickly and silently opened the door.

"Don't forget," Cliff said in a subdued voice, "don't take anything but the cards." He handed Eddy the attaché case. Pete and Eddy went on inside while Cliff stayed outside to keep watch. The cardroom smelled stale, the cigar smoke still thick from the game that had just ended. Loud snores indicated the position of the night watchman. Silently, Pete approached him, a shot-loaded rubber hose in his hand. His instructions were specific in the event the watchman awoke—which, considering his age, the hour, and his penchant for the grape, seemed unlikely.

Eddy approached Burger's safe and knelt in front of it, placing his stethoscope in his ears and, as his long, delicate fingers worked the combination, listening to the tumblers inside. Finally with a click, the safe opened, revealing a large stack of

256

hundred-dollar bills neatly stashed inside. With the money were Burger's personal papers and, at the rear of the safe, stacks of red and blue Bee brand cards, each freshly wrapped in cellophane.

Quickly the safecracker removed all the decks from the safe, opened his briefcase, and began substituting seemingly identical stacks of red and blue Bee decks. In a minute he was done and, closing the safe, twirling the knob off the last number of the combination, stood up.

The old night watchman still snored fitfully, flat on his back underneath the card table in the next room, with Pete standing over him. Of course even if he had begun to wake up, and Pete had had to top him, they'd have figured it was a dumb, unsuccessful robbery attempt, because absolutely nothing would be missing. Gaffed decks didn't talk.

Silently Eddie and Pete left the cardroom and as the first faint pink appeared in the sky over the ocean east of Miami Beach, the three of them were on their way to drop Eddy off at his hotel in South Beach after Cliff had handed him ten one-hundred-dollar bills. "Good job, Karl," Cliff said.

"Thanks, you know where to find me if you need me again," Karl said, getting out of the car.

But the night's work was not yet over. On Collins Avenue at Lincoln Road they stopped at the all-night drugstore. A single sleepy attendant stood behind the prescription counter. "Can I help you, mister?"

"You can if you have any playing cards." Cliff said.

"Sure do."

"How many packs you got?"

"Let's see . . ." The druggist opened a drawer behind the counter. "I got . . . yeah, four decks."

"No more?"

"Sorry, that's all there are in the store."

"I'll take them." Cliff and Pete then drove back to the Roney Plaza Hotel.

As they entered their rooms, Cliff somehow hoped, despite

everything, that Kathy would be there waiting for him, but the bed was empty, they were alone. "She didn't come back." Cliff announced in a hollow voice.

"You really fell for her, didn't you?" Pete said.

"Yes . . . yes I damn well did . . . have."

"I thought she was just going to be the paddle to her old man's ass."

"Maybe it started out that way. It's not that way now."

"Give her a chance," Pete said. "Like you said, she needed a little breathing room. You came on pretty strong, maybe crowded her . . . let's hope her parents are doing the same thing now and—"

"Yeah, sure . . . well, let's get some sleep now," and he pulled the heavy drapes across the windows to shut out the sun until they were ready for it. "We got another tough night ahead of us . . ."

A few hours later Cliff was abruptly awakened by the shrill ring of the telephone, and fumbling the sleep from his eyes, he snatched at the receiver. "Yes?"

"Cliff? I . . . oh, Cliff, my father told me what happened last night . . . I'm so sorry . . . please, Cliff, can't you just *forget* this whole thing with Dad—"

It was the call he wanted, all right, but not what he wanted to hear. "No, damn it, Kathy, I can't . . . not yet. . . . Are you coming back?"

"No . . . you're going to play again tonight, aren't you?"

"Is that what your dad said?"

"He said he only took you for twenty-five thousand last night and tonight he's going to give you a fifty-thousand dollar lesson . . . Cliff, you can't afford it . . . all the money you worked so hard for . . . you'll *lose* it all—"

"Maybe not . . . I might just win—"

"You can't . . . I . . . I don't think my father's playing honestly."

"My, what a surprise."

258

She pretended to ignore it. "All right, Cliff, but *please* . . . be careful? . . ."

"I will, honey. Tomorrow it'll be all over, *everything* we've worked for all these weeks . . . will you come back then?"

"I . . . I don't know. Just be careful." She hung up.

A couple of hours later, after grabbing a bit more sleep, Cliff was hard at work carefully peeling back the tax stamp and slipping four more of Saint Louis Dutch's card decks into the boxes he had purchased the night before at the drugstore. Then he returned to Collins and Lincoln. The night man was off, but he approached the day man at the prescription counter.

"Say, maybe you'd be willing to help me . . ."

"Yes?"

"Yes. You see, last night I bought four decks of playing cards here and by the time I got back to my hotel the other fellows didn't want to play, so I'm stuck with the four decks. What's the chance of you taking them back?"

"We don't make refunds."

"I'm not asking for a refund. Just take the cards back and let me have a toothbrush and some paste, okay?"

The druggist glanced at the four packs of cards and saw the unbroken tax stamps. "I guess that's a fair trade." He put them back in the drawer. "Huh . . . must have taken the last decks we had."

Just before three that afternoon, Cliff and Pete went to their bank and drew out all the money in the account—seventy-five thousand dollars. It was all or nothing now. "Uh, tell me something, Cliff . . . you got to admit that even with your readers in the game, we've got pretty heavy odds against us. What happens . . . if we blow this?"

"We're not going to blow it."

"But that mechanic Toby, even if you read the hands, he won't deal you anything to play with."

"Toby deals one out of six hands. Right?"

"Sure, and in the meantime he's got the deck stacked for Brian and the others."

"Right. But then *I* get to deal one out of six hands. And the others are going to make mistakes. I'll just have to take advantage of them. . . . Besides, nothing's a sure thing, pal."

And so it began . . .

The game started promptly at ten o'clock with three hundred thousand dollars riding on the outcome: fifty thousand dollars of Cliff's money, two hundred and fifty thousand of Brian's, including the fifty Nate Burger had riding on his "sure thing."

Roy Brian was all friendliness as he sat down next to his dealer, Toby. The big paddle was going to be built that night, all right . . . but it was young *Thompson's* ass that was going to get it. The players cut cards for deal. One of Brian's shills won. Cliff concentrated as the shill dealt Cliff an ace and a deuce down and another ace showing—a promising hand. He had the potential of going either high or low. In this game you could win either way—a busted straight could be as valuable as four kings. Reading the cards of the other players he saw that only Roy Brian came close to having as good a first deal, six and a five down and a two up. He was well on his way to a good low, almost a perfect low, that much-desired ace-two-three-four-six busted straight that was the lowest hand you could get —and, so, unbeatable. Cliff's ace entitled him to open and he cautiously put a hundred-dollar chip in the center of the table. Brian, Burger, Toby, and a shill stayed with him. The other shill dropped out.

On the next deal Cliff caught a four, Brian a four and Nate a ten. Nate's other cards showing were a seven and a six, so his chances for a low were cut considerably. Brian with a six-five-four-two low in his first four cards bet a thousand dollars and Cliff called. Nate dropped out. With the next card Brian drew a seven and Cliff a five. Brian now had made his seven-six-five-four-two low. He threw in three thousand dollars—three blue chips. Cliff had a chance to go high with two aces or low with a five-four-three-ace, so he bided his time, calling the three

260

grand, but didn't raise. On the next hand Brian got a jack and Cliff a seven. Now Cliff had a lower hand than Brian. There were two aces out and even if Brian caught one of them, he'd still have a seven-six low to Cliff's seven-five. Brian put five thousand in, Cliff called his five and raised another five and Brian, ahead from last night, called it. The two of them now had fourteen thousand one hundred dollars each in the pot, not counting four thousand Nate had left in when he folded. The down-card was dealt. Brian got a jack and Cliff . . . an ace. A perfect hand—three aces for a high and a seven-five low. Brian had nothing to match him either way—but, of course, Brian didn't know it.

Brian thought a bit . . . after all, Toby hadn't dealt this hand . . . then bet five thousand dollars on his down-card. Cliff matched him and raised him another five, and Brian called with a matching five. It was Cliff's turn to declare. "High *and* low."

Brian stared at the unlikely four cards showing. High *and* low? It couldn't be. Thompson must be bluffing, just like he kept bluffing the night before—and losing. Well, it was time for lesson number one. "Okay, high and low, too." Cliff flipped over his two aces and a three. Son-of-a-bitch, Brian thought. Thompson's seven-five low beat his seven-six, and his three aces high beat his two jacks. Twenty-four thousand one hundred dollars in the first play of the game. Brian's good humor was long gone. It was time to stop playing games.

Except Cliff kept winning, and Brian, no dummy, couldn't understand it. After all, each time the deal came to Toby, the mechanic, he dealt Cliff hands calculated to make him bet—and lose, since at the same time he dealt Roy Brian perfectly concealed slightly better high-low combinations—but Cliff never seemed to rise to the bait. He bet on the good hands and folded on the bad, and all Brian and the other players could do was demand fresh packs of cards with ever-increasing frequency.

By two in the morning, Cliff had frozen out the three shills and Roy Brian was down to his last ten thousand dollars, as was Nate Burger.

Finally Brian sat back and looked angrily at the mound of chips in front of Cliff. "Something smells about these cards." He glanced at Toby.

"Are you saying I'd throw gaffed decks into the game?" Nate said.

"Nah, nothing like that, Nate . . . but these cards just ain't lucky."

"If you want to get some new cards, it's all right with me," Cliff said. "Looks like I can win even *without* my little Lady Luck beside me."

Brian pretended to ignore the dig, pushed back his chair. "Go get some new cards!" he ordered one of his shills.

"Wait a minute," Cliff said. "You think I'm going to let you bring your own cards in from the outside?" He stood up from the table. "I'll just take my winnings and push off."

"Hold it!" Brian said. "This is a freeze-out, Thompson. No-body stops until he's lost his whole pile."

"Then let's go on with Mr. Burger's cards."

"No, we get new decks!"

"Okay, okay . . . but my man goes with your man to get them."

Brian shrugged, turned to his man. "You go with Pete White —and watch him."

The two of them left the cardroom and went out to the car Brian had driven down from Delray Beach. "There's another cardroom on Collins we can get the decks," Brian's man said.

"Nothing doing," Pete said. "How do I know what kind of cards your friends will give you?"

"All right, so what do you want to do?"

"There must be a place open around here . . ." He saw a newspaper vendor on the corner. "Pull up and ask that guy where there's an all-night drugstore."

"Yeah, good idea . . . hey you, where's an all-night drugstore around here?"

"Well, I think there's one about twenty blocks north on Collins, maybe thirty—"

262

"Balls . . . there must be one nearer. We'll catch hell if we keep them waiting." Pete fished a dollar out of his pocket and bought a *Miami Herald*. "Keep the change."

"Thanks, mister . . . say . . . I think there's an all-night drugstore down at Lincoln and Collins. About six blocks away."

"Why didn't you tell us that in the first place," Brian's man growled, and with a jackrabbit acceleration shot forward.

Both men walked into the store together. The druggist looked surprised. "Why, that's funny, I just sold all my cards last night."

"Take another look," Pete said . . . "you must have at least one deck."

"I'll look . . . but I sold them all to another gentleman last night—"

"Will ya take a look, goddamn it?" Brian's man put in.

The druggist went to the drawer behind the counter. "This is where we keep them when we have them . . ." He pulled the drawer open and peered inside.

"Well, doggone me! There they are. Maybe I dreamed it." "Give me them cards," Brian's man said impatiently, pulling five dollars out of his pocket, and then, followed by a grinning Pete, stalked out to the car, and drove back to Nate's.

The game resumed. Roy Brian broke the seal on a deck from the drugstore and put the cards into play, but somehow his luck didn't change.

Soon it was Cliff's turn to deal again—these were the only hands he could be sure were honestly dealt. He dealt a six-five low to Burger, but by the time they had come to the last card, and Cliff had bet into what he could see was the winning hand, Burger obviously didn't have enough chips in front of him to cover the bet.

Cliff leaned forward. "Well I guess that's it, I'm throwing my cards in. There isn't enough money left to make the pot."

"Wait a minute," Burger said. "Hey, Roy, give me fifteen grand to make the pot."

"Hold it!" Cliff's voice was angry. "This was a freeze-out, remember?"

"Give me a break, for Christ's sake . . ."

Cliff gave him a look of disgust and then glanced over at Brian, who was mumbling to himself, plainly nonplussed at Cliff's streak of luck *despite* the fresh cards and Toby, the mechanic. "All right, I'll tell you what I'll do, Nate," Cliff said. "You've got some mineral deeds that belonged to my father, you know the ones I mean?"

"Sure, I know what you mean, Cliff."

"Go get them, sign them over to me, and *I'll* give you fifteen thousand dollars."

"Nate, don't do it," Brian said urgently. "Look, sell them to me—*I'll* buy those leases—"

"You aren't in this hand," Cliff told him. "You were the one who said this was a freeze-out. Only a player in the hand can let new money in. That leaves you *out.*"

Roy Brian was obliged to watch Burger get the leases from the safe, and in spite of his protests sign them over to Cliff. Cliff pushed fifteen thousand dollars in blue chips toward Burger.

So now he had them all—all the oil rights to Grove City Block II. Cliff didn't know quite what to feel. The months and years of scheming and hustling were over—or almost . . .

The game continued, and to Burger's surprise Cliff now backed out of the hand, folded, and Burger happily raked in the chips; the game went on back and forth for another hour or so before Cliff, reading the cards, saw he was the winner once again and this time wiped out the last of the players.

It was over. With Pete's help he cashed in his chips and walked out of the game with two hundred and sixty-five thousand dollars of Roy Brian's money. Now it began to sink in. "Pete, we did it! We've got it! Enough money to drill that wildcat well. . . . Hey, Brian, you think Block I was good? Wait 'til you see my production on Block II!"

Brian, already on his way out of the room was too enraged to look or answer back.

264

"Well . . . good night to you gentlemen, it's been a real pleasure," Cliff said, and walked out into the early Miami morning more than one quarter of a million dollars richer.

He and Pete drove directly to the First National Bank of Miami and with the envelopes they had brought for the purpose, stuck the entire two hundred and sixty-five thousand dollars into the night-deposit slot, plus the fifty Cliff had started the game with, all credited to the joint account of Pete White and Cliff Thompson. Then, euphoric, they drove back to the Roney Plaza. Roy Brian had been well and soundly paddled. And the icing, the final kicker—Cliff savored the prospect privately—was yet to come. . . .

One hour later, as soon as it was late enough, with Pete and Carol still dancing around the hotel suite, Cliff picked up the phone and called Kathy.

"Hello?"

"Hi, darling, it's me. All over, *kaput,* no more vendetta. Are you coming down here or do I have to come up and get you?"

"Cliff . . . what happened?"

"Ask your father, he should be home by now. . . . Honey, I'm leaving pronto for Grove City to drill me an oil well and I want you to come along . . . what do you say? . . . Oh yeah, we'll be married the day after we hit—"

"Cliff! Of course I want to go with you to Grove City . . . but this time . . . Cliff . . . I want mother and dad to feel okay about it. Do you mind?"

"No, of course I don't mind, but Kathy . . . your father will never be happy about it. I guarantee you."

"Oh, I know you're probably right, but I've just got to give it a try. I'll go with you anyway, but to have his blessing . . . all right, Cliff?"

"Sure, Kathy, but let's not wait too long. I want to get started soon as possible."

". . . How much did you . . . win from my father?"

"Not much by his standards, a quarter of a million. Enough

to drill an oil well. Roy Brian's still got his millions left, I guarantee you that too."

"Darling, I'm so glad it's at least all over. I'll call you at the hotel when I've seen Dad and Mother. Wait for my call."

"I'll be right here, love."

Early in the afternoon Cliff was at the swimming pool when a page came by with a message. He had a telephone call. Cliff ran for a phone.

"Darling . . . this is the strangest thing. I . . . I don't know what you did to my father last night, but he seems to have changed his mind about us. He asked me to invite you to dinner tonight. Really! I think he's *seriously* going to discuss our marriage."

"He is? . . . Well, that's great news, Kathy, terrific, but I wonder—"

"Don't question it, Cliff, accept it. Maybe he's finally seen after last night just how smart you are . . . you know, someone good to have on *his* side? *I* don't know, just be happy about it. . . . And Cliff, bring all that scientific information you were showing me. He seemed particularly interested in it, and I want him to see just how much of a real business we're going into. Okay?"

"Sure thing." But Kathy caught the doubt in his tone.

It was a subdued, even polite Roy Brian who presided over the dinner table at Delray Beach that evening, and when dinner was over they all assembled in his study to look at the oil surveys. Cliff went into lengthy explanation of what he planned to do, and Brian was obviously impressed at the seismic reports and the new geological surveys Cliff had commissioned over the years. The best-known names in geological exploration were represented among the reports Cliff had laid out on the desk.

"The problem was," Cliff said, "that when you had your geological surveys made they just didn't have the techniques to develop seismic information that came about during the war. My man at Hammer and Stone in Pittsburgh is Tom Casewell,

266

if you want more information on these reports. I'll leave his card with you . . . Pittsburgh says that we'll hit oil at between twelve and fourteen thousand feet, give or take a couple of hundred feet. As you can see from the report, Grove City II will be a field four or five times as rich in reserves as Grove City I . . . now maybe you realize why I worked so hard to reassemble those mineral deeds. . . ."

Roy Brian nodded somberly. Damn if Thompson hadn't seemed to have done it. He'd jumped too fast getting rid of those deeds . . .

And then, like any other dutiful potential son-in-law, Cliff undertook to tidy up his credentials for daddy's darling daughter's hand . . . "I know you've been concerned about my recent background, but I really had no choice. I hope you can see that now. And after all, Roy, if I may call you that"—Brian nodded uneasily—"we all have to start somewhere. I'm a lawyer specializing in petroleum law and I'm going to put together one of the great oil fields in the West and I'm going to do it all myself. The way you did it, Roy . . ."

Roy Brian figured there was nothing to do but play it straight. With a straight face. "Well, good luck to you, Cliff. I've fought you hard, but after last night, I can see there's no point to it anymore. You're a smart young man, Kathy loves you. All in all, I guess it's time to make the best of it . . . I only hope you can make Kathy as happy as I've tried to all these years." Kathy's mother then rose to kiss the young lovers. . . . "I'm so happy—"

"There's just one thing," Brian interrupted, "Kathy's told me that you sensibly have suggested that the marriage take place *after* you've hit oil. Is that correct?"

"Yes, it is."

"Very well, then. On the proviso that we stick with that— I'd say you two have my blessing—"

"Oh, Daddy, thank you! . . . But I can't let Cliff go out to Grove City alone for the next year, or however long it takes . . . I've got an investment to protect too . . ."

267

"You can go out and visit him from time to time. I'll call friends out there and you can stay with them," Roy quickly countered.

Kathy looked at Cliff, some of the happiness clearly draining from her expression. "When are you leaving for Grove City, darling?"

"In a few days . . ."

"I'm going with you."

"I think it's only right, Roy. Even if we can't be married right away, at least we can be together—"

"I don't think it's proper for Kathy to go out there with you on your first trip, unmarried," Kathy's mother said, ignoring the fact that they'd already spent more than a little time together.

Before Kathy could answer, Cliff said, "Well, I think it's either that, or we get married tomorrow . . ."

"All right, all right." Brian sighed and turned to his wife. "I'll call our friends the Larsens out there in Grove City and ask them to look out for Kathy." He turned to Cliff. "Bull Larsen's the best drilling contractor in Oklahoma, I guess you know that. I'll call him and ask him to give you special service, make the drilling go quick as possible—"

"You think I'd use Bull Larsen? After what he did to my father?"

"Cliff, I know how you feel, but, really, he's still the best driller in Oklahoma. This is a new venture and you'll need help. He drilled all the wells in Grove City I, he knows the area, he's got the rigs and equipment. Anyone else will take twice as long to get the job done."

Cliff appeared to be swayed. "Well . . . maybe you're right, I don't know, I still don't feel good about it, but . . . I *will* need the help."

"That's the spirit. You won't be sorry . . . son." Cliff actually thought Brian might choke on the word. There were deep circles under his eyes and he looked more tired than at any time since Cliff had seen him. "Well," he said, finally, "if you'll

268

excuse me I think I'll go to bed. I'll talk to you some more, Cliff, before you leave for Grove City."

"Sure."

Kathy's mother also retired, leaving Kathy and Cliff alone.

"Kathy, come on, it's been three whole nights . . . let's drive to the hotel . . ."

"Cliff, I'd love to, you know I would . . . but now that we've got everything the way we want, it'd be silly to—"

"I think it'd be much sillier for us not to be making love right this minute." He drew her close and kissed her, long and just a little rough.

"Umm . . . yes, oh God, Cliff, I missed you so much . . . but I *can't* leave. How can we—"

"Seems to me I remember a pool house around here somewhere."

"You're planning on taking a swim, sir?"

"Lady, I plan to dive right in."

30

ANOTHER DRILLING DELAY—but Cliff wasn't surprised when Bull Larsen's field foreman brought the news to Cliff's office shack on Grove City II.

"I'm telling you this is the *fourth* delay we've had in the last month and I'm not going to stand for this harassment anymore. You tell Bull Larsen I want to see him and I want to see him right *now.*"

"Mr. Larsen doesn't just come *now.* He's a very busy man, Mr. Thompson, and believe me, he's doing you a favor drilling this hole—"

"It wasn't *my* idea to have Larsen do me this 'favor' . . . now you tell Larsen I want to see him, and if he's not here by the end of the day the whole Larsen crew and rig goes *out* and we start again with another outfit. You understand?"

"Come on, you don't have enough money to start over again with another outfit. You've got us, you'd better stick with us."

Cliff knew the man was right. "Look, when are we going to hit twelve thousand feet at least? We're more than a week behind, we've had two pipe breaks, equipment failure everywhere and we haven't even hit *ten* thousand feet yet—"

"Don't sweat it, buddy, we're doing the best we can." The foreman turned and walked out of the shack.

Cliff slammed the office door, got into his car and drove toward Oklahoma City and the offices of his lawyer, Mike Sandberg. An hour and a half later he was sitting across the desk from him. "We're in trouble, Mike. I thought we had more than enough money to sink that well, but now . . . hell, I don't know if we'll make it."

"Don't worry about it, Cliff, I've got some good news for you. I was going to call you if you hadn't come by. I took all the Grove City II deeds and transferred them to the SLIMCLIFF Corporation, like you suggested—and we just got our papers back today, approved with authorization to issue one hundred and twenty thousand shares of stock at a par value of one hundred dollars a share. You know, frankly, I was surprised we received permission to capitalize at twelve million dollars so easily—we haven't even hit oil yet."

"We will . . . it's there," Cliff said with conviction.

"Good. I certainly hope so. Well, you can put the issues on the market anytime you want . . . of course, it's easy to put shares on the market. The big question is, can you sell them?"

"We'll sell them. Do you think we can do it fast enough to sink another well with a different drilling company? I tell you, Mike, Bull Larsen is out to get me. Why else would he have so much trouble with my job when all his other jobs are going so well? I knew I shouldn't have listened to Brian . . ." and he looked closely at Sandberg, who nodded briefly and turned away, saying, "Still, it wouldn't make much sense for Larsen to deliberately wreck your drilling program, would it. People would hear about it, they wouldn't use him . . ."

"It wouldn't make sense unless Larsen had a very damned good reason for doing it and I'm beginning to suspect he has. All I know is my Kathy One just plain isn't coming in on time, and what is coming are problems and I'm convinced *they're* coming from Bull Larsen and his outfit."

"Well, these shares should take care of the money problems

for a while . . . when do you want to put them on the market?"

"Next week—and as soon as I get enough cash, Larsen is *out.*"

As soon as Cliff left Sandberg's office, he drove to Bull Larsen's huge house on the edge of town to see Kathy. Altogether the Grove City situation seemed to be a disaster. Not only was his stake diminishing every day with no results, but Kathy was still staying at Larsen's. Pete and Carol thought he was crazy to let her stay there in the first place, and they weren't too happy at the daily dwindling of the stake they'd taken off Roy Brian in the big poker game . . . a stake they shared in.

At Larsen's house the servant rudely, almost reluctantly, allowed him to come in the house and wait in the hall. When Kathy joined him, with a kiss, he said abruptly, "Kathy, come on let's get out of here."

"Cliff, what's the matter?"

"I'll tell you about it at the club. I need a drink."

"Kathy, I'm in deep trouble," Cliff said in the lounge of the Petroleum Club. "I'm running out of money—Bull Larsen is obviously sabotaging my well. He should be at twelve thousand feet right now, we should be producing *oil,* instead we haven't come anywhere near that and I'm down to about my last twenty thousand dollars."

"My God, Cliff, I didn't realize things were that bad. What are you going to do?"

"The first thing I'm going to do is take you out of Bull Larsen's house right now. We're not going back."

"But Cliff—"

"I tell you, Kathy, he's trying to ruin us. When I pay him off at the end of the week I'll be almost broke. I've just capitalized SLIMCLIFF Corporation at twelve million dollars and authorized Mike to put out one hundred and twenty thousand shares, and as soon as I get some buyers for just a few thousand shares I'm going to finish this well and sink Kathy Two—and you can be *damned* sure I won't be using Mr. Bull Larsen to do it."

272

"But if you sell those shares, then you won't own your own company anymore."

"I realize that, Kathy, but I can't help it. It's the only way we're going to stay afloat."

"Oh, God, Cliff, this is awful . . . I'm so sorry—"

"It's all I can do . . . pay off Larsen at the end of this week, tell him to get himself and his men the hell off my land, and let them take their rig. At least we're ten thousand feet down and I can put in a new rig and drill the other two thousand feet in about two weeks. But I'll need at least another hundred thousand dollars for that—realistically, even more."

"Cliff . . . now don't blow up . . . but . . . why don't I ask my father, he'd lend you the money. After all, it's his fault you went to Bull Larsen in the first place—"

"*No,* I'm not going to ask your father for money. I'll get that hundred thousand somehow. As for tonight, I don't want you to go back to Larsen's. I'm sending him a telegram right now. He's off the job . . . I'll get us a room in the hotel."

"No, Cliff. I'm going back to Delray Beach. I want to give my father a piece of my mind for getting us mixed up with Larsen—and I want to tell him we're getting married right away. I've had enough of this waiting around . . . but I want to tell him in person. I'll be back on the next plane, I guarantee it."

"Okay, Kathy, go ahead . . . but *don't* ask him for any money, I don't want his money. I just want to marry his daughter." He took her hand. "Don't worry, baby, we'll get out of this somehow. Just trust me . . ."

"Cliff, you know I do . . . oh, come on, let's go to the airport right now. I don't want to stay in that man's house another minute!"

31

ROY BRIAN LISTENED, barely concealing his satisfaction, as Kathy proceeded to give him, as promised, a piece of her mind . . . "Yes, Dad, Cliff's having an awful time and it's *your* fault . . . Cliff's run out of money, he's fired Bull Larsen but he still has to raise enough money to get a new driller. We know the oil's there, we know Cliff's sitting on the richest field in Oklahoma, but there's nothing we can *do* about it for a while—and it's all because of Larsen and you—"

"I'm sorry, darling, but you must understand, I can't help it if Larsen had trouble. He's the best in the business. If he had trouble, any other drilling contractor would have too."

"Daddy, I don't believe it . . . anyway, now Cliff says we have to raise another hundred thousand dollars."

"Huh . . . more like a quarter of a million, you mean. There's no way a hundred grand's going to save that operation."

"But Cliff's just formed a corporation, it's called SLIM-CLIFF"—Roy winced—"and all he has to do is sell a few thousand shares to start drilling again . . ."

"Shares, huh . . . how much stock is he trying to sell?"

274

"Well, he's got a hundred and twenty thousand shares at a hundred dollars a share—"

"He's trying to sell *twelve million* dollars worth of stock?"

"No, no, Daddy, if he did that he wouldn't own any of the field himself. He just wants to sell enough to finish the drilling."

"Interesting . . . who's his lawyer?"

"A man named Mike Sandberg . . . but I don't think Cliff really trusts him either. He thinks somehow Sandberg's tied up with Larsen."

"Well, you know, darling, the oil business is pretty tricky, especially when you're trying to get into the big league like Cliff is, and this business with the stocks . . . well, you need a lot of experience to handle it, and from what you tell me . . . you know I want you to be happy, Kathy . . ."

"I *know,* Daddy."

"Well, this time I'm really going to do it. I'm going to help your young man—I'll lend him the money. We'll see that he gets that well drilled, okay?"

Kathy kissed him. "You *are* wonderful, Daddy . . . but Cliff made me promise not to ask you for anything—"

"You didn't ask me for anything, baby, I offered it without being asked, right? I really don't think Bull Larsen would deliberately try to hurt Cliff, but since I *did* suggest him and since I guess he *has* been the cause of Cliff's problems, we'll just have to make the problems go away."

"But, Daddy, Cliff won't take a loan from you."

"He doesn't have to. I'll get in touch with this lawyer Sandberg and arrange to buy enough stock so Cliff'll be able to drill his well. Now, does that make you happy, darling?"

In answer she threw her arms around him and kissed him again.

"All right, dear. You stay with your mother and me for a couple of days until I can get this rescue operation under way, then we'll go out to Grove City and make things work. All right?"

A few minutes later, Roy Brian put a phone call through to Oklahoma City person-to-person to Bull Larsen. "Hello, Bull, how you doing? . . . Yeah. . . . Yeah. . . . You *did?*" Brian roared with laughter.

"Yeah, that old trick held him up pretty good," Bull said, "and now I got me a telegram two days ago firing me. Hah! Today I moved all the boys and equipment off the site and he's there with ten thousand feet of pipe in the ground and no money to get another crew and drilling outfit."

"Bull, near as you can say, how much does Thompson actually need to hit oil?"

"According to them seismic surveys, Roy, the oil's down there between twelve and fourteen thousand feet . . . I figure it'd take Thompson a hundred and fifty easy to get down there. Should be worth it though. I just wish to hell we'd had that Hammer and Stone survey ten years ago."

"Funny, Slim always said there was oil down there . . ."

"What do you want me to do now, Roy?"

"Okay, Bull, here it is." He told him about the corporation and the stock. "What we are going to do . . . you, me, some others . . . is buy him out. You call Sandberg and tell him to put it all on the market—everything—what the hell, twelve million dollars? We'll own the biggest oil field in Oklahoma. We should be able to buy those shares on margin, say fifteen down, twenty percent at the most, then when we own SLIMCLIFF— that name gets me—we'll figure some way not to pay off the balance. By the time we're through, we'll have several hundred million dollars worth of oil field. . . . Look, there's just one call I want to make first, just to make guaran-damn-tee sure, and then I'm sending my people out there to buy it out from under Thompson. You work out the best margin you can with the broker involved, hell, *buy* the broker if you have to. I'll go as high as twenty percent cash."

Roy hung up and rummaged through his desk drawer for the card of the Hammer and Stone executive Cliff had given him.

Here it was, Casewell, Thomas Casewell. He put a person-to-person call through to Pittsburgh.

Cliff stared at the empty area where the rig had stood. Now there was just the pipe in the ground. Cliff had contacted three drilling operators so far, and they were all willing to start work . . . as soon as they saw his money. He drove over to Mike Sandberg's office.

"Hey, Cliff, glad to see you—looks like a few people have faith in Grove City II. SLIMCLIFF is selling!"

"Great, I'll go around and see Bill Moss, the wholesaler, see what he says personally—"

"No, no—no need. I talked to him, told him how much stock you wanted to sell. Why don't you leave it all to me?"

"Okay . . . after all, that's what I pay you for."

Cliff left Sandberg's office—and then phoned Bill Moss. They talked at length and Cliff followed it up with a call to Tom Casewell.

"Any more calls, Tom? . . . No? Okay, the deal we made in Pittsburgh stands . . . right, and I'll be your first customer when you start the new firm."

There was nothing more for him to do but wait and hear the results from the sub-brokers selling SLIMCLIFF stock—and wait for Kathy to arrive. She'd called him that morning to tell him that Roy and Eleanor were coming out with her, and then she hadn't been able to resist telling him that Roy had offered to help.

"Kathy," Cliff sounded stricken. "I didn't want your father in this. With the stock sales, I can handle it . . . okay? Great, see you in two days. Carol and Pete will be here too."

As it turned out, it wasn't until four days later that Roy Brian, Kathy and her mother arrived in Grove City. Cliff, Carol and Pete were waiting for them at Cliff's on-site office with several bottles of champagne chilling and champagne glasses waiting.

"Welcome back!"

"Oh, God, it's so good to see all of you . . . mom, this is Carol and Pete, I've already told you so much about them . . . Dad, this is—oh, I forgot you know them already. Cliff, is it really true, do we really have all the money we need?"

"Absolutely, sweetheart, the stock's selling like crazy. Thanks for your offer, Roy, but it looks like we didn't need it after all."

Roy smiled and moved to the telephone.

"Champagne!" Kathy called out. "We really do have something to celebrate, don't we?"

"Hello," Brian was saying into the telephone, "what's our position in SLIMCLIFF? I want the final figure."

"Your position?" Cliff asked.

"Yes. . . . Yes. . . . Good!" He hung up and turned to Cliff. "I *own* it. Lock. Stock. And goddamn barrel—all hundred and twenty thousand shares at a hundred dollars a share par value. We bought the last of them this morning . . . okay, *now* you can open up the champagne . . . what's the matter, sonny, you think skin's the only game I know? . . ."

"What do you mean, you bought SLIMCLIFF lock, stock and . . . I only authorized my lawyer to sell ten percent of the stock—"

"Cliff, my boy, I'm afraid you've still got a whole lot to learn. Sure . . . maybe you can hustle a card game, I'm glad for your sake at least you can do that . . . and you're not too bad at an occasional golf dodge . . . but that's all you're ever going to do in this world. You're a hustler, kid, a short-score artist just like your old man . . . you're also a chump, you know that? You think Mike Sandberg was working for you? He took his orders straight from Bull Larsen, who took them from yours truly. They sold out the entire issue, *every* damn share of it—and I'm the owner. And you know who else owns it? Some old friends of yours named Bull Larsen, Turk, the Ganoffs, George the

278

Greek, Willy Bishop, and Nate Burger . . . now ain't that sweet . . .?"

Cliff looked at him, shaking his head. "You mean to tell me, Brian that you put up twelve million dollars and bought out everything. *All* of Grove City II?"

Brian grinned delightedly. "That's right, sonny, every share of SLIMCLIFF stock, and for only twenty percent down."

Cliff turned slowly to Kathy. "Now do you see? Now do you finally know him for what he really is?"

Kathy broke down and started to cry. Pete and Carol looked at each other and in their eyes were reflected visions of all the crummy whack-out joints they would have to face again, of all the gamesters and hustlers they would never be able to escape —the Turk, George the Greek, the Ganoffs, Willie Bishop . . .

Brian was still laughing as Cliff this time picked up the phone and placed a call. "Hello, Bill, Bill Moss? What did we make, Bill? What did we make on the sellout—lock, stock and barrel? . . . You've got twenty percent, two million four minus broker's commissions? That means two million two net to me. Right? Okay, Bill, keep it in my account. We'll get it banked tomorrow."

And finally he let it out . . . laughing like a crazy man.

The rest of them stared at him and wondered whether the big paddle put to *his* ass had unhinged *him*.

Finally, still laughing and sputtering, he managed to get out: "Roy, *old man,* now *I* can tell *you. There is no oil in this ground.* There never was. You have your people, I have mine. And one of them is Tom Casewell at Hammer and Stone in Pittsburgh, who I know you checked with, and who you can check with now if you want to." And he began laughing again, feeling the relief and delight that, by God, he'd spent damn near a lifetime working for and earning. Worth it all was the expression on Roy Brian's face, and he went on, driving it deeper, as he said, "No, Roy, I'm afraid my father was dead wrong, there just never was any oil under the Grove City II block . . . I spent the last five months of my life finishing off the paddle big enough to fit you, and by God it's tailor-made. You and your *associates* have just been whacked-out for two million four hundred thousand dollars—the price you put down for my stock. Whacked-out good and proper by Slim Thompson and his little boy Cliff . . ."

Brian stared at Cliff, not saying a word, then slumped down into a chair. He could check with Casewell, he would, but he also knew what he'd find. God damn, it had ended like it had begun, except that he was on the short end this time, up the creek *with* the paddle put to *his* ass!

And now it was time for Pete to see the light . . . "Cliff, you mean to tell me all those oil leases we went after, all that time, were just part of the scam?" And as Cliff nodded, a grin splitting his face . . . "Well, I'll be a son-of-a-bitch. Cliff Thompson, for the first time in my life I've been playing a natural straight. Me, the all-pro con of cons. By God, you had me all the way, I just *knew* the oil was there, just like our friend Mr. Brian here, and I . . . well, hell, I've got to hand it to you, old buddy. And I understand you couldn't have let anybody in on it, not even me. What nobody knows, nobody let's slip . . ." He shook his head in admiration. "A masterpiece. A flat-out, for-real masterpiece." And like Roy Brian he too sank into a chair, a dazed look on his face.

Cliff looked at Pete, nodded, and then at Roy Brian. "Better than a masterpiece, old buddy. The Big Paddle . . ."

"Cliff—" It was Kathy. "What are you saying—"

"I'm saying that it's finally, finally over, sweetheart. The poker was just to get the money to get the real money—and make a lifetime dream come true for Slim Thompson's boy. You and I are getting married. I just took your father off for two million four hundred thousand dollars. I figure that should be about enough to get *two* young couples pretty well started in married life, wouldn't you agree, Pete, old buddy? And I sure couldn't have done it without you. . . . So, my love, half my score is yours to do with what *you* want. You've earned it."

He pointed then at Roy Brian, who seemed to be physically shrinking in size as he sank even further into the chair. "I mean it, Kathy, half my score really is yours . . ." He shrugged his shoulders. "You can even give it back to *him* if you want . . ."

Kathy looked at her father, seeing him, as Cliff had said, really seeing him for the first time. Then she turned away, and linked her arm in Cliff's. "You know something, Cliff. Fuck him."

Eleanor Brian winced, perhaps at her daughter's language, perhaps, even more, at her husband as she finally was forced to recognize him.

"I'm sorry, Mother, I don't think I've ever said that before, but it just felt right, under the circumstances. And as for the money, Cliff, we'll give it to our kids, all twelve of them . . . boxcars, I believe you call it . . ."

And this time it was Cliff's turn to sit down in shock, a beatific smile, nonetheless, on his face.